TIME
WITH NORMA JEANE

A Time Travel Novel

Elyse Douglas

COPYRIGHT

ISBN: 9781671646032

BROADBACK BOOKS USA

I am good, but not an angel. I do sin, but I am not the devil. I am just a small girl in a big world trying to find someone to love.

—*Marilyn Monroe*

When you speak of the American way of life, everybody thinks of chewing gum, Coca-Cola and Marilyn Monroe.

—The Russian magazine *"Nedvela"*

I got a cold chill. This girl had something I hadn't seen since silent pictures.

—*Leon Shamroy*, describing one of Monroe's screentests

For all the Marilyn lovers...

TIME
WITH NORMA JEANE

PROLOGUE

Today is a day for memories. It's December 18, 2019, my thirty-seventh birthday. Outside, large feathery flakes drift and glide in a quick, wheezing wind. I've been focusing on one snowflake at a time, following its dance as it sails off on a wild ride, refusing to land on the pristine quilt of snow that spreads out before me and beyond, to the distant trees. How lovely it is. How quiet and full of longing and memory.

I drowse, dream and remember a time in my life that seems more fantasy and fiction than reality. When I think of her—of Marilyn Monroe—I recall something she once said to me.

> "*I've never fooled anyone. I've let people fool themselves. They didn't bother to find out who and what I was. Instead, they would invent a character for me. I wouldn't argue with them. They were obviously loving somebody I wasn't.*"

I'm curled up in an old, brown leather chair in the living room, a comfortable fire blazing, and I'm staring out through the picture window into the white page of

1

the day, remembering, drinking a glass of champagne and toasting myself on my thirty-seventh birthday.

My mind dances with the flakes; it plays and flirts with recollection. It refuses to settle, just like the snowflakes. They glide and they sail, and so does my mind.

Twenty-one years later, I have finally written my story, the story of a journey that changed my life. For years, I had suppressed the memories; I had shoved them aside and hidden them. And then a recent event startled my recollection, compelling me to pry open the dusty boxes that had been stored in the attic of my mind. When I finally allowed myself to remember them, the events and emotions of that journey returned in vivid detail.

So I wrote my story in a kind of nervous fever, my fingers sprinting across the keyboard. I was delirious with purpose, possessed by a hovering ghost that nudged me on. I ate and slept little, a solitary woman at her desk, slumped over a laptop at all hours, no longer imprisoned in my tidy home office, but free of enclosed walls. I was outside, wandering old paths, recalling forgotten faces, inhaling scents, my ears awakened by whispering conversations. I relived the vast, magical world of the impossible and I documented it all—my entire incredible journey—indifferent as to whether it would be believed, or even read.

A gust of moaning wind circles the house and awakens a longing, an inner havoc, a restless need. Though my story is now completed, I still can't rest. I feel a magnetic pull from that other world, a compulsion to vacate my chair and this warm room, this cozy fire, and to wander outside, to find a snow-covered path—a path marked by deer tracks—the same path my dog, Sonny, found years ago, when I was sixteen.

It was a path I'd never seen before, nor have I seen it since. It existed on the narrowest edge of a slope and perhaps on the narrowest edge of the world. That path hurled me back in time to an adventure that had thrilled and matured me, as much as it haunted and confused me.

If I find that path again, who knows where it might lead? Who knows if *he's* still out there under a star-studded sky, waiting for me? Who knows if *she* will appear again, flashing that girlish smile, waving me to come closer, to laugh, to dance, to experience yet another wonderful and life-changing adventure?

CHAPTER 1

Two roads diverged in a wood, and I—
I took the one less traveled by,
And that has made all the difference.

The Road Not Taken, by Robert Frost, was a poem I
was forced to memorize when I was a junior in high
school, a few weeks after I took that path—the path less
taken.

It was snowing on my birthday, Saturday, December
18, 1998. My father and stepmother were arguing.
Nothing unusual, really. They always argued—mostly
about money—Dad shouting that she spent too much—
she shouting back that he was a stingy, lazy man, who
drank too much. I could hear everything downstairs in
the rustic family room while I watched TV.

"You spend more time at Dillon's Tavern than you
do at your office," Carol, my stepmother, yelled. "And
then you tell me I'm spending too much money, when
most of the time I'm spending it on clothes for Darla, or
on groceries for you."

Dad laughed darkly. "Don't make me laugh. When was the last time you bought anything for Darla? I've seen the damned credit card bills. You bought yourself over six hundred dollars' worth of clothes from Macy's and Bloomingdale's. I don't know how that mall would survive without you."

Carol's voice grew strident. "If you'd looked a little more closely at those bills, you would have also seen that I bought Darla a new dress for her sixteenth birthday."

"That she returned," Dad countered. "Darla doesn't wear dresses, Carol. After two years you'd think you would know that."

"Well, she needs to wear dresses. What girl doesn't like to wear dresses? She's just weird, Carl. I've never known a girl like her, and I don't understand her."

"Let's leave Darla out of this. You've never liked her and, let's face it, she doesn't like you all that much either."

"Because she's weird, Carl."

"Don't call Darla weird. She's smarter than you and me put together. Her IQ is off the charts and she has a near photographic memory, like her mother. She's smarter than everyone else in her class. And she's only weird to you because you've never taken the time to really get to know her."

"And how would I get to know her? All she does is sit downstairs watching those old Marilyn Monroe movies, or she's in her room reading, or wandering around taking photos of God knows what. I've tried to talk to her. God knows I've tried. She won't talk. She doesn't even have friends, Carl. I mean, there's something wrong with a girl her age who doesn't have friends."

"Give her some time, for God's sake. We only moved here in September. It takes time to make friends, you know."

Dad had wanted to throw me a Sweet Sixteen party, but I told him I didn't want one. It wasn't my thing, and Carol was right about friends. I had made few in the three months I'd attended the new high school, and they probably wouldn't have come to my party, anyway. So, for my birthday, Dad promised to take me to dinner and a movie—and the movie is what excited me the most.

In 1998, we lived in Connecticut, just outside Weston, a town hidden among thick trees and hilly farmland, looped with stone walls. It had a few red barns and a white church spire, which added a picturesque, peaceful quality that I loved. It's only about 55 miles from New York City, and I occasionally took the train into Manhattan to wander Central Park or visit the Natural History Museum. I also managed to see a movie, if I had the time.

Before my mother died and we moved to Weston, we had lived in Brooklyn, where Dad had his contracting business. I had loved it there. As a family, we were happy. Mom and Dad had met when they were in high school and they got married right after graduation.

When Mom got sick, Dad spent a lot of time at home and then upstate at the mental hospital to be with her. His business suffered, but he never complained. He had to work extra hours to catch up, and I seldom saw him.

After Mom died, he was broken and sad. He began
to drink heavily, and all his energy and time were
poured into his work. As an only child, I learned to be
alone and, since I was a loner anyway, it wasn't so bad.

My stepmother, Carol, had worked as Dad's secretary, and she had been there for him, at least that's the
way she put it. When Dad's father, Grandpa Mike,
died, he left Dad his home and some money, not a for-
tune, but no small amount either. Carol's interest in
Dad seemed to sharpen and, before I knew it, Dad took
me alone to dinner and sprang the awful news: "I'm going to marry Carol, Darla."

Needless to say, I was shocked and disappointed in
him. Carol had none of the warmth, intelligence and
youthful spirit that Mom had possessed in abundance.

"Why, Dad? Mom's been dead just a little over a
year. Carol's not the right woman for you."

"You're too young to know things like that, Darla,"
he'd said dismissively. "You're only 13 years old.
You don't understand what goes on between a man and
a woman."

The anger grew in me. He looked at me with half-
hooded, weary eyes. Dad always did remind me of the
actor Robert Mitchum. He opened his hands, then
closed them.

He wouldn't look at me. "I'm lonely, Darla. I'm
lonely as hell. Carol is there for me."

What could I say? His eyes were filled with pain,
but if he was truly in love, shouldn't they have been
filled with hope and happiness?

The wedding was one of the saddest days of my life.
It rained, the church was cold, and Dad seemed more
resigned than happy. I didn't like the woman, his new

wife, and I didn't trust her. She was effusive, loud and possessive. She clung to Dad's arm all night, ignoring me and my good friend, Patty Baker, who, like me, was rather shy and self-conscious.

As the months passed, I tried to be kind to Carol, as she did to me, but it became painfully obvious that we rubbed each other the wrong way.

Two difficult and frustrating years later, Dad decided to leave Brooklyn and move to an exclusive neighborhood, where I'd attend a high school that challenged me academically. I think he also believed it might help save his marriage with Carol, which had lost all its luster, having corroded into daily arguments or long, dangling silences.

Sometime later, I learned that it was Carol who wanted to live in an area that boasted of movie stars, business barons and famous artists, all living in luxurious, sequestered homes. Ours, though nice enough, was modest by comparison and, as it turned out, we were way out of our class.

What I loved most about the house and the area surrounding it were the grand, swaying trees and the dark forest trails. My daily hikes on those paths were the best way to escape my prison of a house.

My alternate escape was settling into a soft, swallow-you-up couch to watch old videos, or to read books and magazines about retro movies: detective and film noir movies with Humphrey Bogart and Robert Mitchum; and romantic films with Rita Hayworth, Doris Day and Marilyn Monroe. Those movies were golden to me. The actors were my friends.

But my favorite star was Marilyn Monroe. She'd been my mother's favorite actress, and I loved and missed my pretty, damaged mother with a full, aching heart.

On that strange and magical day, Saturday, December 18, my sixteenth birthday, Dad and Carol were having a battling argument. As it grew uglier and more volatile, I increased the TV volume and reached for *FOCUS*, a movie magazine from the 1950s. It had long ceased to exist, but I'd found it at a flea market in Manhattan. I kept it because Marilyn Monroe was on the cover, wearing a fuchsia-colored dress with a bow tied at her cleavage. Her thick hair was a glowing, yellow luster. Her gold hoop earrings, teasing eyes and glossy red lipstick all gave Marilyn the appearance of a sassy, sexy gypsy.

A headline on the right of the page read:

MARILYN MONROE!

LOWDOWN ON HER FIRST BIG FLOP!

I'd seen that flop, but I hadn't thought it was a flop at all. I'd loved it. It was *The River of No Return*, starring Marilyn and Robert Mitchum. I devoured the article, my eager eyes re-reading a section.

The cast and crew departed for Calgary in late June 1953. From there they traveled by special train to the Banff Springs Hotel, which would serve as their base during the Canadian filming.

As they were about to rehearse a scene in the river, Marilyn donned chest-high hip- waders to protect her costume. While she ran through her lines, she slipped on a rock and the waders filled with water. She was unable to rise. Robert Mitchum and others splashed in-

*to the river to rescue her, but she had sprained her an-
kle.*

The argument upstairs beat on, their high, feverish
voices clashing. I closed the magazine and laid it aside,
reached for a video cassette and inserted it into the
VCR. It was *Gentlemen Prefer Blondes*, a 1953 movie
starring Jane Russell and Marilyn Monroe. I'd watched
only about ten minutes of the movie when, upstairs,
something crashed and shattered. I'd had enough. I
couldn't stay in that house one minute longer.

I grabbed the remote and switched off the movie. At
the closet, I pulled on my boots, snatched my coat,
pulled a cap over my long, light brown hair, and called
for Sonny, our tan and white beagle. He brushed my
legs, sneezing, his tail moving, his eyes bright with anticipation. While I snapped the leash to the ring on his
collar, I glanced over at my camera case, lying on a
chair. The camera was a Canon Prima 85n Point &
Shoot 35mm with a zoom lens. I reached for the case
and, with Sonny's leash in hand, started for the back
door.

At that moment, I heard heavy footsteps on the
basement stairs, and turned to see my father duck his
head under the low beam and descend to the carpeted
floor. His face was flushed with distress, his eyes moving, searching for me.

I waited as he approached with uncertain steps. He
ran a trembling hand through his thinning hair and
struggled to steady his heavy breathing. He smoked too
much and drank too much. He had been diagnosed
with high blood pressure and the early stages of heart
disease, and his doctor had warned him to cut his work

hours, the stress and the drinking—especially the drinking.

He was a bear of a man, with a round, florid face, generous belly and large ears. Once a handsome man, he was now overweight, his face slack from booze, and his eyes tired and bloodshot.

Our eyes met, his filled with a vacant sadness. "I'm sorry, Darla. I'm sorry about what happened up there. I try not to shout… get angry. I try to let things go, but sometimes…" He left the words hanging in the air, raised a hand, then let it fall back to his side.

"Where are you going?"

"Just out for a walk with Sonny."

"It's cold out there. Wrap yourself up," he said, reaching to tug my scarf up to my chin. "It's your birthday. You don't want to get sick on your birthday."

"I'll be okay."

"I really am sorry about… well. I hoped things would get better when we moved here…"

"I know…"

He pinched the bridge of his nose, lowering his head. "And they will get better, I promise you. Carol and I are working things out. We're positive about it. You'll see. They'll get better."

That was Dad's usual closing line with me after a tumultuous argument. I'd heard it hundreds of times, even before we'd moved to Connecticut from Brooklyn.

"Yeah, I know."

"Okay, you go for your walk now… It's your birthday and I've got plans," he said, trying to give me a reassuring smile.

"Yeah, sure, Dad. I'll be back soon."

Dad reached and drew me into his arms, giving me a hug. "I love you, Darla. You know that, don't you? You know that you've always been the light of my life; the best thing in my life. You know that, don't you?"

He sounded a little desperate and scared.

"Yeah…"

We held our embrace.

"So make a little birthday wish for yourself. You deserve to have a wish come true. You deserve all the good things life can give you, Darla, and you'll see, honey, I'll make sure you get all the happiness you deserve."

Whenever Dad drank too much, he turned sentimental. Even then I recognized the twisting emotions he wrestled with—his lack of a college education that left him insecure and overly ambitious; despair at the loss of my mother, and his own perceived shortcomings as a husband and father.

I didn't know what to say, so I said the wrong thing. "Dad, maybe you shouldn't drink so much. Maybe you should cut back some… just a little."

He held me at arm's length, and I saw I'd wounded him. I'd made him feel weak and small in the presence of his precious and precocious daughter. I saw hurt and tension. I saw a failing struggle going on behind those watery eyes, and I wished I'd just kept my mouth shut.

When he spoke, his voice was small and overly contrite, a little boy apologizing to a more exalted creature, although I was anything but that.

"I'm sorry, Darla. I should do better. Of course I should. You're right. I should do that. Yes… I should."

But he didn't say, "*I **will** do that.*"

He swiftly recovered, pointing a shaky finger at me, giving me a lopsided grin, looking a little like John Wayne in his last movie, *The Shootist.*

"Don't be gone long now, Birthday Girl. We'll be heading out for dinner soon and I've ordered you something special for dessert."

I gave him a final, quick hug, then shouldered the back door open and fled that stressful house, with Sonny straining on his leash, his nose high in the air.

As we rambled off, I told Sonny that I never wanted to go back. I never again wanted to see Carol. I never again wanted to look at my father's slack and drunken face, with his sad eyes begging for forgiveness. I wanted to fly away to another, more perfect world; to a world of happiness and make-believe. Following my father's advice, I stopped and made a birthday wish, holding it deeply in my heart's core.

When we crossed the backyard, I gulped in cold, clean air, already revived. I aimed Sonny and me toward the distant trees and our adventure began.

CHAPTER 2

Snow whipped about us, already three inches on the ground. As we approached the forest, I released Sonny's leash and we forged ahead into a sturdy wind. I wandered through the trees and stomped through drifts of snow with Sonny beside me, sniffing, alert and happy. I pulled my camera from the case and snapped a few photos of Sonny as he romped and darted about in a crazy circle. He barked, and I laughed.

I turned back to look at the house—the house I'd just escaped. *I'm free and I never want to go back there,* I thought.

I whirled about and marched off into the grove of trees, stopping to lean back and stare up into the moving gray sky, feeling the cold pricks of snow strike my face.

I opened my mouth wide, catching flakes, feeling a deep inner aching, a catastrophic loneliness. I squeezed my eyes shut and prayed to the wind, to the sky and to anyone who could hear me. I prayed that I could escape from it all—from school, from life, from my family; from life in the uncertain world. I prayed with all my heart that I could simply vanish, like my mother had wanted to do.

My sweet, crazy mother. As a young married woman, she'd been a struggling actress for a time, and my father happily supported her. When her career showed little signs of success or promise, she reluctantly gave it up, deciding instead to become the perfect mother and housewife.

I was the first child, and I would have had a younger sister if she hadn't died during childbirth. When Mom lost the baby, she began to lose her mind, one day simply drifting away into mumbles and whispers. We were seldom able to reach her again.

Dad struggled to understand, pleading with her to return to us; pacing the floor most nights, lost in helpless melancholy. When she stopped talking to him, he began to drink heavily. At first, he angrily refused to send her away "to the hands of people who won't give a damn about her."

When Mom grew worse, a kind and soft-spoken doctor finally convinced Dad to place her in a facility in upstate New York, something called supportive housing for people with mental illness. Because of my father's love and involvement, Mom received excellent care, but her mind never recovered from the loss of her baby, a girl she had named Marilyn.

A week before she died, Dad and I drove up for a visit. With dazed, suffering eyes, Mom stared into mine, and I wondered where she was and where she'd gone.

"I'm here, Mom. Dad and I are here."

And then, right out of the blue, she said, "We were sisters, you know."

She sat in a wicker chair in the day room, sunlight streaming through, coloring her pallid face yellow.

"Who?" I asked. But I knew. She'd often repeated the same thing.

And then, from under a shawl covering her legs, she produced a black-and-white photo and handed it to me. It was a portrait shot of Marilyn Monroe I'd never seen before. I didn't know where she'd found it.

I angled Marilyn's photograph into the light, studying it. I loved photographs, imagining myself becoming a professional photographer someday—perhaps even a war correspondent. I wanted to travel, be daring and bold, take risks and snap photos of the rare, the strange and the beautiful.

Of course, this photograph of Marilyn Monroe was beautiful. She had a dazzling showbiz smile, that gorgeous, leonine mane of blonde hair, and startled, laughing eyes. Her appeal was devastating, magnetic, and haunting. In later years, I would perceive more in Marilyn's photo than what she was projecting to the world—a deeper, secret Marilyn, a restless, frightened soul with searching eyes, hiding under all that dreamy warmth, a fascinating creature embodying a strange poetry. Even at twelve years old, though, I thought to myself, *Who is Marilyn, really? What is going on in her inner theater?*

That day in my mother's room, staring at Marilyn's photograph, I made a human connection, direct, stark and binding. Little did I know what lay ahead, and how Marilyn would change my life in countless ways for many years to come.

"Marilyn said I'm prettier than she is," my mother blurted out. Her wandering eyes were glassy from medication, not meeting mine.

"Well, you are prettier, aren't you?" I said.

Dad fought back tears.

"Marilyn came to visit me, you know," Mom said. "Yes... yesterday, I think. Yes. She wants me to be in her next movie. Should I? She and I are such good friends. I love her so much, you know. Should I be in her next movie?"

"Yes, of course you should," I said without hesitation.

And then her eyes slid away toward shadows, and she went silent. Those were the last words I would ever hear her speak.

My mother died when I was 12 years old. When I viewed her lying in her casket, a stabbing heart pain nearly buckled my knees.

A week after my mother's death, I had a dream in which she and Marilyn Monroe were walking with arms linked, laughing, as they strolled through a canopy of snowy trees into streams of dappled morning light. From then on, Marilyn became my favorite actress. In my bedroom is the framed black-and-white photo of Marilyn Monroe that Mom had shown me that day, next to a framed black-and-white publicity shot of my mother. In that photo, Mom's dark eyes are clear and probing, her hair gleams, and her mouth is partially open as if waiting for a kiss. Dad said, "She was a good actress who just didn't get the right breaks."

I did not inherit my mother's natural beauty, except for her full lips. I was tall and gangly, with shoulder-length light brown hair, almond eyes and an oval face.

Pretty? I don't think I was all that pretty, although Dad said I was. But then he would, wouldn't he?

In high school, I recall Bobby Sparks, a senior, telling me once that I had a remote expression and a distant look in my eyes. I liked his description because I thought it made me seem mysterious and exotic.

I certainly didn't have that indefinable charisma that Marilyn had, or even the delicate looks of my mother. I was just ordinary... just a shy, withdrawn teenage girl.

And then I found that path.

CHAPTER 3

There are many reasons I have never talked about that bizarre, thrilling and frightening night, but I'll let the story speak for itself.

When I was 16 years old, I was experiencing a riot of emotions, along with a true teenage crisis. It was nothing unusual. Most teenage girls experience it at one time or other—that teetering on the cusp of womanhood—that longing for an unexpected adventure into maturity, and yet that uneasy fear of leaving behind what is known and comfortable, even if it is frayed and worn.

I would close my eyes and see the image of my two selves. There we were in a face-off—the young girl facing the woman I was yet to be. We were glaring at each other, nose to nose, each frightened, each perplexed, each resisting the inevitable integration and growth. But then, like a young plant, either one grows up, or one withers and dies.

My emotions were unstable; every nerve ragged; every throb of my aching heart seemed a ticking time bomb about to explode. And I wanted it to explode. I wanted to fling the scattering pieces into the wild wind, watch them scatter, and see what happened.

I was alerted to the path by a set of fresh deer tracks. Nothing new; I'd seen many deer and many deer tracks before. They were plentiful in those woods. But these tracks, as strange as it sounds, seemed to glisten, as if lit from under the snow by a bluish light. I was captivated by them.

We had lived in our present house since September, and there were still many trails that Sonny and I had not explored, but I was sure I'd never seen this one. I wanted to pause and snap a photo of it, but as I reached for my camera case, Sonny jolted to attention, his head raised, his ears flicking about, on high alert. His twitching nose struck the air, catching a scent, his body tense, his eyes searching. He barked three times, faced the path and dashed off, jerking the leash from my hand. He went bounding through the snow, bulleting down the path like something possessed. I'd never seen him run that fast.

Startled, I yelled for him to stop, but he didn't stop. He'd never run off like that before, and we'd taken many walks together. We were good buddies, and he'd always been gentle and obedient.

Gripping the camera strap so it wouldn't swing from my shoulder, I scrambled after him, but he was too fast. Soon, he was out of sight. I shouted at him, hearing my voice fall flat, smothered by the pushing wind. Cupping my gloved hands around my mouth, I screamed out his name, clouds of vapor puffing from my mouth. I heard the faint echo of his barking and trudged ahead, following the sound.

In the haze of falling snow, I searched, sliding down little hills, scrabbling up others, picking my way through a grove of trees, searching in all directions. Sonny's barking soon faded into the squealing wind. He was gone.

The white sun was sliding down over the horizon, turning the sky into a bluish mother-of-pearl. The temperature was dropping. I was cold, my toes were tingling, and my hands felt numb. Still, I scurried about, calling and searching for Sonny. I was not going back to the house without him. He would freeze to death in this cold.

Fifteen minutes later, I had left the path and was fighting panic, not knowing what else to do or where to look. And then, abruptly, the snow stopped, and the wind died away. It seemed peculiar that the snow and the wind just ceased, as if someone had thrown a switch and turned them off.

As the light left the day, a strange but beautiful pinkish moon arose over distant hills, sliding in and out of purple clouds. I stopped to stare at it. It was lovely, enchanting. I'd never seen the moon so vivid and so enthralling, its pinkish glow lighting up the trees and highlighting the moon-beamed path I was on. Peering at the path's unseen depths, I thought, *Is that where Sonny went?*

I hesitated, nervous and conflicted. Should I go down that lovely, pastel-lighted path? A moment later, Sonny barked, a haunting echo which seemed to come from a deep cave. His bark had come from farther down the path, a pink ribbon stretched out before me. I took a few steps forward and then stopped. The path glowed and shimmered.

I glanced back up at the moon, a big round ball, radiant and intoxicating, something I'd seen only in Sci-Fi drawings. Breathing in, resigned to finding Sonny, I started off down the path toward the source of Sonny's bark, feeling light-headed and scared.

CHAPTER 4

I gingerly worked my way around trees, down a slope and up the other side, my breath coming fast, Sonny's barking subsiding again, the pink path fading. Night descended and suddenly the sky was a mass of glittering stars, billions of them. I stopped, tossing my eyes up into the sky, my mind briefly distracted by the magical, starry wonder. My science teacher had once told us that some starlight had begun its journey to Earth thousands of years ago, and that some stars had long since flamed out, leaving only their dying light for us to see. He also said that a black hole can gobble up a neutron star and thus cause ripples in space and time.

I thought, *what is time anyway*? My mother's time on Earth was so short, and yet the stars and planets exist for millions of years. Right on cue, Mom's favorite line by the poet Emily Dickinson slid into my thoughts. *"Forever is composed of nows."*

Sonny's bark startled me back to the "now." Newly focused, I fled up the path, gathering speed. The temperature seemed less bitter, and the wind clean and fresh, having shifted direction from east to north.

Snow-heavy trees looked sugary and a little spooky, like something from Grimm's fairy tales.

The moon-lit trail ended just ahead, and I stopped short, blinking, blowing on my gloves to warm my hands. The moon was still visible, but its light had left the path. It seemed odd that the light trail had ended so abruptly. Murky darkness and white tree limbs reached out, hovering, like nefarious beings. Still, Sonny barked.

I inched forward, testing the ground, my throat tightening. Each advancing step scared me, as I stepped around protruding tree roots and jagged rocks that obstructed the unraveling path.

Suddenly, I was jolted by an electric charge. I cried out. The hair on my arms and neck stood up. I heard a clicking sound and my frantic eyes flicked about, searching for the source. When I saw it, I stood still as a rock, enthralled. Racing toward me at light speed, was a horizontal, five-foot, squiggly blue line. Before I could leap away, it engulfed me—a hot, electric shockwave. My terrified scream was hollow, the whoosh of wind circling, stirring snowy tornado-cones into a frenzy around me. I couldn't move a finger or break through the terror, as my body burned on the inside but was cold on the outside.

Dazed, I watched the stringy light vanish into rippling night air, leaving behind shimmering shards of blue light. They were tremulous for a time, spinning fireworks, finally extinguished by a gusting wind that left behind a startled night.

A call for help got swallowed in my throat as the inner burn cooled. I swayed, took one dizzying step and almost fell, recovering my balance at the last moment.

Overhead, the moon flew across the sky in a blur of pink, a stretching ribbon from west to east and east to west. Stars whirled overhead. I reeled, and the earth tilted.

I don't know how much time passed before I returned to my normal senses, and I heard Sonny bark and whine, as if he were calling to me. I tottered about like a kid on shaky legs, eyes burning with fear. When the movement stopped and the heaving world settled, I looked heavenward. The sky was there—the diamonds of stars, the moon, the stringy purple clouds; they were all there, just as they should be.

Had I had a seizure? Was it a virus? Had I been out too long? Was I suffering from hypothermia?

Sonny came galloping toward me, his tongue waggling from side to side, and I shook awake to full consciousness. I was thrilled to see him, my friend, a sure sign that all was well, and would be well. I dropped to my knees as he rushed into my arms, panting and excited. I stroked him and held his head in my hands.

"Where have you been, Sonny? Why did you run off like that?"

His eyes shone like moons and he tried to twist away from me. And then, from out of nowhere, a voice startled me, and I flinched. I still hadn't recovered from that electric jolt.

I released Sonny and leapt to my feet, whirling toward the sound. Astonished, I saw a guy in his early 20s, standing tall on a slope about 25 feet away.

He was bathed in a soft throb of moonlight, as if he'd come from another world.

"Where did you come from?" he asked, obviously surprised.

I didn't know what to say. In that moonlight, he was quite good-looking, hatless, wearing a long, black coat and jeans, his hair closely cropped, like a soldier's.

"You weren't here a minute ago. Where did you come from?"

"What?" I said, trying to understand. I stammered, fighting to get the trapped words out. "I'm out walking my dog."

When he started toward me, skidding down the slope, his arms out to keep his balance, I stepped back, ready to run for it. Sonny's bark stopped the guy in his tracks.

Glancing warily at Sonny, he said, "Does he bite?"

"Yeah," I lied. Sonny's bark was literally worse than his bite. He had never bitten anybody, but I didn't want this guy to know it.

His breath smoked. He didn't advance. "Nobody ever comes out here in the winter, especially on a cold night like tonight."

"Well then, what are *you* doing out here?" I asked.

"I often come out here."

I looked around. "Why?"

"Surely, you don't live around here," he countered.

"Yes, I do. Not far. Just over that hill," I pointed. "What about you?"

"Not far. A few miles. You can't live close by."

I was guarded. "Yes, I do. Not far." I pointed again. "Over that way."

He stuffed his hands into his pockets, his expression thoughtful. "There's nothing over there but a barn and an old, broken-down shack."

"Well, my house is over there, and it's not a barn or an old, broken-down shack."

"No, it isn't over there. I know these woods and there isn't any house over there."

I straightened in defiance. "Yes, there is."

He yanked his hands from his pockets and put fists to his hips. "Okay, I guess you've lived here longer than me, and I know that's not true. My father's construction business has been here 22 years, since before World War II. Since 1932, to be exact, and I was born here in 1933. He almost went bankrupt during the depression but, finally, his company helped to build a lot of the houses around here, and I can tell you for sure that there are no houses over there where you say you live. It's private property, owned by a grouchy, old man named Hubert Wheeler."

I had never been a genius in math, but I *was* a good student. This boy's numbers didn't add up. If he was born in 1933, then he'd be about 65 years old. I stared, doubtful. "Okay, so don't tell me you're only about 21 years old."

"Yes, I am. I'm twenty-one. How old are you?"

I hesitated. Was he joking or being a jerk? "Seventeen," I lied.

He looked me up and down, and I didn't know if he liked what he saw or not. His expression softened, so I supposed he liked at least some of what he saw.

"I'm Eddie."

I was quiet.

"Aren't you going to tell me your name?"

"Maybe. I don't know."

"Just your first name?"

Being around boys always made me nervous and shy. I liked them well enough, but I had the tendency to file them into categories: Jocks—they bored me.

Studious—they were shyer than me and often self-satisfied over-achievers. Bad Boys—basically insecure showoffs. Artsy—mysterious, distracted or gay.

There was one more thing about boys. I tended to get defensive and argumentative around them. Even competitive. A quick perusal of any mediocre self-help book would tell me I was insecure, self-conscious and not comfortable in my own skin.

So, as I appraised Eddie, I worked to slide him into one of my boy slots. What type was he? Not a jock, although he had a good body. Not overly studious and not shy, for sure. Certainly, he wasn't a bad boy, at least on the surface, and he wasn't really an artsy type. He intrigued me.

"I'm Darla. Why do you want to know?"

"Well, why not? Isn't it civilized to introduce one-self?"

I shrugged. "I don't know. Maybe it's more civilized to keep one's mouth shut."

"Is that what you want me to do?"

I looked away into the dark trees. "No."

Why was I arguing with the guy? He seemed nice enough, and did I already say it? He was nice to look at. Yes, I was attracted to him, so I tried to recover. "My father owns a construction business, too. In Brooklyn and Queens."

Now Eddie seemed argumentative. "So why are you living out here then? Does it make sense that a guy has a business in Brooklyn, and he lives out here. Why?"

I turned petulant. "Because we want to live here."

Sonny was trembling in the snapping wind and looked up at me with pleading eyes.

"Okay, well I'm cold and Sonny's cold." I bent over and clipped Sonny's leash to his collar. "I'm going."

Eddie softened again. "I've got my car just down the road. I can give you a ride."

"No. Thanks. I'll walk."

"You said you're cold. It doesn't make sense to walk when my car's close by." I started off and he called to me.

"Okay, suit yourself... but it's a 1951 Ford Customline V8, with a mint green finish. Soft interior, with plenty of heat."

I turned back to him. "1951?"

"Yeah..."

"That's an old car."

"What do you mean, old? It's only three years old. I got a deal on it. My father knew the guy at the dealership."

Another cold wind circled me, stirring the bare branches of trees, slinging snow. I started back to him, uneasy. Something was wrong. He didn't seem to be joking, and he didn't seem like a jerk.

What about that crazy light and electric shock? The impact of the experience hadn't entirely left me, and I was still a bit weak in the knees from it. The inner burning sensation had been real and frightening, and the dying embers of blue light flying around the trees was real.

I stopped a few feet from him, facing him. My smile came and went. "Did you feel it?"

"Feel what?"

"A few minutes ago. A kind of electric shock, over there, just beyond that big oak tree," I said, indicating.

"Electric shock? What are you talking about?"

"So what are you doing out here?" I asked. "I mean, there's nobody around and it's cold. Why are you just hanging around out here?"

He studied me, considering his answer. "Do you like looking at stars?"

"What?"

"Yeah, you know, on a cold night like tonight when the stars and the moon and the planets seem so close you can almost reach out and touch them, do you ever just stop and look up at them?"

Who was this guy? There was no slot for him. My attraction for him grew. "Yeah, I do look at them. I like looking at them. Why not?"

He smiled, a friendly, knowing smile. He made a motion with his head for me to join him. "Come on, I want to show you something."

"I have to get home."

"Ah, come on. It won't take long. You'll like it. I promise."

Still, I hesitated. "I don't know you."

"Darla, do I look like some kind of psycho? Anyway, you've got your dog to protect you."

I glanced down at Sonny, uncertain. His tail was wagging, his eyes on Eddie, suggesting he was all in, having warmed up to this guy. I still wasn't so sure.

I scratched my nose and trudged off, following Eddie's long strides. So far, this had been one strange birthday.

CHAPTER 5

In a clearing forty feet away, I saw tire tracks. Further ahead, a parked car. Eddie hurried toward it, slipped behind the steering wheel of the car and flipped on the dimmer lights.

In the meager yellow glow, I turned and saw them: a tripod and a telescope tube pointed at the sky. Eddie emerged from the car, invigorated, and started toward it, waving me over. "Come and take a look but keep that dog away from me."

"He won't bite," I said.

"You said he would."

"He won't... well, at least he never has. Is that your telescope?" I asked, my eyes sharpening on it.

Eddie approached it proudly, touching the tube like a proud father. "Yeah. It's a De Luxe Skyscope. All metal with a great eyepiece. I can get 60 times magnification. I bought it in Brooklyn."

I dithered, unsure. Sonny was tugging at the leash, wanting to run toward the woods.

"Go ahead, Darla. Look into the eyepiece. The moon keeps sliding in and out of the clouds. It's a full moon tonight. That's why I came out."

I glanced up into the lovely night sky. *Just a little while ago, it was cloudy and snowing,* I thought.

"Go ahead. Don't be scared. Look at it," Eddie said, with boyish excitement. "You can have all the fun of the stars!"

His enthusiasm was contagious. Still a little self-conscious, I ventured over, squinted an eye, stooped and peered in. "Wow... Look at all those stars... And I see the moon. I see the pock marks. Wow... Nice."

"I told you," Eddie said, animated. "On clear, cold nights I can see Venus and Mars, too. Really good."

I watched the ghost of the moon slide in and out of stringy clouds, vanish in a dark moving cloud, reappear in a bright patch of clear sky, and then disappear again.

I lifted up, absorbed.

"Isn't that something?"

"Yeah. Can you imagine what it must have been like to land and walk on the moon?" I asked, in wonder.

The wan light from the car illuminated Eddie's confused face. "What are you talking about?"

"Neil Armstrong. Apollo 11. Hello? He was the first man to walk on the moon in 1969. I recently wrote a book report about it."

Eddie's face passed through confusion, worry and, finally, doubt.

"Come on, Eddie, why are you looking at me like that? You must have learned about Neil Armstrong in school?"

He stared as if a large part of me lay hidden. "Are you talking about a movie or something? Some book? Some Sci-Fi book?"

"No. N e i l Armsssttttrrong," I stressed, stretching out his name. "He walked on the moon, Eddie. What's the matter with you? What planet have you been living on? You can't know about the stars and not know who Neil Armstrong is."

Eddie shoved his hands into his pockets and backed away from me, hunching his shoulders. "You're kooky. You're... I don't know, screwy or, I don't know, you're putting me on. I wasn't any whiz kid in school, but nobody has ever walked on the moon, Darla. Nobody. Did you come here on a flying saucer from the future or something?"

His overreaction unnerved me. "Eddie... Lots of other guys have been on the moon since Neil Armstrong."

Eddie shook his head. "You said he walked on the moon in 1969?"

"Yes... of course, 1969."

His mouth was a hard, thin line as he considered me. "Well then, you are kooky or, I don't know, just crazy. You're just plain nuts crazy."

"I am not!" I shot back. "You're dumber than dumb if you've never heard of Neil Armstrong."

Eddie jerked his hands from his pockets, insulted, pulling himself to his full height. "Well, at least I know what year this is and it sure isn't 1969!"

I was sure that *he* was a little crazy. "Well, whoop-di-do for you. What do you know?"

"What year is it, Darla?" he said, in a challenge, jaw thrust out. "Tell me, huh? What year is it?"

I was defiant. "No, you tell me, if you're so smart."

"Okay. Fine. It's 1954. December 18, 1954 and nobody has ever walked on the moon. I repeat. Nobody. And, frankly, I don't think anybody will until maybe a thousand years from now."

I laughed a little nervous laugh as I studied him—his flashing eyes, his mouth unyielding. He wasn't joking. I saw the piercing truth in his eyes.

I jerked my uncertain eyes from him, as my mind stumbled over thoughts and images, remembering— rerunning what had happened before I met Eddie. The shock. The lights. Either Eddie was crazy, which was a definite possibility, or I had fallen and hit my head.

My obstinate posture was weakening, but I decided to fight on, despite a little shiver traveling up my spine. Calmly, I said, "It's not 1954, Eddie, it's 1998, December 18. I ought to know, it's my birthday."

We locked eyes, neither of us backing down. We held and held.

Finally, Eddie took steps toward me and I back-stepped. My worried eyes watched him reach into his back pocket to retrieve his wallet. From a plastic sleeve, he tugged out a square piece of paper and held it up. "I know you're putting me on, pretending to be some star girl because of my telescope, but this is my driver's license," Eddie said, pointing at the date with his index finger. "See? I renewed my license four months ago. Right there it says Connecticut, 1954. Come on, take a real good look if you don't believe me."

"I can't see it in this light."

He marched to his car, stooped in, switched on the headlights and returned. He nearly shoved the license into my face. "You can see the date now and don't say you can't."

He turned, pointing to his front license plate. "And look at my license plates. In the light, you can see them, too! It's 1954, Darla. Proof! Now, show me your proof."

I stared at the driver's license. I glanced over at the front license plate. I saw, but I didn't see, because my head seemed stuffed with feathers.

Both clearly stated that it was 1954 but, of course, it couldn't be 1954. I didn't speak as Eddie returned the license to his wallet. He glared at me. The car's head-lights glared at me, and the night suddenly seemed a threat.

In my feathery head, with feathers blowing in windy chaos, I refused to allow those feathers to settle. I needed the chaos, the stormy disorder. My frightened brain refused any clarity: the impossible cannot just suddenly become possible. Dogs can't fly. Dead peo-ple aren't raised from the dead and life only goes in one direction: straight ahead. You're born, you grow up, you die.

"So, what's the matter with you?" Eddie asked. "Why are you joking with me and making all this up?"

I couldn't process the reality. I was in the grip of something beyond me, some beast of a thing that lived between sanity and insanity.

I pushed it all away, turning sharply around, ready to march home to my waiting father and my birthday cel-ebration.

"I'm going home. I need to get home. I'm late."

And off I went, wanting as much distance from Ed-die and his telescope as I could get.

He shouted after me. "Darla! Where are you going? I really wanted us to get to know each other. I wanted to share my telescope with you and the night sky with you. What you did is not so funny."

I kept going, Sonny trotting ahead, sniffing and exploring. Eddie's words boomeranged back on me, bouncing around in my head.

At the crest of a hill, I recalled the electric shock. I recalled the clicking sound and the burning, shimmering blue light that had passed over me—through me. I tamped down a mounting anxiety.

Eddie had not been standing there before the shock. I was sure of it. Nobody was around, and it was snowing and the wind was strong and sharp. All that changed after the shock; after the dancing light. And the weather had abruptly changed, as if I'd stepped from one room into another.

Something was wrong. Increasing my pace, my strides lengthening in the wet snow, I became aware of a new quality of light; a new tone to the quiet. It was as subtle as the shift in music from a major key to a minor key. A different sound, a different pitch.

Panic arose. Eddie wasn't joking. He was dead serious. The impulse to run for it—to run blindly—to scream out for my father to come save me—burned through me like a grease fire. I fought it. *Get a grip,* I thought.

My legs grew weak, rubbery. Breath was getting trapped in my chest, fear squeezing my heart.

Yes. Something was very wrong.

CHAPTER 6

I ran back toward my house the way I'd come, except nothing looked quite the same. There were more trees than I remembered; different slopes; wider vistas. Though I expected to see two homes off to my right as landmarks, I didn't see either. Still, I pressed on, disoriented and weary. Sonny looked up at me and barked. He was tired, too. We'd been out a long time, and it was late. Dad was probably worried sick. I glanced at my glowing watch. It was almost 7 p.m.! How could it be that late? Sonny and I had left around 3:30.

Night settled in, the clouds had parted, and the stars were vivid. The distant moan of a train comforted me some. I'd often heard that train whistle.

As Sonny and I climbed the last hill, I stopped, breathing hard. I expected to see our house in the middle distance; lights glowing from the window; a Christmas tree shining from the living room picture window. The house wasn't there, but a solitary gray barn was, its peaked roof white with snow. The surrounding land was desolate, with tall, withered, brown grass poking up out of the snowy blanket.

Terror filled me like a cold liquid. I turned in place, walked in a circle, searching, squinting in the darkness, willing the house to be there. It had to be there somewhere! Surely, that crazy guy, Eddie, was just that: crazy.

My teeth chattered, and Sonny looked up with pitiful eyes. "I don't know, Sonny. I just don't know. I don't know what's going on."

I tilted my head back to see the moon, round and white. That odd shade of radiant pink was gone. My first thought was: I am going insane like my mother. I am completely losing my mind. None of this could be happening. None of this could be true. How could it be?

A movement to my left drew my eye, and I pivoted. On the summit of a hill, about twenty yards away, was the silhouette of a man standing firm, his legs apart, his hands on his hips. The moon cast moving, eerie shadows around him. I shuddered, sure it was Eddie. He was a psycho. A stalker.

I tore off in the opposite direction, yanking poor Sonny along. I sprinted across the field, past the barn where my house should have been, my lungs burning from the cold. I ran up and over the next hill, heart thumping, escaping past a line of trees into another open field. Where were the houses? Where were the people?

Winded, exhausted and cold, my legs finally gave out, and I fell sprawling into the snow, my camera case bouncing away, the leash ripped from my hand as Sonny charged on in full panic mode, not looking back. He just left me there. I shouted at him to stop, pounding the ground with my fist in frustration, but he bolted off, vanishing into the darkness.

I was close to tears when I sat up, slapped the snow from my jeans and coat and glanced back over my shoulder. There was no one there. I struggled to my feet, grabbed my camera case, swung the strap over my shoulder and staggered on after Sonny.

Minutes later, the sky darkened, snuffing out the moon. It began to snow, and the wind picked up, a rasping, nervous wind, tossing the trees. I didn't see the drop-off until it was too late. My feet slipped away, and I plunged down a steep hill, tumbling, reaching, sliding. I thought it would never stop. I thought I would fall off the edge of the world into infinite darkness.

At the base of the hill, I crashed to a stop, blunted and dizzy. As I was catching my breath, the sharp, piercing glow of car headlights stabbed my eyes, coming straight for me. I gasped, glancing about, seeking escape. I was lying on the narrow shoulder of a two-lane road. Where did that come from? The glaring headlights grew large, approaching fast.

Straining, I struggled to my feet, but a knifing pain seized my left ankle and dropped me hard to the ground. I grabbed at it, pain grinding into me. The headlights were close. Frantic, I raised my arm, hand waving madly, hoping the driver would see me. With my other hand, I clawed and dug at the ground, trying to get away.

The car closed in. I shaded my eyes from the blinding headlights as it whizzed by, missing me by two or three feet. I heard the brakes squealing, the tires skidding, seeking traction on the snow-covered surface, the car finally coming to rest at an angle in the middle of the road. If another car had been behind it, they would have collided. If a car raced by now, it would broadside the angled car.

I sat panting, cold and in pain, waiting. Sonny was nowhere around, and I'd lost my camera when I'd fallen down the hill.

A car door opened. Snow was boiling around me, little flakes flitting across the headlights, looking like insects.

Someone approached, footsteps crunching the snow. I looked up into a young woman's concerned face. She wore a royal blue jacket with a fuzzy collar, and a red cap with ear flaps; one turned up and one down. It was a pretty face, with big, startled eyes, glowing skin and a soft mouth, with no lipstick.

"Are you all right, honey?" she asked, in a concerned voice.

I blinked up at the woman, focusing. A few wisps of blonde hair were visible under the turned-up ear flap.

I stared in dazed wonder at the woman, feeling a swelling knot of unease as I examined her face. She was beautiful and entrancing; her voice familiar. Even in my battered, confused state, I knew who this woman was. I'd seen her countless times in photographs and movies.

For a few startled and impossible seconds, I thought I'd been knocked silly. Surely, I was hallucinating or dreaming; some mad dream that comes with a fever. I recalled Eddie and what he'd said about the date and year—that it was December 1954—but I refused to take it in. I was too spacy and lost, and my ankle throbbed. That was real if nothing else was. Pain is real.

The woman stooped toward me. "Honey, what are you doing out here on a night like this? Can I help you?"

"I'm so cold," I said. "I hurt my foot… my ankle."

She reached for my hand. "Take my hand. I'll help you up."

I took her gloved hand, and with the help of her firm grasp, I managed to stand, favoring my left foot.

The woman glanced around. "Are you alone?"

I nodded, again searching the woman's face, confirming again her unmistakable identity. My grip on reality seemed to have slipped away. And then I remembered Sonny, and I turned, searching the night.

"My dog ran away. I have to find him."

"Honey, we have to get you inside. You're freezing, and you've probably sprained your ankle."

"But I can't leave Sonny out here. He'll freeze to death."

"I'll take you to the house and you can call your family from there. Someone will search for him and then come by and pick you up."

She supported me as we started for the car. That's when I caught a glimpse of the rear license plate. It was illuminated by the taillights: bold black letters on a silver background. **A8081N**. Beneath that was a red square, **54**, and **CONN**.

I was teetering on the edge of reality. What reality, I wasn't sure. My world, my Earth, had suddenly gone spinning off its axis, and I was hanging on for dear life.

It was a sleek, black sports car, with two seats and a red and cream interior. She helped me ease down into the passenger seat, closing the door gently. Feeling the warm breath of heat, I leaned back and shut my eyes, exhausted.

I heard the woman slide in behind the wheel, close her door and drop the car into gear. The car lurched ahead and gathered speed—a lot of speed. Why was she driving so fast on this snowy road?

I had to have confirmation. I had to know, once and for all, where I was. I had to know who this woman was. I had to know if Eddie was right. Was it 1954? Had I flipped out? Had I slipped back in time?

I opened my eyes and summoned courage. Calmly, I said, "You're Marilyn Monroe, aren't you?"

She threw her head back and laughed. It was a girlish laugh, just like I'd heard in the movie *Some Like It Hot*, one of my favorite Marilyn movies.

"Oh, honey, not tonight I'm not. I won't be Marilyn Monroe again until after the New Year. For now, just call me Norma Jeane."

.

CHAPTER 7

Marilyn drove fast along the winding, two-lane road, swerving through hilly country, the world a motion-blur of dark shapes and swirling snow. Was I alone with a ghost? Was I a ghost, a shadow tossed haphazardly into another world? If so, why?

On the car radio, *Earth Angel* was playing, a song by The Penguins, or so the DJ announced when it had finished. As we shot ahead into the unknown night, I instinctively felt for a seat belt, but didn't find one.

"I like that song," Marilyn said.

"I can't find my seat belt," I said.

Marilyn glanced over. "Seat belt?"

"Yeah, don't you have seat belts in this car?"

"Why?" Marilyn asked. "It's a safe car, a 1950 Pontiac."

Here was yet another confirmation of time and place. This was a world before seat belts, and even though I was in pain, confused and disoriented, the idea of not having seat belts in cars seemed absurd to me. *Reality—true reality—is made up of silly details*, I thought, not knowing where that thought had come from.

Elyse Douglas

In a sudden shock of motion, Marilyn swung the car left onto a gravel driveway that unraveled to a large, rambling house, where every window blazed with light.

"My friends, the Greenes, own this house. They left because Milton's father had to have a heart operation. They probably won't be back until after Christmas."

I still did not trust my senses nor fully believe in this shadowy, night reality. I looked at Marilyn with some surprise. "Are you going to spend Christmas alone?"

We skidded up to the house and came to an abrupt stop. Marilyn laughed again, as she rammed the gear shift into park and killed the engine.

"Alone? Oh, yes. I'll be alone, but I don't mind it. I love being alone, and I'll call all my friends. I'd rather be here than kicking off my shoes to samba at El Morocco half the night. Here, nobody is gawking at me or grabbing me or pulling me in all directions. I can just be me, Norma Jeane."

Her eyes studied me. She seemed to see me for the first time and she smiled; a beautiful smile, a warm smile.

"What is your name?"

"Darla..."

She eased back, looking me over. "What a pretty name, Darla... Yes, it suits you. You have a very pretty face. It's an honest face, I think. How old are you, Darla?"

"Sixteen... Today's my birthday."

Marilyn lit up. "Today's your birthday?"

I nodded.

"Oh, how wonderful! Happy birthday! And you're sixteen!"

I looked down, shyly. "Yes..."

"Sweet Sixteen! Now that is a special birthday and it must be celebrated. Okay, let's get you inside and take care of your ankle. Then you need to make that call to your parents. They must be worried sick... especially since it's your birthday."

Marilyn nudged the door open and got out, slamming the car door shut. She rounded the front of the car, opened the passenger door, extended two hands, and helped heave me out.

"Okay, honey, we'll take it slow."

I shut the door and, with Marilyn's gentle arm about my shoulder, I limped ahead, viewing the house and the surrounding wooded area, awed by the size and privacy. "It's a big house."

"It has fourteen rooms and a rustic-style kitchen that I just love. The Greenes own eleven acres and, in summer, they have vegetable and flower gardens all over the place. And the trees ramble on for miles, with hidden pathways and beautiful splashing streams. When I'm here, I feel so wonderfully lost and away from the world."

Once inside, Marilyn held my arm, guiding me into the wide living room that had comfortable brown and green furniture, a cozy stone fireplace, a mounted globe of the world, and floor-to-ceiling bookshelves. With a painful sigh, I sat down into the deep, soft couch and pulled off my hat. Marilyn helped me remove my coat, boots and socks, and she winced when she saw my swollen left ankle.

"Oooh, that must hurt. I'm going to get some aspirin and look for an elastic ankle brace. I'm sure they have one around here someplace. Then I'll make some tea to warm us up, and I'll open a bottle of champagne to toast your birthday. Your sweet sixteen birthday!"

I brightened at the thought of drinking champagne. I'd never tasted it.

Marilyn placed her hands on her hips and smiled. "How does that sound, Darla?"

"Good. Thank you."

"Okay, now I'm going to bring you the phone. Call your parents and tell them what happened and that you've lost your dog. What's his name?"

"Sonny."

She beamed. "I love that name. When I was a little girl, I had a black and white dog named Tippy. Every day, Tippy would go to school with me. And he would wait and play with me at recess. I loved him so much. Don't worry, Darla, we'll find Sonny. If your parents can't find him, then we'll go out again and look for him until we find him."

When Marilyn pulled off her cap, all that luscious, blonde hair bounced to life, gleaming under the lights. Even with minimal makeup, she was enchanting, her smooth skin lucent, like a pearl. Under the halo of light, she truly looked like an angel lit from within, and I couldn't pull my eyes from her.

Marilyn indulged in an arched back and a full wing-span stretch and yawn, then she shed her jacket and tossed it on the couch next to me. She wore a royal blue men's crewneck sweater, denim pants rolled up to her bare ankles, and pumps, damp from the snow. I wondered if her feet and legs were cold but, if they were, she didn't seem to care.

When she handed me the telephone, having stretched the coiled, black cord to its limit, I accepted it, hesitantly. She noticed my conflicted expression.

"Is everything all right?"

I nodded.

"Don't worry, the Greenes don't have a party line. It's private. Make your call and I'll be right back with the aspirin and ankle brace."

I stared down at the black, rotary phone that sat heavily in my lap. It was just like the ones I'd seen in old movies. Who could I call?

The cold had seeped into my bones, bringing a quivering loneliness that chilled my soul. I felt like a helpless swimmer cast adrift in the ocean, frantically slapping at the water, searching for land, for a lifejacket, for anything familiar to grab onto, but all I had was this bulky telephone that felt more like an anchor than a lifejacket.

If this was December 1954, I was alone. Or was I? I nervously removed the receiver from the base and inserted my index finger into the rotary circle. Methodically, I dialed my home number and tentatively held the receiver to my ear, waiting, swallowing.

It rang four times before an ugly, funky ring-back tone pulsed and assaulted me. I pulled the receiver from my ear and replaced it on the base.

I stared ahead. Should I try someone else? Maybe old friends in Brooklyn? I dialed their number and got the same result, only this time I also heard the recording of a pinched and thin woman's voice saying, "*If you'd like to place a call, please dial the number or call your area operator. Thank you.*"

I made four calls, and none went through. It was yet another blow to my rational mind. None of what I was seeing and experiencing made sense, and yet...

I wasn't stupid. There was proof all around me: Eddie and his car; my non-existing house; the license plate, and Marilyn Monroe. If I was dreaming or hallucinating, then it was the most detailed, believable dream or hallucination of all time.

And my ankle hurt—and it was a *real* hurt. Pain anchors experience. I had been shivering from *real* cold, and the heavy, retro telephone could not connect me to my parents or my friends because they weren't there.

Acceptance came slowly. First was the feeling of someone's hands coiled around my brain, strangling it. Had I blundered into this time like an explorer who blunders into an old cave, discovering artifacts and riches from a bygone era?

If this was 1954, was I a ghost, a shadow, or a real flesh and blood human being who could make choices, and from those choices, change and remake events?

Minutes later, Marilyn returned. She was barefoot, moving easily across the carpet toward me, one hand holding a glass of water, the other holding a dangling, beige elastic bandage.

"Look! Success. I found both aspirin and the elastic bandage in the downstairs bathroom."

She handed me the glass and, from her partially enclosed hand, she dropped two white aspirin into my palm.

"Swallow those, Darla, and then I'll wrap your ankle. Later, when you get home, you should soak your ankle in warm water and Epsom salts. My Aunt Olive used to say that the best thing for a sprained ankle is a good soak in Epsom salts. Of course, she also used to soak her whole body in it, because she said it helped her lose weight."

Marilyn sat crossed-legged, gently lifting my left ankle. "Ooh. Your foot is so cold, and your socks are damp. I'll have to find you some dry ones. I'm sure Milton has a drawerful in his bedroom."

I gazed at her with wide new eyes as the walls of disbelief began to crumble; as reality replaced fantasy; as the possible replaced the inconceivable.

The woman holding my foot, my aching, swollen foot, really *was* Marilyn Monroe.

CHAPTER 8

Marilyn went to work on my ankle, wrapping the bandage around the ball of my foot once, keeping it comfortably taut with a light pull. After this first wrap, she adroitly circled the arch of the foot in a figure-eight pattern.

"I learned how to wrap a sprained ankle from my first husband, Jimmie. He was in the Merchant Marine and he knew first aid. Once, when my mother sprained her ankle, he showed me how to do it. Mother didn't like the thing, and she kept taking it off. So I just kept wrapping it. I got pretty good at it."

"What was your first husband like?" I asked.

Marilyn was thoughtful for a moment, as she pulled the bandage diagonally from the bottom of my toes across the foot's top and circled it around the ankle.

"Jimmie was a nice boy. I was your age when we married. Only sixteen."

I knew that, of course, because I'd read biographies about Marilyn's life. But seeing her alive before me, wrapping my ankle, I couldn't imagine being married at my age, and so I asked a question I already knew the answer to. "Why did you marry him?"

Marilyn sighed. "We decided to get married so I wouldn't have to go back to another foster home."

"Did you love him?"

Marilyn grew quietly reflective as she continued wrapping my ankle and foot in a figure eight, working down toward the heel and up toward the calf. The bandage soon covered my entire foot and several inches above the ankle.

"Yes, Darla, I did love Jimmie. He was good to me. We didn't have much to say to each other, but he was a nice boy." She looked at me. "It's not too tight, is it?"

I shook my head.

Marilyn continued, her expression pleasant with memory. "For our honeymoon, we went to a lake in Ventura County. We had fun. We laughed a lot. I don't remember what we laughed about, but I was so happy not to be stuck in another foster home, that I was a little silly."

Marilyn laughed as she took a little metal clip and secured the bandage.

"There. How does it feel? Not too tight?"

With care, I flexed the ankle. "No... Good."

Marilyn eased back, pulled her knees up to her chest and hugged them, gently swaying.

"We moved into a studio apartment in Sherman Oaks, with a pull-down Murphy bed, and I became a housewife."

"Did you like being a housewife?"

Marilyn shrugged a shoulder. "I think so, at least for a while. I wanted to make a home. I'd never really had one, so I thought, yeah, Norma Jeane, let's make Jimmie happy and let's have the perfect home. I wanted children and pets—yeah, I wanted it all."

Marilyn smiled wistfully. "That seems like such a long time ago."

There was a sadness in her eyes that touched me. I wanted more. I wanted to know everything about her, the stories about her past, the stories about her movies, and all her personal secrets. Being with her, staring at her, and listening to her were an impossible dream. Not knowing how long I'd be with her, I wanted to make the most of it.

And then Marilyn's eyes cleared. "Did you call your parents, Darla?"

I was silent.

Marilyn turned her eyes aside, obviously suspecting something was wrong. "Did you know, Darla, that no one ever told me I was pretty when I was a little girl?"

"Really? But you *were* pretty. I've seen so many photos of you."

Marilyn stared at me, her eyes flashing humor, or was it irony? "Honey, nobody thought I was anything special when I was a kid."

"But you were," I insisted. "You were a pretty little girl."

Marilyn reached out and touched my knee. "You are so sweet, honey. And *you* are pretty."

"I'm not so pretty. Anyway, nobody is as pretty as you. That's why you became a model, isn't it?"

Marilyn nodded. "When I first started modeling, Jimmie was away because the war had started. Well, I got some modeling jobs, and Jimmie used to say that my modeling cost him more money than I made, because I emptied our bank account buying the clothes I needed."

Marilyn laughed again. "Yeah, Jimmie was good to me. I was sorry we divorced."

Marilyn looked deeply into my eyes. "Darla, all little girls should be told they're pretty, even if they aren't. But you *are* pretty."

And then Marilyn returned to the previous subject, the one about my telephone call to my parents. "Honey... did you run away? Is that why you're not calling your parents?"

I looked down and away. I finally removed the telephone from my lap and set it aside.

"Yeah, something like that. I can't go back... at least not now."

Marilyn stared at the telephone. "So things aren't good at home?"

I faced away from her. "I can't talk about it. I just can't call anybody right now. Nobody's there."

Marilyn nodded in understanding. "Do you know, Darla, that when I was a girl, I lived in a lot of foster homes, and even in an orphanage? Well, you know that, don't you? You've read a lot of movie magazines, haven't you?"

Marilyn's mouth tightened as memories rushed in. "God, how I hated that orphanage. I felt so alone. And the foster homes were never really my home. I never felt a part of those families. I always felt like a sort of outsider."

She looked at me, and I met her eyes.

"Have you ever felt like that?"

I nodded.

"You know, Darla, I didn't really have a real house until, oh, let's see, maybe 1933. My mother bought a house, and I went to live with her. I was so happy to be with my mother. We were happy for a time... a short time, it turned out."

I watched as Marilyn's expression clouded over and turned dark. "But then, my mother had a kind of mental breakdown."

The memory sharpened Marilyn's sorrow, and she picked absently at the carpet. "I became a ward of the State. Anyway, I married Jimmie so I could finally make my own home."

Marilyn and I had something in common, and I wanted her to know it. I wanted her to like me and bond with me.

"My mother was in a mental facility."

Marilyn's beautiful blue eyes widened and then misted over. "Oh no. Was she? Is she still there?"

"No, she died a few years ago."

Marilyn's shoulders sank. She got up, shoved her coat and the telephone aside, and joined me on the couch, wrapping an arm around my shoulder and giving me a little hug.

"I'm so sorry, Darla. I'm so very sorry."

We sat there for a time, neither speaking. When Marilyn released me, a thought struck, and she stood up.

"Wait a minute. We have to go back outside and find Sonny."

Marilyn had read my mind. I had been fighting a towering fear that Sonny was freezing to death out in the frigid night.

With sudden urgency, Marilyn said, "If you haven't called anyone, then poor Sonny is all alone out there. He'll die. We have to go. Can you walk?"

I nodded vigorously. "Yes. Yes, I can walk."

Marilyn helped me to my feet, and we shouldered into our coats.

At the front door, I paused. Was Eddie out there? The thought of seeing him again both scared and fascinated me. He was handsome, after all.

CHAPTER 9

Under a light snowfall, with the windshield wipers slapping, we sped back to the area where Marilyn had found me. We were the only car on the road, and I was uneasy about that. After Marilyn had picked me up and we drove to the house, I hadn't seen any other car pass or drive by. We were always entirely alone.

Marilyn and I craned our necks, searching, squinting out into the snowy night, until we found the spot where I'd fallen.

She yanked the car right, slammed on the brakes, and I braced my hands against the dashboard as the car skidded to a stop on the narrow shoulder of the road.

Marilyn kept the engine running and the headlights on, their eerie beams shooting out into the ghostly, swirling world. After she burst out, she rounded the car, opened my door and helped me out.

"Is the ankle painful? Can you stand?"

I nodded, but my ankle pulsed with pain. I didn't care. I had to find Sonny. We crossed the road, anxious as we scanned the area, throwing darting glances into the darkness.

"Is this where you last saw him?" Marilyn asked, her breathy voice loud, snow settling on her red cap and shoulders.

I pointed. "I fell down that hill. He was up there when he ran off."

Marilyn nodded. "Okay, I'll circle around the hill toward those trees and call for him. You stay here and call for him. I'll be back in a few minutes."

After she was gone, I hugged myself with my arms, scanning the area nervously. I called for Sonny, but my voice fell into an empty cavern of wind and snow. I called out repeatedly, just to keep myself company. Hopping on my good foot, I ventured along in the moody silence, peering around. When I saw movement, I froze. No, I didn't imagine it. Something moved. Was it Marilyn? I called to her. No answer.

Ahead, I could make out a half circle of trees. I kept to the shoulder in case a car approached, and curiosity kept me shambling forward.

And then I saw him emerge from the trees. At first, he was just a silhouette, but as he drew closer, I saw Eddie! I made a little sound of surprise and took a couple of clumsy steps backwards.

"It's okay," he shouted. "Don't run away."

Like I could run away. And then I saw that he was cradling something in his arms. As he closed the distance between us, I saw it was Sonny. Eddie was carrying Sonny!

Forgetting my sprained ankle, I started toward them, but the sharp pain seized me, and I fell, grabbing the ankle in pain.

Eddie hurried over, bending to release Sonny. He galloped toward me and I managed to sit up and gather him into my arms, hugging and kissing his cold body as Eddie stood by.

I lifted my eyes to Eddie, thankful, again surprised by his height and handsome face. He both scared and attracted me.

"I thought you might come back," Eddie said.

"Where did you find him?"

"Over there by those trees. He was crouched down, shivering. He let me hold him. I took him back to the car, blasted the heater and we both warmed up. I gave him part of a chicken sandwich. He loves chicken. He even likes mayonnaise. He licked it like it was ice cream. I never knew a dog who liked mayonnaise. He's all right, this Sonny," Eddie said, grinning. "Anyway, I brought him back here, sure you'd come looking for him."

Eddie swung the camera case strap from his shoulder and handed me the camera. "I found this too. I thought you might want it."

Sonny left my arms as I reached for the camera case, trying not to snatch it. I held it gratefully, my eyes taking Eddie in with new warmth. "Thank you. Thank you so much. I was afraid I'd never see it again."

I examined it, concerned, running my hands over the water-spotted leather case.

"The camera's fine," Eddie said. "I looked it over, and I even snapped a couple of photos of my car."

"Do you know about cameras, too?" I asked, swinging the camera case strap over my shoulder.

"Some. That's a good camera. Never seen one like it."

"Well, thanks again for Sonny and my camera. That was nice of you."

"You're welcome."

Eddie grinned mildly. "Tell me something. Why did you joke with me back there? I mean, about it being 1998. I kept thinking about it. Why did you do that?"

I gently rubbed Sonny's ears to warm them, working to invent a story. "I don't know. I've had a weird day."

We were silent for a few moments.

"I knew she was living around here," Eddie finally said.

"Who?"

"Who?" he said, lifting his hands with impatience. "Marilyn Monroe, of course. Who else? You're with Marilyn Monroe. *The* Marilyn Monroe. The one and only Marilyn."

"Yeah... So I am," I said casually.

"Look, Darla, you're really confusing me. I followed you, you know. I followed you to where you thought your house was. I saw how you ran away. You really did believe your house was there, didn't you? So who are you, really, and what's going on?"

I couldn't come up with an answer, so I didn't say anything.

Frustrated, Eddie gave a little shake of his head. "How's your foot? I saw you fall."

"It's sore, but it'll be okay."

He bent over, offering me his hands. "Come on, I'll help you up."

I reached, and there was strength in his grasp. He helped me to my feet. We stood there, his eyes watchful and cautious, mine shyly taking him in, his hair mostly white from snow. He was a good six inches taller than I. Even in his long coat, he appeared lithe

and trim like an athlete. I was impressed by his intelli-
gent eyes, his powerful gaze, his determined jaw and
his muscular neck.

"You need a hat," I said.

"Does that mean you like me? You care about me?"

I grinned, not answering.

He grinned. "I never wear a hat. It's not my style.
So, back to basics. Where's your house? Why are you
with Marilyn and what's going on?"

"I don't know!" I blurted out, sharply. "I don't
know anything right now, okay? Stop it with the fifty
questions. I don't know. Why aren't *you* out with your
girlfriend or something?"

Surprised by my sudden emotion, he took a moment
to pocket his hands and gather himself. "We broke up a
couple of days ago. She doesn't like star gazing. She
thinks the moon is boring. She says 'It's up in the sky.
I can see it whenever I want.' She likes hanging out
with her silly girlfriends who spend all day blabbing
about makeup and hairdos, and swoon over Eddie Fisher."

I perked up. "Eddie Fisher? Oh, you mean Carrie
Fisher's father?"

Eddie screwed up his eyes in confusion. "There you
go, off to the land of Oz or something. Who is Carrie
Fisher?"

"Carrie…" I said, then stopped, time and place returning. Carrie Fisher probably hadn't been born. "Oh,
never mind."

"Okay, so forget the whole thing," Eddie said, irritated again. "Do you know what? I don't want to
know what's going on anymore. I don't give a damn,
all right?"

I turned defensive. "Yeah, sure. Fine. All right. Forget it."

Eddie huffed out a breath and worked on a change of mood. "I don't know about you, Darla. You make me mad and you make me want to do something like, I don't know, kiss you."

That stopped me and stunned me. Kiss me? We'd just met. I didn't like it at first, and then I did like it. I liked it very much. I was so off-balance and confused I didn't know anything, except, I *wanted* him to kiss me.

He didn't move or make a motion to kiss me. Instead, he pointed down at my foot.

"So how's your foot now?"

Sonny snuggled next to my leg, his eyes on me, making whimpering sounds. I thought, *Eddie, why don't you kiss me?* Instead, I said, "I'm okay."

"Are you going to stay with Marilyn Monroe?"

The question stunned me into sudden excitement. That's right, I was with Marilyn Monroe! *The* Marilyn Monroe. If this was 1954, and it sure seemed like it was, then fine! I'd get into it and have the adventure of a lifetime.

When I'd left my house those long hours ago, I had prayed for an adventure. Okay, so my prayer had been answered. How? Who knew? Why? Who cared? I was here. Now. I had time traveled back to 1954 and I had met Marilyn Monroe. I was actually *with* Marilyn Monroe. I was living my sweet Mother's longed-for fantastic dream, and in honor of my dear, loving and sensitive mother, I would take full advantage of it.

I glanced down at my camera case. I could document every amazing event. My head boiled with possibility: the people I would meet, the places I would go and the photographs I would take.

Eddie breathed out a jet of vapor and startled me from my daydream.

"Okay, so maybe I could come by and we could go out for a movie or something? Maybe we could just look at the stars through my telescope? You don't seem bored by the night sky. You seem to love it as much as I do."

How crazy was this? I thought. I'd just time traveled to 1954 and I'd already been asked out on a date, and I was staying with Marilyn Monroe. I didn't care if the entire world had flipped out. I was going to make the most of this dizzying, surreal adventure.

"Hey, who knows?"

I saw disappointment in his face, so I added, "Well, yeah, maybe."

He was still trying to figure me out. Eddie had keen, smart eyes and a listener's attention. "Okay, Darla. So maybe I'll come by soon."

I lowered my gaze, pleased and still wanting that kiss. "Okay... So come by."

Then Eddie surprised me. "Well, I'm going to leave now. I'm not sure what I'd do if I saw Marilyn Monroe in the flesh. I'd probably faint or something."

"Darla!" Marilyn called, a silhouette looming out of the darkness toward the light.

"Goodbye, Darla," Eddie said, quickly. "I'll see you around."

And then he was gone, sprinting off in the opposite direction to Marilyn. He ran with surprising speed up a slope and disappeared into the darkness of trees.

Sonny barked after him while I pondered, staring into the darkness. If I returned to the woods, would I stumble upon the same time portal that had magically dropped me in 1954? And if I did find it, would I return to the exact moment in 1998 from which I'd left?

I turned away. I didn't want to find it. I didn't want to go back to 1998. Maybe I never would. Why would I go back? There was nothing to go back to.

Marilyn came toward me. "You found him! Sonny!" she said brightly, her face a sunburst of joy.

She crouched, rubbing his ears, nosing into him. "Oh, your ears are so cold, Sonny. Let's get out of here and back to the house."

Rising to her feet, she noticed the camera case swung over my shoulder.

"Where did that come from?"

I stammered. "Oh... It was... you know." I pointed. "It was over there where I fell. Thank God it's okay."

Marilyn accepted my lie and we were soon on our way.

As we drove the quiet, dark road, I thought of my father's sad face and the birthday surprise he'd planned for me. Yes, I missed him, but I pushed the image of him from my mind, feeling like a bird who'd flown from a cage.

Dad wouldn't miss me because he'd only recently been born, in May of this year, 1954. He was just a baby. Mom wouldn't be born until 1955. How could I be missed if I'd never been born? The thought chilled me a little.

If I wasn't born yet, in 1982, then who was I? The Darla I had been was no longer me. That Darla didn't exist.

I didn't dwell on it. I glanced over at Marilyn and smiled, ready for whatever this wild adventure would bring me.

CHAPTER 10

In the large, rustic kitchen, Marilyn opened a can of
Campbell's tomato soup, prepared grilled cheese sandwiches and poured each of us a coupe glass of champagne. I was thrilled that she didn't care if I was only
sixteen.

As she poured my glass full, she said, "I have to
quote Coco Chanel at times like this, 'I only drink
champagne on two occasions. When I'm in love and
when I'm not.'"

With a naughty laugh, she lifted her glass, and we
chimed a toast.

Marilyn's hosts had a dog they'd taken with them, so
fortunately there was dog food in the house for Sonny.
Marilyn slipped into the walk-in pantry, found a can
and opened it with one of those old manual can open-
ers. While she spooned the food into a plastic red dog
dish, Sonny looked on, tail swishing, eyes bright. Marilyn lowered to her haunches, watching in pleasure as
Sonny chomped away.

"I'm so happy tonight, Darla," Marilyn said, rising
to her feet. "I'm so happy you're here and that you
found Sonny. What a wonderful Christmas present."

As we ate our dinner, Marilyn was full of plans and excitement.

"Tomorrow I'll take you to see Dr. Ellen Miles and she'll make sure your ankle is okay. Maybe she'll have some crutches for you."

"I don't need them. I can manage. The sprain isn't that bad."

"Whatever you think, Darla. I'll leave it up to you. After we see Dr. Miles, we'll buy a Christmas tree, some groceries and..." Marilyn glanced up, mid-thought. "Darla, you don't have any extra clothes, do you?"

I shook my head, stirring my bowl of tomato soup.

Marilyn sat back, worried, a hand touching her neck. "Honey, are the police looking for you?"

"No... Not at all," I said, quickly. "No. Nobody's looking for me."

"You do have family, don't you?"

I didn't know what to say. "Right now, I don't have anyone. That's why I left."

"Left where?"

I decided to lie. "An orphanage."

Marilyn teared up. "Oh... God, honey."

She pushed her chair back, got up and came to me, offering a hug and a kiss on my cheek. "So you ran away from there?"

I continued the lie. "Yes... and I don't want to go back."

Marilyn hugged me again. "No, honey. Don't go back. Don't ever go back." She paused, considering her words. "Are both of your parents dead?"

What could I say? I'd have to lie. "Yes..."

Another hug. I decided to use what I knew to deflect from my story. "You know what orphanages are like, don't you, Marilyn?"

Marilyn straightened, her face turning sad, her eyes downcast as the dark cloud of memory changed her from a pretty woman to a shy girl. She wandered back to her chair, but she didn't sit. She stood behind it, staring into the middle distance, remembering.

"Yes... I know. I was born on June 1, 1926, in the charity ward of the Los Angeles General Hospital. That has always bothered me. It shouldn't, but it does. It was like I didn't have a home when I came into this world. It's not right that a baby is born into this world without a home."

"Didn't your mother get sick?" I asked, watching Sonny trot over and lie at my feet, warm and contented.

"Yes... Yes. When I was eight, she had a nervous breakdown and was committed to an asylum. I was sent to live with my mother's best friend, Aunt Grace. She was good to me, but when she lost her job with Columbia Pictures in 1935, she was forced to take me to the Los Angeles Orphans Home Society."

"How old were you?"

"Let's see... I think I was nine years old."

"How long were you there?"

"On and off, about a year and a half. We called it 'The Home'. The ladies that took care of us were kind, but I couldn't help feeling abandoned and lost."

A little smile formed, and she went into a private silence. When she spoke, her voice was dreamy, just above a whisper. "And do you know what, Darla? That orphanage was only seven blocks away from Tom Kelley's Photography Studio."

She paused, and I waited, rapt, our soup getting cold.

Marilyn lowered her eyes. "Well... you know... Tom Kelley's was where I posed for calendar photos in 1949. When I modeled, I changed my name a lot. I was Jeane Norman for a while and then Mona Monroe."

She giggled. "I was never shy about my body, and I loved looking into cameras. Sometimes I think I'm a better model than actress. I don't know why, but I feel more comfortable doing stills than doing a scene in front of a movie camera."

She sat, scooted her chair toward the table and reached for her soup spoon. She dipped the spoon into the soup but didn't eat, looking instead into the distance beyond me.

"There were twenty-six other girls in that orphanage dormitory, and we went to school at the Vine Street Elementary School, a few blocks away. But what was so magical to me at the time was that I could look out from my dormitory window and see the RKO Studio's water tower. That really excited me."

Her beautiful, sad eyes took me in. "You know what, Darla? I would stare at that water tower and dream of someday becoming a world-famous movie star. Yes, I did, nearly every night."

I thought how incredible that was. How strange and wonderful that little Norma Jeane, born in a charity ward, turned out to be one of the most renowned movie stars of all time. Had it been fate—written into the script of the world?

Marilyn absently dipped her spoon again and held it up, still wandering in the past.

"Darla... as I looked out into the Hollywood night at that RKO Studio's water tower, I thought, there must be thousands of girls sitting alone like me, dreaming of becoming movie stars. But I said to myself, I'm not going to worry about them. I'm dreaming the hardest."

"And you became one," I said. "You're like the biggest movie star in the world."

Marilyn finally swallowed some soup and didn't seem to notice it was cold.

"You know what, honey? Do you know what I have found out? That dreaming about being an actress is more exciting than being one."

We ate for a time in silence, while Sonny slept below me, and the aspirin finally helped ease my ankle pain. When Marilyn looked at me, her eyes held questions.

"Darla, you'll have to go to school. You'll have to finish high school."

I bit into my grilled cheese sandwich, pulling the bread away, stretching the cheese. I chewed, wrapping the hanging cheese strings with my finger.

"But I don't need to think about school until after the new year," I said. "I'll figure it all out then."

Marilyn nodded, laying her spoon aside. "What about you, Darla? What were your parents like? What do you want to do with your life?"

I shrugged. "My mother wanted to be an actress. You were her idol."

Marilyn's eyes were warm. "How sweet. I wish I could have met her. I'm sure we would have become best friends. What about your father?"

"He was a good dad, but he drank too much, and he and my stepmother were always fighting. They should have gotten a divorce. It would have been better for everyone."

Anticipating Marilyn's next question, I had already composed a third act in my head, finishing my parents off with a dramatic flourish so there wouldn't be the need for further explanation. "But then... well, they were killed in a train wreck out west."

Marilyn's eyes held tears.

I despised lying, but my choices were limited.

"I'm so sorry, Darla. I guess neither one of us has had a happy childhood. And about your parents fighting, well, a marriage is a hard thing to make work."

The mood had turned gloomy, and I wanted to lift it. "But marriage can be a good thing sometimes, can't it?"

Marilyn's smile transformed her face for just a minute, and then it faded. She gave a little shake of her head. "Well, I'm sure you know that me and Joe... Joe DiMaggio and I are separated and we're getting a divorce. And do you know what, Darla? I told myself that I'd make that marriage stick no matter what I had to do. I said to myself over and over, that since I had to divorce Jimmie, I was never going to let that happen again. And I love Joe... And he loves me."

Marilyn picked up her spoon and dipped it into the soup, but then left it there, gazing into it. "So you say to yourself, what happened? How can you be in love with someone and then you wind up unhappy and apart? And then I can't sleep because I keep thinking about it. What happened, Darla?"

Of course, I knew what happened. Marilyn and Joe had marital problems right from the start. Most of the fan magazines blamed it on Joe and his jealousy. He was a retired baseball player who had lost some of his shine, and Marilyn was the most famous and the most beloved woman on the planet, who glittered like diamonds. People wanted to be around Marilyn; they wanted to know about Marilyn; they were crazy over Marilyn and not so interested in Joe.

Marilyn folded her arms, her eyes moving. "Do you know what? As soon as *There's No Business Like Show Business* wrapped, I didn't take a break. I should have spent some time with Joe, but I didn't."

"You made *The Seven Year Itch* right away," I said.

Marilyn glanced up. "Yeah, I did. And that's when our nine-month-old marriage got all busted up."

"I love that movie," I said.

Marilyn shot me a questioning look, blinking. "But, Darla, honey, we only wrapped that movie in November. It won't be released until sometime next year. How could you have seen it?"

I dropped my chin, going into recovery mode. "Well, what I mean is… I mean, I've read about it so much in the movie magazines that I feel like I've seen it."

Marilyn accepted that. "Oh, well… Of course Joe got all upset about that scene where I'm standing over a subway grate and my dress blows up around my legs. Back in our hotel room, he got physical with me. That's when I decided to file for a divorce."

Marilyn took a long sip of champagne. "And you know the funny thing about that, Darla? We shot that scene in Manhattan on Lexington Avenue at 52nd Street, but because the crowds were so loud, the director, Billy Wilder, couldn't get a good take. So guess what happened? The original footage isn't even going to be used. Wilder re-staged the scene back in a Hollywood studio and he said the scene is better. So go figure. Joe and I are busted up because of a scene that could have been shot in a studio."

I was chewing a piece of the grilled cheese sandwich, seeing a faraway look in Marilyn's eyes. I wanted to say something clever or funny to break the serious mood, but I couldn't think of anything.

I had read a lot about *The Seven Year Itch*. I knew that Marilyn's bouts with lifelong depression and self-destruction had taken their toll during the filming of that movie. She frequently spoiled scenes, forgetting her lines. Sometimes they had to shoot as many as forty takes before a scene was completed.

Marilyn was also late every day, something that drove Billy Wilder crazy. But what Marilyn couldn't know, but I did know, was that she would work with Wilder again on one of her most successful and famous movies, *Some Like It Hot*.

And then Marilyn said something that completely shocked me.

"I'm going to call Joe in a few minutes. Would you like to speak to him?"

I recalled from an old fan magazine that Joe would escort Marilyn to *The Seven Year Itch* premiere in June 1955. They would never completely stop seeing each other, I knew that.

I shook my head. "I don't think so."

Marilyn seemed disappointed. "Don't you like baseball, Darla?"

"No, not much."

Marilyn laughed. "I don't know a baseball from a football, but I love Joe. I know you must think I'm crazy, like everybody else, but I know I can count on him, and I need somebody to count on. We all need some-body to count on, don't we?"

"Yeah... Yeah, I guess we do."

Marilyn propped her chin in the palm of her left hand. "Do you have anyone you can count on, Darla?"

The question caught me off-guard. "I don't know..."

Marilyn brightened, lifting her head from her hand. "Well, you can count on me then, honey. I'll be here for you."

It was music to my young, teenage ears.

"So what do you want to do with your life, Darla?"

"I want to be a photojournalist. I want to travel eve-rywhere and take pictures of people and places and events. And I want to tell stories—true and gripping stories. And then I want to write books about all my experiences and fill them with all the photos I've taken. Maybe I'll even make documentaries."

Marilyn's soft eyes came to mine. "I think that's wonderful and exciting. I think you'll be a great jour-nalist and photographer. I feel it. I feel something spe-cial about you, Darla. I feel as though you're smart and wise."

I lowered my meek eyes. "Not so wise... Maybe a little smart sometimes, in English class, and history class and photography."

Marilyn boosted herself up, a decision made. "Okay, that settles it then. You'll stay here with me, and we'll shop, and have your hair done, and we'll cook, and maybe we'll even go into New York and have some fun. How does that sound?"

I felt the sudden burn of excitement. I wanted to see what New York was like in 1954. "I'll take my camera," I said, suddenly feeling buzzed by the champagne.

"Of course bring your camera, Darla. Of course. You can take all the photos you want."

"Can I take some of you?"

Marilyn laughed. "Darla, you know how much I love cameras. The man who lives here, Milton Greene, takes lots of photos of me. Of course you can take photos of me."

After dinner, we were both tired. Marilyn led me into her bedroom, handed me an unused toothbrush from her travel bag, as well as a nightgown and a pair of new silk panties. I took them shyly, but Marilyn didn't seem the least bit uncomfortable.

She escorted me to a rear guest bedroom, pausing to retrieve a towel and washcloth from the corner closet.

My bedroom was large, with a rose theme, a double bed and a spacious bathroom. Marilyn fixed me with a stare as we stood in the center of the room.

"Now listen, honey, when you wash your face, you should rinse it about fifteen times, and when you're not wearing makeup, you should apply lanolin or olive oil. It helps to protect your skin. There's some over there in the bathtub rack. Now, do you have everything you need?"

I nodded.

"Okay, Darla. Get some sleep and I'll see you in the morning."

She gave me another little hug. "I'm so glad you're here. We're going to have a lot of fun."

With a peck on the cheek, she left, not closing the door.

I washed in the sink. I couldn't shower because of my wrapped foot. With teeth brushed, hair combed and moisturizer on my face, I returned to the bedroom, overhearing Marilyn in the living room, laughing and talking to Joe DiMaggio.

It truly was a surreal moment. I slipped into Marilyn's soft underwear and silky, peach-colored night gown, and sat down on the edge of the bed, my head whirling with images and ideas. Sonny had made himself at home and was curled up beside the bed in the large blue cotton towel that Marilyn had arranged for him. He was soon asleep.

Exhausted, a little drunk, with a throbbing ankle, I switched off the light and flounced back onto the soft bed. I tried to sleep but couldn't. I was sure I'd awaken in the morning and find myself back in my own bed in that prison of a house.

I awoke late into the night, sat up and glanced about for a clock, finding its green hands illuminated. It was 3:40 a.m. The room was cave dark and the house loud with silence. My attention was drawn to the window. I folded back the quilt and swung my feet to the carpeted floor, careful not to disturb Sonny and his raspy little snore.

How long had I slept? Over four hours. I was still in the house with Marilyn. But I wanted proof. I left the bed, limped to the window and parted the curtains.

A buttery moon and swirling stars filled the sky. Of course, I thought of Eddie.

Yes, I was still in the house with Marilyn Monroe in 1954. What strange magic had brought me here and what was I going to do?

CHAPTER 11

The next morning, I was awake by 8 a.m. I sat up, put feet to the floor and examined my ankle. It was less swollen, but stiff and still sore. At the window, I peered out into the flood of sunlight glistening off the snow. What a glorious winter day.

I took Sonny outside for a few minutes, then busied myself until Marilyn awoke a little after 10. Sonny and I were in the kitchen when she came in, he busy sniffing and exploring new corners, me munching cornflakes at the long, wooden table.

Marilyn entered dressed in a sheer gown, holding a fist to a yawn, her hair askew, her eyes small, struggling to focus. And yet, she was still a beauty; a magnetic vision of a drowsy goddess. Even at my young, naïve and inexperienced age, I wanted to protect her. In that startling instant, I felt the overwhelming desire to save her from all the events that she would experience: another bad marriage, to Arthur Miller; mental illness; too much champagne; too many drugs; addiction; and finally, death, and no one would ever know if it was by suicide or accidental overdose.

Once again, I realized my power. My boundless, unequaled power. I held the knowledge of the future, not only of Norma Jeane's future, but also the future of the entire world. Even if I wasn't the greatest student of history, I knew the basics of coming events: I knew that in 1955, rock-and-roll music would become mainstream, and Elvis Presley would begin his rise to fame.

Men would land on the Moon in 1969. The Vietnam war would be a disaster. Ronald Reagan would become President of the United States. Would anyone listen to me or believe me if I told them not to escalate the Vietnam war? Should I tell people about personal computers and cell phones?

And on a more personal level for Marilyn, I knew that Marilyn would have an affair with President John F. Kennedy, and that he would be assassinated in Dallas in 1963 by Lee Harvey Oswald. Should I tell her, so she could warn him?

Power? Yes, I held great power. I was a wild card. I was a crazy, teenage kid who could change the entire course of history if I wanted to. But did I want to?

Marilyn was watching me. "Are you feeling all right, Darla? You look strange this morning."

I snapped out of my rambling daydreams. "Yes... Yes. I feel fine."

"How is your ankle?"

"Better. Not as sore. It's going to be fine. I don't need to see a doctor."

Marilyn raked a hand through her tousled hair. "I called Dr. Miles just a few minutes ago. Since it's Sunday, she's not in her office, but she said to bring you over anytime today to her house. I think we should go, just to make sure."

Sonny was at her feet, staring up, tongue out, tail wagging. She crouched and pulled him into her arms, hugging him. "Good morning, Sonny boy. You are such a good dog. A sweet dog, aren't you?"

Sonny seemed to be smiling his agreement, but then I'm sure that was just my imagination.

She looked at me with a new pleasure. "I love dogs so much, Darla. I'm so glad you found him." Then she had a thought. "By the way, how did you find him?"

I shrugged. "I don't know. I called, and he came. It was just luck, I guess."

Standing, Marilyn went to the stove and put on a kettle. "Want some tea?"

"Sure."

"I talked to Joe last night. I told him about you."

"Oh, really," I said flatly. I didn't want Joe DiMaggio to come. It would complicate things.

"He's so silly sometimes," Marilyn said. "He's coming to New York, and he wants to come by. I told him to wait until after Christmas, but he said no. So he's coming, I guess. If I'm honest, I want to see him, maybe for just an hour or two, but I don't want things to get all steamed up and angry. And I don't want him demanding I do what he wants. That's what always seems to..." And then her voice ran out.

I stayed quiet.

She turned to me, tilting me a look. "Sometimes I don't really know who I am, Darla. Does that ever happen to you?"

I nodded, feeling the pressure of fate. It was time to own my power. I had to come up with some way to help Marilyn improve her life.

I watched Marilyn standing barefoot, leaning casually against the stove, and I wondered what I could do or say to stop her from taking an overdose of barbiturates in August 1962 at her home in Brentwood, Los Angeles. That was more than eight years away.

I drank tea and Marilyn nibbled on a graham cracker, humming, as she left for her bedroom to dress. A half hour later, she appeared, wearing a flare tan jacket, a man's white shirt, blue jeans and a babushka covering her hair. She wore red lipstick, but no other makeup.

By one-thirty, we were on our way, speeding along a two-lane road, traveling to Dr. Miles' home. Just as we passed an old, rickety-looking store with the sign Weston Market perched on top, Marilyn swerved sharply left into the parking lot.

"I love this little place," she said, slamming on the brakes. "I want to get some smoked salmon and the *New York Times*."

I was excited. I was about to meet people from 1954. We left the car, and I noticed the car next to ours was orange, with a cream-colored top. Marilyn said it was a 1952 Chevrolet. I liked it.

The store could accommodate about six people at a time, including a young, bubble-gum-chewing cashier, and a gray-haired, florid-faced proprietor, who was smoking a cigar.

"Hey, Marilyn," the portly, pudgy-faced proprietor blandly called. Wearing a white apron, he was hunched at the narrow counter, dithering over a crossword puzzle. He was friendly but distracted, as if Marilyn were just an ordinary customer.

But the cashier lit up like a flash bulb when Marilyn tossed her a hello. I was pleased when the cashier passed me an envious glance, as if to say, *"Who are you, a nobody, to be hanging out with Marilyn Monroe?"*

I straightened, proudly erect at 5'9", taller than Marilyn, who was 5'6".

I'd never seen anything like the place—a small mom-and-pop grocery store. It was surrounded by woods, and the dark interior clashed with the dappled sunlight pouring through the slats.

There were mostly liquor bottles on the shelves, and very little food. Marilyn found what she was looking for, paid the giddy cashier and left, with a warm smile and a raised hand. Soon, we were off again, flying along the countryside, Marilyn humming along with the radio.

We followed a narrow, winding road, passing dilapidated barns and colonial houses that dotted the land on either side. Eventually we approached a line of bare maples, white with snow, and a roadside, free-standing, metal post box.

Marilyn turned right into a short driveway that led to an impressive, two-story colonial house, with a trio of dormers and a two-car garage. She parked behind a black and white Cadillac in the circular drive, keyed-off the engine, placed her hands on the top of the steering wheel and glanced over. "Well, Darla, here we are. Let's get your ankle checked out."

"I really am all right."

"I'm responsible for you now, so I insist. Dr. Miles is a good doctor and her husband, Bert, is a dentist. They are both kind and skilled. Ellen has been the family physician for the Greenes, and I saw her once for a bad cold when I was visiting a few months ago. You'll like her."

We left the car and wandered up the stone pathway that led to the oak front door. Before Marilyn could press the doorbell, the door swung open and an older man, with gray, flattop hair, black-framed glasses and lively dark eyes, smiled happily at Marilyn. He held a pipe, wore gray dress pants, a white shirt and a dark blue cardigan sweater. He was *Father Knows Best* incarnate, and thanks to cable, I'd seen many episodes on *The Family Channel*.

"Hello, Marilyn," Bert said, "Ellen said you were coming. How nice to see you again."

Marilyn's eyes sparkled; her smile welcoming. "I'm so glad to see you, Bert," she said, in her small, breathy voice. She kissed him on both cheeks as I stepped to her side.

I studied Marilyn. It was the first time I'd heard that voice—that breathy, wisp of a voice she used in her later movies. She hadn't used the voice with me, the voice she used as part of her "Marilyn act." Her true voice was actually quite resonant and unaffected.

Bert ushered us into the house through a short foyer, which led into a spacious living room with lovely, powder-blue furniture, a deep white carpet and a rustic rock fireplace, the fire low and gleaming.

From the windows, I saw a dormant white bird fountain, a wall of shrubbery that wrapped the front of the house, and distant, sloping hills, white with snow.

After introductions and small talk, a blue-uniformed maid entered, carrying a silver tray with a teapot, cups, saucers, and a rose-patterned plate holding an assortment of cookies.

"Thank you, Gwendolyn," Bert said. Then turning to Marilyn and me, he said, "Gwendolyn bakes the best Christmas cookies I have ever eaten."

Gwendolyn was a sturdy, African-American woman, with a kind face, easy smile and delicate hands that worked with focused care.

She smiled when she saw Marilyn, who stood to greet her.

"You are my favorite actress, Miss Monroe," Gwendolyn said, taking her hand. "Except for Hattie McDaniel. I was so sorry when she passed away."

"She was one of my favorites too," Marilyn said. "Especially in *Gone with the Wind*. We will all miss her. Now, why are you here, working on a Sunday?"

Gwendolyn made a gesture with her hand and uttered a little laugh. "Oh, Dr. Bert did me a favor. My husband was having some friends over after church so I called Dr. Bert and said I was sure he needed more Christmas cookies, and he said yes, to come on over and bake some. So I told my husband and two daughters that they were in charge because I'd been called into work." She laughed again. "I escaped!"

"And tomorrow she can stay home and have the house all to herself," Bert said.

Dr. Ellen Miles soon appeared, a tall, statuesque woman with short, graying hair, a pleasing expression and the soft, pious eyes of a missionary. She wore a white smock, buttoned up the front, and had a stethoscope about her neck.

Her smile to Marilyn was warm, not effusive. "Good to see you again, Marilyn."

Standing, Marilyn held the doctor's hand gently. "Thank you, Dr. Miles, for seeing my friend, Darla, on a Sunday."

Dr. Miles held her smile and placed her hands into her pockets. "I am happy to do so. I trust all is well in Hollywood?"

Marilyn laughed. "Hollywood is doing just fine, and it's a good place to get out of. It's a place where they'll pay you a thousand dollars for a kiss and fifty cents for your soul."

Bert laughed, but I saw the truth of Marilyn's words in her glowing eyes.

After I was introduced, Dr. Miles glanced down at my wrapped ankle. "Well, let us scrutinize your foot, Darla, and see what's going on."

While Marilyn and Bert continued their conversation, Dr. Miles led me down a long, quiet hallway to her home office.

She closed the door behind me and indicated toward a high-back chair that stood before her heavy oak desk. I sat obediently while she lowered into her desk chair, reaching for a leather notebook and a fountain pen. She began to write, so I glanced about, hands folded and moving.

The meticulously clean room looked out on a patio, a blue, tarp-covered swimming pool and manicured gardens, now brown and snowy.

I smelled a cinnamon/rose sweetness in the room and, casting about, I spotted a side table and a lovely ceramic, rose-colored bowl, filled with potpourri.

Wearing one of Marilyn's cream-colored blouses with my jeans and sneakers, I felt confident and poised.

Marilyn had also helped me apply some light makeup and had braided my hair. I felt like a new person.

Dr. Miles straightened, resting her clear eyes on me. "All right, Darla, let us begin. What is your full name?"

"Darla Fiona Gallagher."

"Age?"

"Sixteen."

"Address?"

I hesitated. Dr. Miles' pen waited.

"... Well, I'm kind of away from home right now. I mean, I don't have an address right now."

Dr. Miles lifted her eyes, appraising me. "All right... Where are your parents?"

I squirmed. "... They're both dead."

Dr. Miles thought about that. "When did you and Marilyn first meet?"

I fidgeted. "Oh... just a... well, yesterday. Yes, yesterday. It seems longer."

Dr. Miles did not write that down. She considered, took a breath and laid the pen aside, folding her hands. Her eyes were cool and direct. "How did you sprain your ankle?"

"I was walking my dog and I fell and tumbled down a hill."

"Where?"

"Not too far from here. Maybe two or three miles away."

"Where were you coming from?"

I blinked rapidly, thinking. "Where?"

"Yes. You and your dog must have come from somewhere. A house? An institution?"

I looked away toward the ceramic, rose-colored bowl. I didn't know what to say. "Well, we came from a friend's house... Yes."

"And have you contacted that friend?"

My mouth got sticky. "I thought you were going to look at my ankle. It's sore."

Dr. Miles' lips tightened. "Are you related to Marilyn?"

"No."

"Does Marilyn know your friends?"

"No."

I had to deflect the conversation. I pointed at my left ankle. "I think it's more swollen today. And it's sore. I hope it's not broken." Of course it wasn't broken, but I had to create urgency and stop the probing questions.

Resigned, Dr. Miles retrieved her pen. "All right, Darla. Do you have any allergies?"

"No..."

"Any recent operations?"

"No."

"Are you taking medications?"

"No. Well, just aspirin."

"Were you alone when you fell?"

Again, I hesitated. "... Well, yes."

"Except for your dog?"

I nodded. "Yes. Well, I mean, Sonny had run away."

"Why?"

"I don't know. He was scared, I guess."

"Scared of?"

I swallowed. The woman was making me nervous. "I don't know. Who knows why dogs get scared?"

"Were you in the woods when he ran away?"

"Yes."

"Were you alone in the woods? Was there anyone else around?"

My mind was getting tangled up. "There was a boy there."

Dr. Miles nodded.

She stared. I stared, our eyes level. I looked away. Dr. Miles didn't. I could feel her eyes boring into me.

"Did he scare you? The boy?"

I glanced around, crossing my arms. "Yeah... well... yes."

"Were you there to meet him? Was it a date?"

I jerked her a look. "No... No way. I was just walking Sonny and we..." I stopped, confused. "Sonny ran off down a path and then I followed him. And then I felt this kind of electric shock or something. Then I saw the boy. We talked for a while and then he scared me, and I ran. I fell down a hill and twisted my ankle. That's all I know. Dr. Miles, my ankle really is hurting."

Dr. Miles' eyes opened fully. "Electric shock... In the woods? A path...?"

I nodded. "Yes. I guess it was from a storm or something."

I was getting in way too deep. I'd already said more than I'd wanted to. The woman intimidated me. I felt like a murderer, getting the third degree. "Dr. Miles, my foot really is sore."

Dr. Miles lowered the pen. She folded her hands again and then sat studying them, staring in a kind of motionless trance.

"How did you meet Marilyn?" she asked, not looking at me.

"I fell down the hill onto the road. She was driving by and saw me."

"And all of this happened yesterday?"

"Yes…"

Dr. Miles lowered her eyes and stood, coming around the desk to me. "All right, Darla, let's take a look at your ankle."

Relieved, I relaxed a little while Dr. Miles drew up a chair, sat opposite me and carefully took my foot into her hands. She methodically unwrapped the Ace bandage, her hands warm, her manner gentle.

She didn't look at me as she spoke. "Darla, did your dog, Sonny, discover a new path?"

She must have felt my foot tense up. "A new path?"

"Yes, in the woods. Did he find a path, and did you follow him down that path?"

My eyes twitched uncomfortably. "I don't know. Yeah, maybe. Yeah, I followed him."

She carefully held my ankle in her hand, examining it. "Yes, it is swollen. And you said it is still sore?"

"Yes…"

"Have you been soaking it?"

"Yes, in Epsom salts."

She tenderly worked the ankle to make sure nothing was broken. "All right, Darla, it is just a sprain. There is nothing broken. I'll rewrap it for you. You should use an ice pack or ice slush bath for 15 to 20 minutes, several times a day. Rest it and don't perform any strenuous activities."

"Okay…"

After she'd rewrapped it, she stood up, moved the chair aside and then sat on the edge of her desk, studying me.

"When did your parents die? What year?"

I didn't want to answer. There was a remote strangeness in her eyes, and it scared me.

Dr. Miles left her desk, wandering to the glass patio doors, keeping her back to me.

"Did your mother die first? Your father? Did they die together?"

"It wasn't my idea to come," I said, defensively, trying to evade her questions. "I didn't want to come. Marilyn insisted I come."

Dr. Miles turned to face me. "I'm glad you came, Darla," she said, soothingly.

Something was wrong. I could feel it. There was tension in the air; a kind of rising, sting of heat, and my temples began to throb. Dr. Miles knew something she wasn't telling me. I fidgeted with my jeans and shifted in my chair, trying to get comfortable. Had I said too much? Was I guilty of something?

"Darla, will you do me a favor?"

I hesitated. "Okay... Sure."

"What year were you born?"

My mind locked up. I hadn't calculated that. Hadn't thought of it. Normally, I could have delivered the answer in a flash. It was simple subtraction. But my brain had been scrambled by endless interrogation.

Dr. Miles waited while I labored, feeling the pressure—feeling like a turtle lumbering across a narrow, hot road as a semi approached.

"That's easy," I said, delaying, thinking, fumbling with simple math.

"Was it 1938?" Dr. Miles offered, mildly. "You are sixteen, are you not?"

I jumped on it. "Yes, of course. I was born on December 16, 1938. Yes... I just haven't been thinking so well. My ankle and everything."

"What day was that, Darla? Did anyone ever tell you what day of the week you were born on?"

My breath was uneven, my pulse in my throat. I closed my eyes, as if to shut this woman out, then I cleared my throat. I had no idea, but I decided to blunder ahead with confidence, although my confidence had been deflated by the math debacle.

"It was a... It was a Saturday. Yes, I'm sure of that. My father told me that."

My face grew hot.

Dr. Miles' voice was alarmingly low. Her eyes narrowed. "Darla, there is something about your manner that is... well, just a little different. Your speech... your demeanor. When you were in the woods, when you felt the electrical shock, had the moon pinkened? Was the path lighted by, shall I say, moon petals? Did you feel as though you had passed through something, such as an invisible doorway?"

My pulse jumped; my tongue was thick and unmovable.

Dr. Miles gave me a sharp, searching look.

CHAPTER 12

How did she know? How *could* she know?

Dr. Miles' eyes suggested turmoil or wistful surprise. I wasn't sure. Though I tried to decipher her look, it eluded me.

"Darla, I can see from your expression that you know what I'm talking about."

I felt a jolt to the gut. I let the silence speak, finding no words.

She began with a long, slow breath. "In 2032, my parents and I lived in a lovely home about three miles from here. My father was a doctor and my mother an attorney. It was not a happy home. My parents were not happily married. It was a home I escaped from often by taking long walks in the woods with my dog, Cookie, a Cocker Spaniel. One cold night, in December, it was snowing. Cookie found a path through the woods I'd never found before. I followed. Clumps of clouds fled across the sky and the full moon swam in and out of them, peeking through them now and then, turning from a pure white to a light shade of pink. I chased Cookie, hearing only the sound of his barking. Moments later, I felt it. A stinging shock."

Dr. Miles lifted her eyes toward the ceiling. "Well, Darla, you can guess the rest, I'm sure. I'm sure you know what happened immediately thereafter."

Dr. Miles' eyes traveled down to meet mine. I sat rigid; eyes moving; then searching her face.

"Do you mean…?" I stopped, struggling to take it in. "Then you…"

"Yes, Darla. Yes. I entered the past. I time traveled."

In that icy silence, I pondered. "What year?" I asked. "I mean, what year was it?"

"It was 1930, and I was sixteen years old."

I let that settle, but it didn't settle. Her words bounced around in my head like a pinball.

Dr. Miles continued. "As you can imagine, I was scared, lost and confused. Luckily, an elderly couple who lived in an old, shabby house, about two miles from here, took me in. To make a long story short, after the depression of the 1930s, I was able to attend medical school, not an easy thing to do in those days. There weren't many women doctors. But I had knowledge that the men and the instructors didn't have. I had learned much from my father in 2032 and, of course, I had had the internet, where a lot of medical knowledge was available. Still, it was a hard road, but I never gave up. Finally, I became a doctor."

I managed to swallow away a lump. "Did you ever want to go back? Did you try to go back to your time?"

Dr. Miles smiled reflectively. "Yes… I tried several times, but I never found the doorway, so to speak. I never did find my way back home and, finally, I gave up."

With a look and a gesture, she said, "So I made a good life for myself here. I married a good man and we have a wonderful daughter and son, and none of them—not one of them—knows what I have told you."

I sat like a cold, marble statue, stunned to my core.

"What time are you from, Darla?"

"1998."

"So it's true then? You came from the future?"

I nodded.

Dr. Miles seemed amused. "And by caprice or luck, or by something neither of us understands, you were found by Marilyn Monroe. How fun and fortunate for you."

I looked up. "But you know… Well, you know the future. You know more about the future than I do."

She nodded.

"Do you ever try to change things? Have you ever tried to change the world?"

Slowly, sternly, she shook her head. "No… Never. Oh, I'm sure I've changed things, inadvertently, in small ways, just by being here… or maybe in not so small ways, but I don't know for sure because the future is always unraveling, isn't it? Will it be the same future you and I know?"

Dr. Miles shrugged. "Who knows? And, I've given birth to two children who have grown up and have lives of their own. Surely they will change things. Who knows what those things will be? But, sometimes I think…"

She let the words go, and the room fell silent while she contemplated. "In any time or place, life is a mystery, isn't it, Darla? Where do we come from? Why are we here, and where do we go when we die? Those remain mysterious, so perhaps I have added a little more spice to the bubbling cauldron of human mystery and history. And, now, perhaps, you will do the same."

When I spoke, my voice sounded strange and faraway. "But... well, what if I want to go back?"

"Do you... want to go back?"

"My father..." I said, the remaining words falling away.

"Do you love him?"

"Yes... but."

I placed my forehead against my knees. "I'm so confused and so weirded out."

A minute later, Dr. Miles' hand gently stroked my head. "I know, Darla. I know. You're going to have to give it time. Once your ankle is healed, who knows, maybe you'll return to the woods and find it. That doorway. Who's to say?"

I lifted my head. "What is it? What is that doorway?"

"I don't know. As I said, I have never, ever discussed this with anyone else before."

"Do you think we're the only two people who have ever experienced this?"

She shrugged. "I just don't know. Perhaps there are others roaming around out there, but I don't know."

We sat in a bizarre, uncertain quiet.

"Are you all right? Can I get you something?" Dr. Miles asked.

"No, I don't think so. What am I going to do?"

"Well, Darla, my dear, as I used to counsel my daughter when she had to make a difficult decision... I'd say, think of it as a unique adventure, never before taken by anyone else in the history of the world. Take a few cautious steps ahead, explore, experiment and then see what happens."

I stared into her kind face. "Thank you. If I need you, can I call or come by?"

"Of course, Darla, but please remember, do not mention any of this to anyone. It must remain a secret between the two of us. Agreed?"

"Yeah... sure. Who would believe me anyway?"

Standing by the door, with fingers gripped around the doorknob, I had a thought. I didn't turn around. "Dr. Miles, when you searched for the doorway, was Cookie with you? Was your dog with you?"

Dr. Miles' voice was muted. "No... Unfortunately, Cookie died soon after I arrived in 1930. He was an old dog, a sweet animal. I missed him terribly and felt so lost and alone without him. And then I tried so hard to find that doorway back home, but I never did. Good luck, Darla."

When I limped into the living room with Dr. Miles at my side, Marilyn and Bert stood up.

"Well, will you be dancing again soon, Darla?" Bert asked.

I smiled demurely.

"It's just a sprain," Dr. Miles said, softly. "Darla will be fine in a few days."

"Thank you, both," Marilyn said, giving them each a quick hug.

"Yes, thank you," I added, following her toward the foyer.

As we approached the front door, I turned. Dr. Miles was waving. "Merry Christmas you two," she said. "Come back anytime," she added. And then she gave me a quick, knowing wink.

As Marilyn drove back to the house, I was quiet, my thoughts grazing the fields of possibility.

"Is everything all right, honey?" Marilyn asked, glancing over.

"Yeah. Okay. Good. I like Dr. Miles. She's nice. Thanks for taking me."

Marilyn slowed down, rounding a curve in the road with easy skill. "Of course. Now we can both relax and enjoy the holidays."

She drove slowly for a while, and then thoughts seemed to race past her eyes, and she had a swift change of mood. She swung the car out into the left lane, gunned the engine and passed a slower car.

As she whipped the car back into the right lane, she sighed audibly, shaking her head. "Joe's coming for a visit for sure. I talked to him this morning. I told him not to come, but he never listens to anybody once his mind is made up. Certainly he doesn't listen to me. But you'll like him, Darla, I just know it."

I stared out the window, still shaken by my conversation with Dr. Miles. The last person I wanted to face was Joe DiMaggio.

Marilyn grew animated. "Look, we need some cheering up. I say we go back to the house and have brunch. We'll whip up some scrambled eggs with the smoked salmon, and then we'll open a bottle of champagne. How does that sound?"

My smile was my answer.

"Good. Then, after brunch, we'll just be lazy for the rest of the day. You need to rest your ankle and I'll make some phone calls."

"Sounds great." I especially wanted to rest and have time to think about everything Dr. Miles had said.

"Have you done any Christmas shopping, Darla?"

"No..."

"Okay, then, tomorrow, we'll drive into Bridgeport to Read's Department Store and buy you some clothes and do some Christmas shopping. Then we'll drive back to Weston and go to a drugstore where we can buy cosmetics and other female necessities, and then we'll have dinner at a little restaurant right next door to the drugstore. They serve meatloaf, peas and carrots, and mashed potatoes, with a lot of thick gravy. Won't that be fun?"

"I don't have any money, Marilyn."

Marilyn laughed extravagantly. "Oh, honey, don't you worry about money. Norma Jeane has plenty of money and she loves to spend it. Now, let's sing a Christmas Carol to cheer us both up. Which ones do you know?"

I scratched my head, thinking. "I know *Rudolph the Red-Nosed Reindeer.*"

Marilyn laughed, a great happy sound that pleased me and helped me forget the strangeness of the day.

She started the song and I jumped in, stumbling over the words and missing notes, but we sang at the top of our voices and laughed, while Marilyn drove as if she were racing; as if time were running out, and she wanted to live life to the fullest and enjoy every single moment.

CHAPTER 13

After brunch, I was a little high from the one glass of champagne Marilyn had allowed me. We were in the kitchen and Marilyn was dreamy and talkative. She insisted I sit with an ice pack around my foot, as Dr. Miles had suggested. Meanwhile, she started making turkey stuffing. She put on a record of her favorite song, Judy Garland singing *Who Cares,* and cranked up the volume. Since I'd never heard the song before, I listened closely to the lyrics.

> *Who cares if the sky cares*
> *To fall in the sea?*
> *Who cares what banks fail in Yonkers,*
> *Long as you've got a kiss that conquers?*
> *Why should I care?*

While the song repeated, I dozed off and the ice pack melted and slipped from my foot. Marilyn hummed and cooked, and I hobbled off to my bedroom and flopped down on the bed, soon falling into a deep sleep, with Sonny curled beside me.

I slept like a rock, awakening to wonderful aromas that lifted my nose. I swung out of bed and went to my door, opening it a tad, enough to overhear some of Marilyn's conversation with Joe. She was emotional, her voice louder than normal.

"No, Joe. I'm not going back to California for a while. I don't think… Not now. I'm not going back to San Francisco after Christmas. You know what happened. You know how we are when we're together. You know what happened to us during *The Seven Year Itch*. You know how crazy you got. Joe… listen to me. Just listen for a minute. All your passion turned into obsession and jealousy. I'm not going back to that. All we do is argue and shout. That's why we busted up and why I filed for divorce in October. I need rest now. I need time to think about things. No… No, Joe, not now. Maybe later. Joe… why did you come to New York? No… Joe… You don't need to come here."

Ashamed for intruding on Marilyn's privacy, I closed the door.

In bed, Sonny seemed dead to the world. I'd never seen him sleep so much and so deeply. Maybe the time travel had worn him out. I rested my head back onto the pillow and closed my eyes.

In the safety of my own thoughts, I pondered my predicament, still overwhelmed by it all. Maybe Dr. Miles was wrong. What happened to her might not happen to me. Maybe I'd wake up soon in my own room, in that quarreling house, wishing I were somewhere else.

My mind spun out fantasies, as if I needed more. Maybe I'd wake up in a hospital bed, and a young, kind doctor, like *Doogie Howser M.D.*, would study me lying there and say, "Hey kid, you fell down a hillside looking for your dog and you hit your head. But don't worry, you're going to be okay."

I'd tell him my crazy dream about Marilyn Monroe and we'd both laugh and flirt, and he'd write down my phone number.

Dad and Carol would be there, she sullen, and he all smiles, holding a beautiful bouquet of lilacs, because he knows lilacs are my favorite flower.

Maybe he'd hand me a beautifully wrapped Christmas box filled with the new videos I'd requested for Christmas, mostly Marilyn Monroe movies that many people aren't even aware of. *Ladies of the Chorus* was a 1948 movie that featured Marilyn in her first major role. *Clash by Night,* a 1952 movie with Barbara Stanwyck, featured Marilyn as a tomboy fish cannery worker, who wore jeans and a bikini top and drank a beer.

A movie I'd seen on the late show and fallen in love with was a 1952 movie entitled *Don't Bother to Knock.* It was Marilyn's first co-starring headliner role, and she played a young, mentally deranged woman. I thought she was brilliant in it, but there was one scene that terrified me. The character ties a little girl up and gags her so she won't interrupt her flirtation with the actor Richard Widmark.

I'd found some promo for *Don't Bother to Knock* in an old movie magazine, along with the written voiceover lines from the movie trailer, dramatically spoken by Richard Widmark. It was over-the-top, and I'd laughed out loud.

"The screen has never shown this kind of woman before. The kind that reaches out into the loneliness of the night to a stranger passing by. But I should have seen the warning of danger in her eyes. She's silk on one side and sandpaper on the other."

These were movies Marilyn made before she took on the persona of "Marilyn Monroe" and, in many ways, I loved those movies more than her more celebrated ones.

A light knock on the door shook me from my thoughts. I lifted up, eyes open.

"Darla… Darla, are you okay?"

"Yes… I'm fine."

"Are you hungry? It's already after seven."

Oddly enough, I was hungry, even though I had eaten a hefty brunch.

"I'll be right out," I said.

Marilyn was at the kitchen stove, barefoot, dressed in jeans rolled up to her ankles and wearing a red and white polka dot top. She was all smiles when she saw me enter.

"You look so much better, honey," she said, her eyes twinkling.

"I didn't know you could cook like this," I said.

"Oh yes, I love to cook. Can you smell the turkey?"

"Yeah, from my bedroom."

"It's only 12 pounds. I put it in the oven while I was on the phone, and I made my own stuffing," she said, reaching for her coupe glass of champagne and stealing a sip. "I hope you like it. I told the Greenes they'd have lots for leftovers. Would you like to peel some potatoes?"

"Yeah, sure."

"And take out some carrots. I love raw carrots. I usually eat four or five raw carrots with my meal. I must be part rabbit; I never get bored with raw carrots."

We worked side by side, each munching a raw carrot, listening to the radio play Christmas music. We laughed a lot, mostly at nothing, but it was natural and joyful—the sound of carrot crunching; Sonny barking for snacks; Marilyn dancing about in a tight red apron and me, doing an impression of Bette Davis, with bug-eyes and my half-eaten carrot dangling from my mouth like a cigarette.

I finished the impression with an expression of volatility and danger, shooting off a line from the 1950 movie *All About Eve*. "We're all busy little bees, full of stings, making honey day and night. Aren't we, honey?"

Marilyn shattered into laughter and said I was perfection.

And, as the kitchen filled with heavenly aromas and the stove warmed the room, we sang along with the radio. Happiness blossomed. I relaxed into safe contentment for the first time since I was a nine-year-old, baking Christmas cookies with my mother.

"So what do you put in your stuffing?" I asked. "It smells so good."

"Well, it's kind of different, Darla, because being married to Joe, I picked up some Italian flavors. So besides all the other stuff, I use raisins, pine nuts, turkey livers, hard-boiled eggs and a hefty amount of Parmesan cheese and oregano. Oh, and it's made with sourdough bread."

"I'm excited to taste it," I said.

Then out of the blue, Marilyn turned to me, lifting her greasy hands in the air, her expression tender. She moved toward me, wrapped me with her arms and hugged me, careful not to touch me with her greasy hands. "I'm so glad you're here, Darla. I'm so glad you ran away from that orphanage and that we're going to spend Christmas together."

I stared into her gorgeous blue eyes and could only squeeze out a tiny, emotional, "Me too."

When we went back to work, I felt giddy and high, and I hadn't touched any champagne. Marilyn was nothing like I'd thought she'd be. She was warm and gentle, moody yet fun, smart and creative; both woman and girl. I was literally breathless with happiness. In that shining moment, I began to think of her as my older sister.

An hour later, we ate voraciously, the turkey tender and juicy. The stuffing was the best I'd ever eaten, the canned peas and mashed potatoes and raw carrots delicious, and the champagne alive with bubbles. I was sure I was the happiest girl who had ever lived.

While we were spooning in mouthfuls of chocolate ice cream, Marilyn giggled. "I know I'm going to gain weight over Christmas, but I don't care. I'll lose it in January before I begin acting classes with Lee Strasberg. Do you know who Elia Kazan is, the movie director?"

I knew he directed one of my favorite movies, *On the Waterfront.* "Yeah, I know who he is."

Marilyn smiled. "He said I should study acting with Lee, so I thought, why not?"

"Why take acting classes?" I asked, not knowing much about this part of Marilyn's life. "You're already a great actress."

In her resonant voice, she said, "Oh, honey, you are so sweet, but all Fox wants me to do is just wiggle, not act. I want to be a true actress and not some dumb blonde movie star. Being a sex symbol is a heavy load to carry, Darla, especially when I'm tired, hurt and bewildered."

And then the words left my mouth before I could stop them. It was another stupid mistake.

"But you were so good in *The Misfits*."

Of course, Marilyn didn't make that movie until 1960, and it wasn't released until 1961.

She stared at me strangely again, her soft eyes clearing, almost as if she were waking up.

"*The Misfits*? I didn't make that movie, Darla. I've never even heard of it."

I quickly recovered, with a squirm and an awkward shrug of a shoulder. "Oh, right. Yes... Yes, well, I'm all mixed up. Not the *Misfits*, I mean *Niagara*."

Marilyn laughed a little. "It sounds like the kind of movie I might do, because so many times that's the way I feel... like a misfit."

And then she grew quiet, and in that brief intimate moment, I wanted to do what so many other people had wanted to do—I wanted to save her from taking her own life on August 5, 1962.

An inner excitement began to blossom. Again, I wondered. Could I save her? Was there something I could do or say that would change her mind; change the course of her life and save her from an early death, only eight years away?

While Marilyn savored the last of the ice cream, I screwed up my courage in preparation for a declaration of the truth. I would tell Marilyn everything. The whole truth and nothing but the truth. I would tell her I had time traveled and how it had all happened. Why not? It might jar her. Shake her. Change her.

Who wouldn't be shaken and changed by the truth of time traveling? I could divulge the future and reveal the movies she would make. I'd detail her failed marriage to Arthur Miller and why she should avoid it. I'd even describe her relationship with President Kennedy. And then after she recovered from all that, I'd pop the big one.

Don't take so many pills and drink so much, I'd say. *All that stuff will kill you.*

I'd conclude with, *Marilyn, you will be one of the most popular and recognized people in the entire world, even in 1998.*

Surely, all that knowledge would shock her into altering her behavior and prevent her from killing herself. And, best of all, when I returned to my own time, how electrifying it would be to learn that Marilyn had survived and had lived a good, long and happy life—a life she attributed to me, Darla Gallagher.

When I returned home, I would contact Marilyn, and, of course, she'd remember me and celebrate me. Marilyn would be 72 years old in 1998.

My over-active teenage mind was dangerously alive and sprinting out of control like a stampeding herd of buffalo. Lost in one fantasy world, I was churning out another, like some mad scientist in a basement laboratory.

"What are you thinking about, Darla?" Marilyn asked, studying me curiously. "Sometimes you seem a million miles away."

I'd been staring off into space and my ice cream had melted into a soft mound, with a chocolate lake surrounding it.

I snapped awake, back to the glorious world where *the* Marilyn Monroe was gazing at me, her pretty smile transforming her face into that of a woman of incomparable beauty and innocence. I didn't know which dream was best, the one in my head that was yet to be, or the one sitting across from me.

In that instant, I was certain of it: I was going to save Marilyn Monroe's life, and I had the power to do it.

"Darla, you are in some other world, I think. Share it with me."

In my mind, I thought. *Why not? This is the time to tell her everything. This is the moment when Marilyn and the entire world are about to change forever.*

I swallowed some water, working to corral my stampeding thoughts. Marilyn leaned back in her chair, waiting, the hint of a girlish smile on her lips.

"Marilyn… I want to tell you something. Something that's going to sound a little crazy. Something that is really going to blow your mind."

"I like crazy, Darla. I live with crazy all the time," she said, with a little laugh. "Go ahead."

I inhaled a breath and blew it out. "Okay…"

The phone ringing in the living room shattered the moment. Marilyn turned her head toward it, made a face of annoyance, and pushed up.

"Hold that thought, Darla, I'll be right back."

CHAPTER 14

I sat waiting at the kitchen table until I realized that Marilyn was going to be on the phone for a long time. As I cleaned the table and washed the dishes, I began to think twice about telling Marilyn the truth. What if she thought I was crazy like my mother, and like her mother? What if she stole off to some private room and called the police? I had no identification and no friends or family, at least none who'd know me, because my father was born in May 1954 and my mother in March 1955. So I'd have to contact Grandpa Mike, who was a career Army officer, a very practical and no-nonsense guy, who would never believe me if I told him I was his granddaughter from 1998. He would swiftly have me tossed into an insane asylum.

No, of course I couldn't take a chance and tell Marilyn the truth. I'd have to warn her another way. To save Marilyn's life, maybe I could gently nudge her off into another direction. But what direction? By the time I'd finished the cleanup, I'd convinced myself that the time travel story was a bad idea.

When Marilyn finally returned to the kitchen, she was dispirited and low.

"Is everything all right?" I asked, wiping my hands on a blue dish towel.

"You didn't have to clean up, Darla. I was going to do it. You're my guest."

"My mother used to say, 'Guests are pests, if all they do is rest.'"

That brought a smile. "I would have liked your mother. I just know it. She would be so proud of you, Darla. You are a very special young woman. I feel it, and I feel things very deeply."

I lowered my eyes, pleased and touched. "What is your mother like?"

With a little shake of her head, Marilyn eased down onto a chair. "My mother is not so well. She struggles in her mind. When she was just seven years old, her father died in the California State Hospital for the mentally ill. But she's a good mother, really."

I had never read about that anywhere. I stared, waiting for more, and Marilyn didn't meet my eyes.

"Yes… she is a good mother, but she gets excited sometimes and I have to find ways to calm her down. She doesn't like to talk much and so when we're together, we just sit quietly or, as funny as this sounds, we clean the house or do things like that."

The silence lengthened while she stared down at the table. "I do love privacy. I don't get much of it anymore."

She gave me a side-long glance. "Well, who has a great childhood, anyway? I'm not the only one, am I?"

"What about your father?"

Marilyn went into a kind of moody trance. "My father wasn't around, but that's another story. But my mother tried hard to be a good mother. When I was seven years old, she was finally able to put a down-payment on a two-story house for us near the Holly-wood Bowl. She even bought me a piano, a black Franklin grand. It was so pretty, and I was so happy then. Mom was a film-cutter at Consolidated Film Industries, and she had worked overtime so she could save money. So you see, she wasn't a bad mother."

I sat in the nearest chair, but Marilyn didn't seem to notice.

"But then there was a strike at Consolidated and things went bad for her, and she had a breakdown."

Marilyn looked up with sad eyes. "Like your mother, my mother had mental problems. She was diagnosed with paranoid schizophrenia. Well, the house had to go, didn't it?"

"And then, well..." Marilyn stopped, not finishing the sentence. She gave me a look and a gesture, as if to say, "*I've had enough of this.*"

Marilyn changed her mood. The sadness left her eyes, and she brightened. "Let's not have any more of that. Do you see how thoughtful I get when I'm away from home?"

She held me gently in her eyes. "I'm so glad you're here. Did I already say that?"

"Yes..."

"Now I've said it again. So let's talk about you now. You said you want to be a photographer and journalist?"

"Yes..."

"Do you know what else you could be? An actress. You do funny impressions, and you have good cheek-bones and nice legs and lovely, thick hair."

I blushed, running a hand through my hair self-consciously. "I don't know about that…"

"Yes, you could. Do you have boyfriends?"

"No… not really."

"I don't believe it. You are so pretty. Stand up," Marilyn demanded, rising to her feet. "Go ahead, stand up. Don't be shy. I want to look at you. I mean, really look at you."

I slowly got up. Marilyn put a thoughtful finger to her lips, moving her head left and right, measuring me with her eyes. "Okay now, tilt your head to the side and make a silly smile."

"I don't know…" I said, stiffening up.

"Go ahead. Let's just play a little."

I obeyed, but I felt my smile was more of a grimace than a real smile.

"A silly smile, Darla, not a painful one. Go ahead. You can do it."

When I parted my mouth and grinned, imitating Marilyn's sexy smile, she laughed and applauded. I laughed too, feeling utterly ridiculous.

"Good, Darla. Good. Now, bend one knee so you look a little curvy. I learned this when I first started modeling. A photographer taught me the stance and my good friend Shelley Winters taught me the sexy grin."

It took me a couple of tries, but I finally managed to perform to Marilyn's satisfaction.

"Good! See how sexy you look? You'll have every guy you meet eating out of your hand."

Before bed, we took Sonny for a walk in the cold night air, under a sky crowded with stars. There was still plenty of snow on the ground and a low moan of wind stirring the trees.

Peering into the night sky, I thought about Eddie and his telescope. I liked him, even though he had run away, afraid to meet Marilyn. He hadn't been shy around me, but then I was a nobody. Marilyn was... well, Marilyn was the star of stars.

Marilyn shoved her hands deeply into her pockets and breathed in, blowing air out toward the sky. "Oh, Darla, how I love the quiet. Sometimes when I'm in California, I think I'm going to go crazy with everything I have to do."

"But you like making movies, don't you?"

"Yes, but I want to be an artist, an actress with integrity. I don't want to be a movie star who can't act. And then there's fame. With fame, you know, you can read about yourself, somebody else's ideas about you, but I'm learning that what's really important is how you feel about yourself."

"I've never felt very good about myself," I said. "I don't know why. I just don't get most people, and I don't understand this crazy world. But when I see you in a movie, you seem so happy, confident and carefree. I want to be like that. I want to be like you in the movies. There must be so many women out there in the world who wish they were Marilyn Monroe."

Marilyn took my hand and squeezed it. "Oh, honey, all that movie stuff is just an act. When it's all said and done, what good is being Marilyn Monroe? Why can't I just be an ordinary woman? A woman who can have a family. I'd settle for just one baby. My own baby. I thought I could have all that with Joe, but things just didn't work out. He had such fixed ideas about what he wanted me to be. I wanted to be a wife and a mother, yes, but I still wanted to be an actress too."

I wanted to make Marilyn feel better, so I said, "You'll find the right guy. I know you will."

Marilyn's voice was mild, her smile loving. "And so will you, Darla. I just know it."

My thoughts returned to Marilyn and saving her life. I contemplated the precise words that might have the impact to set her on a new life course. "Marilyn, have you ever thought of leaving Hollywood and all that stardom? Maybe you would feel better about life and things."

Marilyn tilted back her head to the sky. "You don't know how many times I've thought about it. That's why I'm here, to get away from that place. Anyway, we are all of us stars, and we deserve to twinkle. And that includes you."

We walked on around the house, crunching through the snow, hearing the distant hooting cry of an animal. I stopped short, shooting a look toward the trees.

"What was that?" I asked, frightened.

"It's nothing. Probably a fox or an owl or something."

I shivered. "I'm cold."

"Let's go in. It's getting late, anyway."

Later in the night, when my bedroom door squeaked open, I sat up with a start, my heart pounding, my wide eyes searching the darkness.

"It's me, Darla... Marilyn. I'm sorry to wake you."

Dim light from the hallway leaked into the room and I saw Marilyn standing in a weak shaft of light.

"Is everything okay?" I asked.

Marilyn padded across the floor in bare feet and sat on the edge of my bed. Beside me, Sonny lifted his head, sniffed at the perfumed air, and then settled back into sleep.

Marilyn was mostly in shadow, and I couldn't read her expression.

"I can't sleep. I guess you can say I have the blues."

I leaned back against the headboard. "What time is it?"

"It's after three."

Her voice sounded dreamy and I could tell her eyes were wandering the room as if searching for something. I concluded she'd taken sleeping pills. I could hear it in her slurred words.

"Darla... That phone call at dinner..." She stopped, and I waited.

"It was from a friend... well, no, not a friend. A man I hired. I shouldn't have, but I did it anyway. I was in a funny kind of mood when I did it. I was angry and confused, and I was curious, all at the same time. Does that make sense?"

I wiped a strand of hair from my eyes. "Yeah, I guess so."

"It's about my father, Darla. The man I hired found my father. I want to go see him. I need to see him. You see... I've never met him. I've never met my father; I mean my real father. Will you go with me? Will you go with me to meet my father?"

CHAPTER 15

On Monday morning, before leaving to go shopping in Bridgeport, Connecticut, Marilyn sat me down at a makeup mirror and began to teach me about makeup.

"Now listen, you should always use a lipstick brush. You can't control the line if you apply lipstick with a tube. A lot of women never learn this one simple trick. Now, if you want to, you can use the brush with an ordinary tube of lipstick, and you can save money, because the brush can dig out the last drop. When I first started modeling, I learned that I could get twice as much lipstick for my money by using the brush. Okay, now the first step is to outline your lips in a darker color, then shade with a lighter color. Here, I'll start it and then you can finish."

We became two mad artists working away on my canvas face. Marilyn was strictly business, her eyes focused, her hand calm and assured, her attention acute.

I sat still and enthralled while she showed me how to de-emphasize my imperfect features and accent my good ones. She dabbed lipstick onto my cheeks, blending it, saying I could use the lipstick instead of rouge. She applied a darker shade of lipstick to make my cheeks appear hollow, and a lighter shade on my thin lips to add fullness.

"Now be sure to make yourself some little eyebrows like this…" And then she drew a delicate feather line down each temple where my eyebrows were sparse.

"The eyebrows are so important, Darla. You can also use the eyebrow pencil to make a beauty mark," she said, as she demonstrated, placing a little black dot to the right of my right lip, near the cheek. "See?"

I did see, and when she'd finished, I inched forward, gazing in startled wonder at a face I had never seen before. I actually looked… well, pretty, maybe even a little sexy.

Marilyn crossed her arms, smiling proudly at me through the mirror. "What do you think? Do you like the look?"

I smiled broadly. "Wow! I love it. I just love it. It's like I have a whole new face and it's so much better than the old one."

Marilyn's laughter burst out. "We're not finished, honey. Tonight, we're going to put rollers in your hair. In the morning, you'll have the prettiest bouncing curls you ever saw. But for now, let's experiment a little bit."

She took a comb and parted my hair on the left side, a much deeper part than I'd ever tried. Then she brushed the hair down close to my face on the right and pinned just a few strands back, leaving the rest to fall heavily around my face.

"Just what I thought. You could be Lauren Bacall's sister," she said, twisting the long strands on the right side of my face around her finger to give them a slight curl. Then she applied some hair spray. "I loved working with her and Betty Grable on *How to Marry a Millionaire.* Anyway, your hair is just about the same color as Lauren's."

Marilyn then twirled the hair on the left side of my face around her finger and sprayed it. Next, she took the brush and curled the back hair under before spraying it, too. She stepped back and appraised her work with pursed lips and a little nod. "They call this the peek-a-boo hairstyle," she said, placing her hands gently on my head and tilting it down to the left.

It was a simple style, but amazingly effective. It revealed an enhanced, sexy Me, more feminine and softer than I could have ever imagined. I looked up with slightly raised eyebrows, as if I were Lauren Bacall posing for the camera. We both laughed.

"Just what I said before. You could be an actress," she said.

I loved the peek-a-boo look. I loved the new Me.

I turned toward Marilyn. "You're a magician," I said. "How did you learn to do that so fast?"

Marilyn hugged my shoulders. "I've had a lot of different hairstyles in the movies, not to mention photoshoots. And I've watched a lot of other actresses get their hair done. I'm so glad you like it. I told you you're pretty. Sometimes, it just takes a little flick of the comb, some lipstick and an eyebrow pencil to bring it out."

She straightened and stretched. "Now, I need to make some calls before we leave. You keep practicing the sexy, peek-a-boo look."

While the living room radio played pop tunes and Christmas music, Marilyn chatted on the phone, roaming the house barefoot, clutching the base of the phone in one hand, the cord stretched, the handset wedged between her shoulder and chin.

She spoke to Joe DiMaggio, her agent, and Milton Greene and his wife, the owners of the house. She told them about me, and I wished she hadn't. I couldn't make out what they said to her, but I heard her say, "We're having so much fun together."

Finally, in late afternoon, we piled into the Greenes' 1952 Ford Country Squire station wagon with light wood panels, and we drove to Read's Department Store in Bridgeport, Connecticut.

There was a festive holiday atmosphere in the air. The entire store was adorned with Christmas decorations and Christmas specials, and it was those specials that drew Marilyn like a magnet.

"I just love to shop," she said, eyes shining, casting about at the many displays, the mannequins, and the racks of clothes. Thanks to my makeover, I strolled with a confidence and pride I'd never before possessed. I'd never looked so good—so sophisticated and sexy. Wishing all my friends in 1998 could see me, I vowed to master Marilyn's techniques and, if I returned, to wow the boys and snub the girls.

But here and now, I was with Marilyn Monroe, even though no one had recognized her. She'd managed to dress down so successfully that people flowed around us without a glance. How was that possible?

Wearing big framed glasses, flats, dark slacks, and a pale blouse under a drab olive winter coat, she appeared ordinary. Without red lipstick or her blonde curls, Marilyn simply looked like an average blonde with her hair combed back and a red and black scarf pulled over her head.

As we picked through racks of the 1950s styles, which were brand new vintage clothes to me, my happy eyes wanted to buy everything. For me, Marilyn selected the stylish and expensive, holding up clothes to match color and tone. Marilyn and I smothered giggles at our secret triumph. Only once did a middle-aged store clerk turn around and stare at Marilyn, as if he recognized her. Marilyn swiftly ducked her head, hiding behind a rack of dresses, tugging my arm, suggesting I give her cover.

Several times I had to sit down to rest my ankle, but Marilyn shopped close by, her back to the crowds, thoroughly enjoying herself. She sifted and examined blouses, tops and pants, nodding or shaking her head, absently humming a tune.

We swept out of the store clutching shopping bags filled with underwear, bras, slacks, tops, sweaters and two dresses. A young, eager clerk helped us carry the shoe boxes and hat boxes, me gripping a dandy-looking box containing a perfume bottle of Rose Geranium Toilet Water.

We laughed at nothing as we stuffed the bags and boxes into the station wagon's cargo area, Marilyn keeping her head turned away from the young clerk who, to my delightful surprise, kept giving me the eye and a come-hither smile. That was new to me and I loved it!

When he was gone, two middle-aged men passed, stopped short and glanced back over their shoulders, their startled eyes finding Marilyn. Recognition dawned.

I slammed the heavy tailgate shut as Marilyn skipped along to the driver side, yanked the door open and slid behind the wheel. She cranked the engine and waved me in. I bounded inside, slamming the door as she shot away from the parking space, arm extended out the window, hand waving as she flashed her dazzling, Marilyn smile.

The men stared dumbly at Marilyn, and we sped away. As the car retreated, they pointed excitedly at it, as if they'd just seen the eighth wonder of the world. To my thinking, they had.

Yet again, we sang Christmas carols as we drove toward the town of Weston, me a little off-key and Marilyn singing harmonies. As we fell into silence, I turned to Marilyn with a question I'd been wanting to ask since the previous night, when she'd crept into my room.

"Marilyn... Where is your father?"

She kept her eyes on the road. Gray clouds traveled the sky, as darkness crept in and snow flurries flitted by.

"I'm so sorry about last night. I get blue sometimes at night and I get a little crazy in my head."

I had read snippets of articles containing information about who Marilyn's father actually was, but many were conflicting and, I suspected, not accurate.

"You said you've never met your father?"

Marilyn was quiet for a moment. "Most people don't really know who he is. They think they do, but they don't. Well, anyway, I shouldn't have told you all that. Sometimes at night, I'm not myself. I get lost and feel alone."

Marilyn gave me a side glance. "I'm sorry."

"You don't have to be sorry. I'll go with you to see him if you want."

She smiled weakly. "Go see him? Honey, in the light of day, I'm not sure I have the courage."

"But he's your father. Wouldn't he want to see you?"

Marilyn's eyes played across the dashboard as if she were searching for something. She wasn't watching the road.

A little scared, I said, "It's getting dark out on the road."

Marilyn's attention refocused outside. We crept up on the tail end of an old black Ford pickup, and Marilyn slowed down.

"Darla, I'm here, and away from Hollywood, because I'm trying to find myself. Here, there are no reporters, photographers or publicists. Whatever I do will be a secret and never written down. I want to stop living a story and start living my life. Do you understand what I'm saying?"

"Yeah, I think so. But if you go see him now, no one but you and me and him will know. It won't be written up in some newspaper or magazine. And it might be a good thing. And maybe he'll be happy to see you."

Marilyn pondered that. "But if I do go see him and talk to him... Of course I don't even know if he wants to see me... And, if he doesn't want to see me, I'm afraid I might break into pieces."

I shifted my body to face her. "I'm sure he'll want to see you and, anyway, it's Christmas. I'm sure he'll want to see you at Christmas. Where is he?"

Marilyn breathed in nerves. "He lives in California, but he's originally from Newport County, Rhode Island. The man I hired told me that my father is in Rhode Island visiting relatives over Christmas. Isn't that something? I mean he's so close, isn't he? Rhode Island isn't that far."

"So you never met him in California?"

"I tried once... Well, let me put it this way. I tracked him down once. I called him. Do you know what he said? 'Look, I'm married, and I have a family. I don't have anything to say to you. Call my lawyer.'"

I was incredulous. I couldn't imagine my father ever saying that to me. "How could he say that to you?"

"It's the big, bad and real world, Darla, not the Hollywood version of father and daughter, like Spencer Tracy and Elizabeth Taylor in *Father of the Bride*. Well... you know, the whole father thing has been on my mind lately, so I came to New York to be quiet. I restore myself when I'm alone."

She flashed me a pretty smile. "But I'm happy you're here. Now I can pretend you're my little sister, or my daughter."

I liked that, and I shrugged a shoulder. "Sure, why not?"

I should have let the subject drop, but I was a snooping teenager and I wanted to know more.

"What do you know about your father?"

The pain returned to Marilyn's face. "He worked with my mother at Consolidated Film. He was her shift supervisor, and they had an affair. It's funny how life goes, isn't it? It's all so mysterious and confusing. Just when you think you've figured one thing out, another one hits you and you're all confused again, and hurting again."

Darkness had settled in, and the car's headlights tunneled into the night, the glare of oncoming headlights flashing by.

"I shouldn't be telling you these things, Darla. I don't tell anyone these things. They're so hurtful and, yes, private."

I sat back and faced ahead, deciding not to push any further. I could hear the stress building in her voice, a voice that was similar to Marilyn's movie voice, breathless, small, sounding helpless.

"His wife sued him for divorce," Marilyn continued. "I managed to get a copy of the divorce petition. She charged him with addiction to narcotics, abuse, and associating with women of 'low character.'"

Marilyn laughed, but there was no happiness in it. "Can you imagine that? And to make it worse, I heard that he deserted my mother on Christmas Eve in 1925, when she told him she was pregnant."

Marilyn dropped into silence and we didn't speak again until after we parked at the curb near Allen's Drugstore.

After she shut off the engine, she turned, looking at me in a pleading way. "What should I do, Darla?"

I was frank. "Go see him. We should go see him."

CHAPTER 16

We didn't linger in the drugstore. Marilyn said she was hungry and thirsty, so we quickly shopped and locked our purchases in the car.

Next door to the drugstore was the square, quaint Busy Bee Restaurant with its blue letters stenciled in an arc across the plate-glass window. Well above the entrance door was a fat, smiling bumble bee, buzzing in neon yellow.

Inside, the room was nearly full. A stout female hostess managed to find us a two-top in the rear, near the jukebox. I sat facing the room, and Marilyn sat with her back to the front door. The hostess didn't recognize Marilyn, and few diners glanced up as we passed, most being lost in conversation.

Marilyn, who had become one of the most recognized people in the world, had an uncanny way of finding shadows and hiding her face, and of throwing a kind of inner switch to turn off *the* Marilyn Monroe.

The place had hardwood floors, red and white checkered tablecloths, and flickering candle globes that made the room romantic. A lighted glass display case featured delicious-looking homemade cakes, pies and muffins, and two young boys had their noses smashed against the glass, peering in hungrily.

White Christmas lights were strung around the crown molding, and a Christmas tree blinked near the front window. Colorfully wrapped presents were arranged around it.

Our toothy young waitress swayed over, chewing gum, her black hair in a ponytail, her attitude one of practiced indifference. She wore bright red lipstick and a light blue uniform with white trim and puffed sleeves. She stared over our heads as she scribbled down our orders, asking if we wanted peas and carrots or beans, baked potato or mashed. I was amazed that she didn't venture a look at Marilyn. If she had, I was sure she would have recognized her, as the dim overhead light bathed her in a soft glow. In that gifted light, there was no mistaking Marilyn's natural innocence and beauty.

For her part, Marilyn stared hard at the menu, never looking up, speaking in a rich alto, a voice I'd never heard.

After the waitress hustled off, I said, "Where did that voice come from?"

"Did you like it? I used it in *Clash by Night,* in a scene with Barbara Stanwyck. My line was 'I hate people bossin' me. You marry a fella and the first thing he does is boss you.'" Marilyn snickered in personal pleasure. "Did you see that movie?"

"Yes, on the late show, after *Nick at Night,*" I said, my speedy mouth again galloping ahead of my cautious brain. Was there a late show on TV in 1954? I didn't know, but I knew for sure there was no *Nick at Night.*

"What's *Nick at Night*?" Marilyn asked. "That's such a funny name."

I stammered out a couple of words. "Oh... Well, you know, just a show where I live. Just a local thing." I hurried on, before she could think about it. "I loved you in that scene where you and some guy leave the cannery where you both work, and you're eating a candy bar. You're real feisty."

Marilyn smiled with recollection. "Yes, I liked that scene. I felt comfortable in that role. I wasn't anybody yet, just an actress trying to make it."

"And you did."

She nodded, but her expression and distant eyes implied secrets. I wanted to know those secrets but, before I could form questions, she changed the subject.

"Do you like this place?"

I nodded. "Yeah... The waitress isn't so friendly though."

"She probably has man trouble," Marilyn said, with a little laugh. "I know that look."

A tall, string bean of a boy in his 20s drifted over to the jukebox, dropped in a coin and selected the bouncy tune, *Papa Loves Mambo*, by Perry Como. Marilyn tapped a finger on the table.

"I love this song. Joe and I danced to it at El Morocco."

I raised my voice over the music. "You miss him, don't you?"

She sighed. "... Well, sometimes. I know he cares about me. So maybe he cares too much. Maybe our bust-up brought up a lot of things. Maybe that's why I'm thinking about driving up to Rhode Island to see my father. Part of me is just so angry at Joe and my father. Sometimes I wish my mother had never told me the truth about my father. Why didn't she just say he'd died or disappeared? That would have been the end of it. And then she told me never to tell anyone who he was... so I never have, and I guess I never will."

I leaned in closer. "Like I said, if you decide to go, and if you want me to, I'll go with you."

As the dishes rattled and the conversation buzzed around us, Marilyn stared blindly through the cigarette smoke at the garish jukebox lights. She gave me a transient grin. "I couldn't go alone, Darla."

I sat up. "Then we should go. Just do it."

Maybe this one event—going to see her father—would change her entire destiny.

At that moment, the front door opened and, to my shock, Eddie entered, with a pretty, pouty-mouthed blonde hanging on his arm. My breath caught. He didn't see me.

"What is it, honey?" Marilyn asked, reading my startled expression, stealing a quick peek over her shoulder.

"Oh, nothing," I said, my voice tight with stress.

Marilyn was concerned. "Is it the police? Are they looking for you?"

"No... Not the police."

"Is it someone from your orphanage?"

"No. Not that."

"What then?"

The hostess approached Eddie and his date. As they were escorted through the dining room to a table nearby, Eddie spotted me. His eyes went wide with recognition. I glanced away.

"Darla, tell me. Who are they?" she asked, glancing over.

"It's nothing... Really."

Marilyn sat up, her expression firm. "Well, don't you worry about it. Whoever they are, if they try anything, I'll stand up, pull off my scarf and let everybody know who I am. That will stop them."

My nervous eyes shifted back and forth. Why was I so upset? Eddie and I had just met. He was nothing to me. But then again, he had asked me out, hadn't he? My face got hot, my stomach sour. I stole a glance at Eddie's table. She was probably the girl he'd recently broken up with. The girl who didn't like looking through telescopes. So why was he with her then?

"Do you want to leave?" Marilyn asked.

"No... No way."

Marilyn gave me a measured look. "Honey, if you're in trouble, I can help you. I know a lot of important people."

"It's not that... It's..." I stopped, holding her gaze.

She looked at me with sturdy determination. "Don't worry, nothing's going to happen to you."

And then, in a sudden change of mood, she said, "I've just made up my mind. You and I and Sonny are going to make that trip to Rhode Island to see my father, and nothing's going to stop us."

CHAPTER 17

I ate my dinner much too fast. I was preoccupied and felt Eddie stealing looks at me. It was irritating. If he was with her, he should be with her and not be looking at me. I had half-a-mind to push up, march over and tell him that, but I was restrained, not wanting to make a scene and draw attention to Marilyn. Again, to my amazement, no one had recognized her.

Marilyn sipped her white wine, observing me. "Darla, you are a mystery. I can almost hear your brain working. I've never seen anyone eat so fast."

"When do you want to leave for Rhode Island?" I abruptly asked.

Marilyn went back to eating, chewing the last of her meatloaf, draining the rest of her wine. She left the question hanging. "Let's buy a Christmas tree on the way home and decorate it tonight. Doesn't that sound like fun?" She was uncertain again. I could see it in her eyes.

"Yeah. Sure."

"Good. I saw a sidewalk Christmas tree stand when we drove in. I'm sure the trees are fresh."

From the corner of my eye, I saw Eddie's date, the pretty, preppy blonde with tight, bouncing curls, whirl about, her face filled with dreamy-eyed shock. Eddie grabbed her forearm, alarmed. It was obvious he'd just told her about Marilyn Monroe.

From the jukebox, Bing Crosby and the Andrews Sisters launched into their hectic and spirited rendition of *Jingle Bells*.

Blondie shot up and started over. Eddie seized up— a deer in headlights.

Marilyn read my face and followed my eyes. Blondie was on us in seconds, standing over Marilyn, breathless and gawking.

"Oh my gosh! I can't believe it. Are you really Marilyn Monroe?"

Marilyn lifted her eyes blandly, frowning, not speaking. Now Blondie wasn't sure. Had Eddie played a joke on her? Was this frumpy, headscarf-wearing woman really Marilyn?

A couple at the table next door heard Marilyn's name. Both man and woman swiveled around like bird dogs, faces on high alert.

Marilyn realized there was no escape. Resigned, she artfully removed her headscarf, shook out her blonde curls, removed her glasses and pivoted to face the dining room.

I watched in rapt wonder as she arose, flipping the Marilyn Monroe switch from "off" to "on," suddenly shining like a Broadway marquee. Drenched with sexy appeal, she aimed her magnetic personality at the room like a floodlight.

Overwhelmed by reality, Blondie backstepped, stumbling into Eddie, who was on his feet, hoping to haul her away.

The room's reaction was immediate: heads twisted around, silverware clinked, and chairs scraped across the wooded floor as astonished eyes stuck to Marilyn. Jaws dropped; torsos lifted. There were gasps and then a startled, crescendoing hum of conversation, as people shot to their feet, pointing.

Waitresses stopped short with trays poised. Water glasses, once balanced, now skated to edges, teetering, water sloshing. A cook in a white apron burst from the kitchen door, bug-eyed, just as a woman exclaimed, in a gushing, adoring voice, "It's Marilyn! My God, it's Marilyn Monroe!"

Pandemonium set in. Within seconds, our table was engulfed by an adoring crowd, all staring at Marilyn with dewy, worshipping eyes. Marilyn radiated sheer joy, tossing her head back, flashing an alluring, media-worthy smile.

Women wiped away tears while men gawked, as if caught in a dream.

"Hello, everyone!" Marilyn said, in her breathy, wistful voice. "Merry Christmas, and may you all have the happiest of New Years!"

A frenetic woman thrust out a camera and began snapping away. A man with a camera picked his way through the crowd, leveled his camera and clicked, the flash strobing the dimly lit room.

Our waitress miraculously appeared, elbowing her way to our table, her face stretched with ecstatic antici-pation. When she saw Marilyn, she fainted, dropping like a sack. She was caught by Eddie before she hit the floor, and he half-carried/half-staggered her to an empty chair, where a female customer fanned her and reached for a glass of water.

Marilyn posed and beamed, laughing merrily, scribbling autographs and speaking to people as if she'd known them her entire life.

I stood up, feeling crushed by the crowd, not knowing what to do. A girl about my age glanced my way and asked, "Are you famous?"

I shook my head. "No..."

"Well, get out of the way then," she said rudely, shoving me left as she edged closer to Marilyn.

I fought the animal urge to scream and run, amazed at Marilyn's cool and gracious demeanor as even more people rushed her, as people from the street, who'd heard Marilyn was inside, shouldered in and surged.

Thankfully, just when I thought the mass was going to overwhelm us completely, a man shouted, "All right, folks, back away. That's enough! Back off. Let her breathe!"

A heavyset, balding man, with a lingering fringe of gray around his bald dome, appeared, pulling his way through the throng. "Step back!" he demanded, finally drawing up to Marilyn, first with an apologetic expression, and then with bright, school-boy adoration.

"Miss Monroe, I'm sorry for all this." He extended his broad, meaty hand. "I'm Don Taylor, and I own this place."

Marilyn fixed him with a sweet smile. "Hello, Don. I am so glad to meet you," she said, giving his hand three shakes. "You have a lovely restaurant, and I just adore your meatloaf and mashed potatoes with all that sumptuous gravy. I just love it."

He blushed with pride. "Well, thank you. I'm sorry my guests nearly trampled you. They mean well. I guess they're just so surprised to see you here. I'm sorry nobody recognized you till now."

"I think you're all wonderful and sweet, and I love you all," she said, throwing them a smiling kiss.

The crowd erupted into cheers and thunderous applause.

I felt a strong hand grip my upper arm, and I flinched. It was Eddie.

"I'm sorry, Darla. I'm really sorry. I tried to stop her."

In a reflex of panic, I wrenched my arm from his grasp and propelled myself into the crowd, leaving him searching for Blondie, who had been bumped, elbowed and shoved aside by the heaving mass.

Marilyn waved me over and I managed to tuck myself next to her. With a broad, welcoming smile, Marilyn said, "My friend, Darla, and I have to go now. We have so much to do. We're behind on our Christmas shopping. I'm sure you all understand."

Don spoke up. "I'll escort you out, Miss Monroe, and don't you even think about paying your check. Your dinners are on me."

Marilyn rose to tiptoes and kissed Don's right cheek; his entire head blushed scarlet. The room exploded into shouts, whistles and more applause.

Two stern patrolmen in tan uniforms, peak caps and black leather jackets appeared, taking Marilyn in with a stoic fascination. She entertained them with a wave and a "hello" and they, along with a delighted Don leading the way like a general, cut a path through the elated crowd and shepherded us outside to our car.

Inside the car, I heaved out an audible sigh as Marilyn started the engine. Eddie and Blondie had wrestled free from a sea of waving hands and ecstatic smiles. They appeared on the right fringe of the crowd, Eddie's expression gloomy, hers euphoric. I turned my head away from them, and Marilyn noticed.

When the car left the curb, she cranked down her window, flashing a final smile and a wiggling-fingers wave. I crouched down, grateful to have escaped. We followed the two motorcycle cops out of town and waved our thanks as we turned onto the state highway and they left us, the motorcycles growling off into the night.

I sat trembling as the glowing eyes of cars passed in the opposite lane, and I didn't relax until we were the only car on a two-lane winding road, flanked on both sides by snowy trees. We followed a road that rose and fell through a night of curves and shadows.

"I don't know how you do it," I finally said, feeling exhausted and drained.

Marilyn had both hands on the top of the steering wheel, her expression somber, showing none of the glittering charm she'd expressed in the restaurant.

"You've got to tell me what you're running from, Darla," she said. "I need to know if I can help you. Look, honey, I know people. Joe knows people. Frank knows people."

"Frank?" I asked.

"Frank Sinatra. I can help you, Darla, but you've got to tell me what kind of trouble you're in. I'm your friend, and I want to help."

I wanted to tell Marilyn the truth, but how could I? "Everything's fine, Marilyn. Really."

"Then who was that boy who grabbed your arm and spoke to you. I saw the look in your eyes."

"He's a nobody… just some guy I met."

I struggled to come up with a good answer. "He's a kind of new boyfriend. I mean, I sort of know him."

Marilyn looked doubtful. "You're hiding something, Darla. Why?"

"No, I'm not. He's somebody I met when I ran away from the orphanage."

Marilyn fixed her attention on the road, lowering her voice. "Darla, I know you're not telling me everything. I feel it and I'm very intuitive about things. In time, I hope you'll trust me and tell me who you really are and what you're running from. I hope you'll tell me if the police are looking for you."

"They're not. I promise. Nobody is looking for me. I don't have anyone."

Marilyn glanced over with a sympathetic smile. "You do now, honey. You have me."

I shifted in my seat, feeling dirty and low for lying. The last thing I wanted to do was lie to Marilyn, who seemed so vulnerable.

I'd read that she'd been an easy target for those who wanted to take advantage of her and thought she was rolling in dough. People would charge her two or three times the normal amount for things she purchased, from groceries to clothes.

A charity had asked her for a donation, and when she wrote a check for one thousand dollars, they looked at her in disappointment and said, "Is that all?" She ended up giving them ten thousand dollars. No, I didn't want to take advantage of Marilyn.

"Marilyn, let's go see your father. Can we leave to-morrow?"

Marilyn's eyes blinked, noting a sudden shift of thought, but she surprised me with her answer. "They were nice people back there, weren't they?"

"Yes... They love you."

"I never want to disappoint people. I have this big fear of disappointing the people I love. It really scares me. Of course they see me as Marilyn Monroe and not as Norma Jeane, but that's okay, isn't it?"

"You didn't disappoint them. You were fabulous. I couldn't believe how fast you changed. All you did was remove that headscarf and glasses and you became *the* great and gorgeous Marilyn Monroe."

Marilyn smiled sweetly, but as headlights approached and flashed by, I saw Marilyn's eyes were glistening with tears.

"Did I say something wrong?"

"No, not at all. I just feel so lonely sometimes. I feel so very alone, and I don't know why. I have so many problems all the time. Just so many problems."

I didn't know what to say. I wanted to hug her, but I didn't. I was just a 16-year-old girl, and I didn't know what to do or say.

In a small voice, I said, "I'm here. You're not alone."

Marilyn sniffed and blinked. "Of course you are, Darla, and we are going to make this the best Christmas we have ever had. We are going to pack our things to-morrow morning and start off on our Christmas adventure to Rhode Island. It's time I faced him. It's time I face my father once and for all, and what better time to do it than on Christmas Day?"

CHAPTER 18

That night, as Marilyn and I slept, the woods filled up with snow. By morning, the world was white, clean and sparkling under a yellow sun in a sharp, blue sky. I held Sonny in my arms as I stood at my bedroom window, glancing about, looking at the glory of the winter day.

The night before, after Marilyn and I had arrived home from the Busy Bee Restaurant, we'd wandered the nearby woods gathering up evergreen branches. Inside, near a comforting fire, we decorated the living room with evergreen branches and Christmas ornaments Marilyn had found in a back closet. The scent was glorious, the atmosphere warm and Marilyn's mood was natural and playful. Again, I was aware of her swift mood swings; her face clearly revealing happy thoughts one moment and, a little later, depressing ones. Despite her moods, her kindness and warmth were always evident; her sensitivity apparent.

As we transformed the room into Christmas, we sipped champagne, sampled an assortment of chocolates Marilyn had received from Joe, and listened to Christmas music on a record player.

Later, we lounged on the couch and sang Christmas carols until the champagne brought the need for sleep.

As I hugged Marilyn goodnight, I asked if she was going to bed too.

"Not now. I'm going to make some phone calls."

Sometime after midnight, I got up and started for the bathroom. Through my partially open door, I noticed light leaking out from underneath Marilyn's closed bedroom door. I left my room and padded over to check on her, leaning an ear close. She was crying, anguished, gentle sobs. I drew a breath, wondering if her phone call to Joe had brought the tears. I'd learned that she locked her door every night, wanting privacy. After a few minutes of thoughtful debate, I decided not to intrude.

At eight the next morning, I left the bed, dressed, brushed my hair and went into the kitchen, letting Sonny out for his morning pee.

By nine o'clock, Sonny had eaten and was asleep on the hearth near the low fire. I was on the living room couch, sipping tea, with a bowl of *Wheaties* on my lap, inhaling the fresh evergreen scent.

By ten o'clock, I had washed my dishes, taken a shower, practiced the makeup techniques Marilyn had taught me, fiddled with my hairstyle—not a sterling success—and set aside the things I'd need for our trip.

By eleven, Marilyn still wasn't up. I went to her door and pressed my ear against it. Silence. No sound. I knocked softly.

"Marilyn? Marilyn... Are you awake?"

No sound. Fear began to rise. "Marilyn?" I said, louder, now hammering on the door and then jiggling the doorknob. It was still locked. "Marilyn, it's Darla. Are you okay?"

Still no sound. I backed away, hands trembling. "It couldn't be," I said aloud, overreacting and thinking the worst. "No way this could be. Not now. Not in 1954."

Marilyn would live until August 1962! I let the thought go, fighting for calm. I knocked repeatedly, then pounded. Nothing.

My pulse jumped and my thoughts went into spasm. Had I done something to alter the course of history? Had I said something or done something that had depressed Marilyn, triggering her to swallow more pills than usual or drink more champagne?

"What ifs" sprang up in my head like geysers. Should I try to break down the door? Should I call the police? Should I call Dr. Ellen Miles and her husband? Should I call Joe DiMaggio or Frank Sinatra, if I could even find their numbers? What about the neighbors? I stood staring, thinking, swelling with emotion.

Finally, determined and taut, I took steps back from the door, sucked in a bracing breath and hurled myself against it, bouncing off, jamming my shoulder. I bent, wincing and cursing, electric pain shooting up and down the length of my arm.

I recovered and, as adrenalin pumped through my body, I tried again and again to muscle the door open. I kicked, pushed, heaved and slammed my body against it, but it wouldn't budge. I pounded it with both fists, spitting curses. Why didn't the damned door burst open, like it always did in the movies?

I gulped in air, exhausted, sore and defeated, my bum ankle now knotted with pain. Sonny trotted over, fixing me with a curious, sleepy stare, his tail wagging.

"Should I call the police, Sonny?" I asked, hearing wildness in my voice.

No, Marilyn would hate that, I concluded, especially if she was just in a deep sleep. The press would descend like locusts. No. No police yet.

I raced into the living room, frantically casting my eyes about, searching for an address book. Surely, Marilyn had an address book with all her phone numbers in it. I covered every inch of the living room, the kitchen, the back rooms and every other room in the house but found nothing. The book was probably with her in the bedroom. I couldn't wait any longer. Marilyn could be dying. I had no other choice.

I rushed to the front door, yanked it open and ventured outside into the crisp morning air. Wrapping my arms about myself for warmth, I listened and watched, white clouds of vapor puffing from my mouth. Both vehicles were coned with snow; the driveway was an undulating carpet; and gusts of wind stirred the trees, shaking limbs, slinging showers of snow to the ground. No one was around. It was as silent as a graveyard, an unfortunate metaphor.

I cupped my hands around my mouth, inhaled and shouted at the top of my voice. "Help! Help!"

I waited, eyes alert, scanning the white landscape. No response. I shouted for help again. I tramped out into the snow in my new Keds tennis shoes and immediately felt the shock of frigid impact; it chilled me to the bone. My teeth chattered. I screamed into the surging wind. "Help!"

I waited, raised a hand against the sun, shading my eyes against the diamond-bright glare of snow, searching, straining ears and eyes.

What happened next will be forever branded in my memory. A car approached from the road, a dark sedan, a wink of sun sparking off the windshield. It turned into the unshoveled driveway and crawled toward the house.

I watched, still as a stone, until the car stopped and the engine went silent. With no other thought than to save Marilyn's life, I ran for the car, sliding, balancing, desperate. As I arrived, skidding to a stop, panting like a racehorse, the driver's door opened, and a big man emerged.

I stared with round eyes; mouth open.

It was Joe DiMaggio!

CHAPTER 19

Joe DiMaggio was tall and austere in his black over-coat, eying me up and down, sternly suspicious. I worked to steady my breath, chest heaving. I struggled to find my voice, feeling floaty and detached, fighting for clarity.

"Who are you?" Joe asked. "Are you the girl Marilyn told me about?"

I heard myself croak out. "Yes... Marilyn... Marilyn is locked in her room. All morning. She won't answer. I'm scared."

Joe broke for the front door. He was inside the house before I could move. Minutes later, I found him at Marilyn's door, calling for her.

"Marilyn! It's Joe, Marilyn. Open the door! Open the damned door, Marilyn."

He waited only seconds before thrusting a big shoulder against the door, ramming it three times. The lock snapped. The door burst open and slammed hard against the wall.

Joe rushed in and I followed. The scene froze me. Marilyn lay across the bed on her belly, partially covered by a sheet, the phone receiver in her hand.

Joe sat down on the edge of the bed and gently turned her over. I inched closer for a better look. She was pale, eyes closed. On the night table next to her bed were several pill bottles, and a half bottle of champagne.

Joe gently shook her. "Marilyn... Marilyn. It's Joe. Wake up. Wake up, Marilyn!" He slapped her lightly on either cheek, then shook her again. "Come on, Marilyn, wake up!"

When her breath caught, I threw a hand to my mouth, tears stinging my eyes. She was alive! Thank God, she was alive.

Joe turned to me. "Get a glass of water. Hurry."

I rushed off, returning shortly with a full glass, handing it to him. Joe had Marilyn sitting up, her back propped with pillows. Her head was slumped to one side, and she mumbled incoherently. Joe carefully tipped the glass to her mouth. She swallowed a little; some dribbled from her lips and she clumsily tried to slap the glass away.

Joe glared at me. "Make some toast. No butter," he said in his commanding, breathy voice.

I snapped to attention and left for the kitchen. When I returned with the toast, Marilyn's eyes were slit open and she was breathing, but her breath was coming in shallow puffs. Joe was speaking softly to her, lovingly.

I stood in the doorway, watching a rare, poignant scene: Marilyn Monroe and Joe DiMaggio alone together. Reality struggled with fantasy. Joe DiMaggio was alive in 1998, but he was a white-haired old man of 83. I had seen him in coffee commercials shown in the early 1990s and in photographs when he was interviewed about baseball.

This Joe DiMaggio was young, vital and charismatic. He wasn't anxious, troubled or ruffled, there being a remote silence about him. His big hands tenderly stroked Marilyn's brow, and she responded with little murmurs of pleasure and the innocent, comforted smile of a little girl.

He sensed my presence and turned. "Bring the toast," he said crisply.

I did so, then backed away. I wanted to ask if I should call for a doctor, but I was too scared, so I stood there, waiting for further orders like a tenderfoot Girl Scout.

My near photographic memory woke up and I recalled a section of an old magazine article that had featured Marilyn. A line about Joe had stuck in my head. It went something like,

"Joe DiMaggio had a purity and a natural grace that few others possessed. His magic was born on the baseball field and abandoned him once he left it."

Watching him being so mild with Marilyn, I sensed there was still a rare magic about him. He was masculine, yet tender. Gruff, yet caring. I'd also read that he was the only man who didn't use Marilyn or feed off her fame. One writer said that he was the only man worthy of her.

Joe turned and glowered at me, and I got the hint. I slunk out of the room, closing the door softly behind me, though it inched open, damaged by the shattered doorframe.

In the living room, I sat on the couch for a time, stroking Sonny's head as he lay beside me, my thoughts flitting about from one thing to another. I had been humbled; my confidence dented; my brash courage deflated. Had Marilyn nearly died?

Now that Joe was around, I figured my time with Marilyn was up, and maybe it was for the best. I was shaken by what had happened and shaken by what I'd seen. Marilyn was sensitive and unstable. Did I want the responsibility of caring for her; feeling a constant gnawing angst about whether she would overdose because of something I had inadvertently said or done?

How fast the world had changed. I had good intentions, but my father often spoke about good intentions, saying, *"Most of the evil in this world is done by people with good intentions."*

I glanced at the front door, contemplating my escape from the house, knowing I should bolt before Joe emerged from Marilyn's room. No doubt he'd pepper me with a hundred questions I couldn't answer. That was another thorn in my side; always trying to cover up the truth about who I was and how I'd arrived in 1954. I just wasn't that good at lying.

But where could I go? Back to the woods to search for that hidden doorway? I couldn't count on that. Dr. Miles had never found it. Then where could I go? My only real option, as I saw it, was to hitchhike to the Miles' house and ask her for advice.

But I sat there, immobile, like a ticking clock, the pendulum swinging left, saying "GO" and the pendulum swinging right, saying "STAY." I massaged my sore ankle for a time, resisting the needling urge to leave the house.

The truth was, in our brief time together, I'd grown fond of Marilyn. Despite her volatile moods and emotions, I began to see her as a sister—sometimes even as a mother. She was fun and unpredictable, but she laughed easily, which made me laugh, and I didn't laugh often or easily in my teenage years. Marilyn opened my heart and brought provocative, exotic music. She was dangerous, mysterious, delightful and warm.

Meeting her was the most exhilarating thing that had ever happened to me, and I knew, without any doubt, that my life would never be as exciting and impulsive and wonderful again. Nothing would ever compare to this adventure.

So I sat on the couch, turning occasionally to stare at the front door, which seemed to be waiting impatiently for me. I turned away from it, obstinate, ready to face Joe.

When he appeared from Marilyn's room, dressed in his smart dark suit, white shirt and royal blue tie, he left the door ajar. He didn't move; his head was down, his expression somber, as if he were praying. It was obvious that he didn't want to leave Marilyn alone for a minute. When he straightened and turned, he glared at me with a certain suspicion and reluctance. His eyes were not friendly. He made a motion with his head toward Marilyn's room.

"Marilyn wants to see you. I told her not to, but she's insisting."

"Is she okay?" I asked. And then impulsively, I said, "I mean, should I call a doctor?"

"She doesn't need a doctor," he said brusquely. "All we need is for some damned fan-crazy doctor to come in here, messing around, fawning all over Marilyn." He made a gesture with his hand. "Then all this, and more, will be in the evening papers before you can snap your fingers. To hell with that. No, if I need a doctor, I'll call my own. But right now, I'll take care of Marilyn. Can you make me some tea?"

I sat up, and Sonny jumped down, sensing agitation. "Yeah. Sure."

"They should have some tea in this place. Lipton. Not too strong. Then go in and see Marilyn... Make it fast and don't tire her out."

I put the kettle on the stove, turned up the flame and waited fretfully, pacing the kitchen and hoping Joe wouldn't venture in, and he didn't. He stayed with Marilyn.

Carrying the tea precariously, I met Joe at Marilyn's bedroom door, my hand trembling, the cup rattling against the saucer as I shakily handed it to him.

He looked at me, eyes narrowed. "Who are you? Marilyn won't say."

I heard Marilyn's weak voice call my name. "Darla... Darla. Come in. Come in and see me."

I didn't answer Joe. I lowered my head and entered Marilyn's room, with Joe keeping vigil at the door.

"Close the door, Joe," Marilyn said. "... As much as you can."

He mumbled a curse. "All right, but I'll be right outside."

Reluctantly, he closed the door.

Marilyn was sitting up, and I was delighted to see that some of her color had returned.

Either she or Joe had combed her hair back and, to my further surprise, she had smoothed on some red lipstick. Ever the star, I thought.

I felt my heart expand into happiness and I flashed a broad grin. "I'm so glad you're all right," I said, stepping toward her bed.

She opened her welcoming arms wide, beckoning me, smiling, tears holding in her eyes. All my doubts and all my qualms vanished, and I rushed to her, stooping into her arms. We embraced, rocking and crying. From the absolute joy bubbling up from the depths of my hungry-for-love soul, I knew I could never leave her. I, like so many others, had fallen hopelessly in love with Marilyn. She *was* my sister. She *was* my mother. She *was* my best friend, and I vowed I would never leave her.

After we broke the embrace, I sat on the edge of her bed, wiping tears. "What happened, Marilyn?"

She gave me a sweet, sad smile while she reached to touch my cheek. "I couldn't sleep. I had so many bad memories and I couldn't sleep. I have to get my sleep, don't I? I'm sorry, honey. I am so sorry I scared you."

Reflexively, my eyes stole toward the bottles of sleeping pills. "Don't take so many of those things," I said earnestly. "Please, just don't take so many at one time. And maybe you shouldn't drink champagne when you take them."

Marilyn's eyes glistened with tears. "I know, honey. But, you know, I have so many problems and they all get together and come at me in the night."

"I'm here, Marilyn. Whenever you feel that way, come to me. You and me can talk and laugh until we fall asleep. Sonny will join us, and you can pet him until you get sleepy."

"You are sweet, Darla. Do you know I have an older half-sister?"

I shook my head.

"She is thoughtful and kind and good, like you. So now I have an older sister and I have a younger sister. How lucky I am."

I took her hand and squeezed it. "I'm so glad Joe came when he did," I said.

Marilyn's face changed, and I couldn't read it. She averted her eyes. "I shouldn't say this to you, Darla, but if it weren't for Joe, I probably would have killed myself by now."

"No, don't say that," I blurted out. "You have everything to live for. You have millions of fans all over the world who love you. And you're beautiful. You're wonderful. Please don't say that or even think it."

Her expression changed again, and she flashed a merry smile. "You, Darla, are a dear one and you make me feel stronger and better."

I sat up, hopeful, wiping the last of my tears. "Are we still going on our little journey?"

Marilyn thought about it, at first unsure.

"It will be good for you," I said. "Good to get away. And it will be fun to take a road trip, won't it? Who knows what might happen? Who knows what will happen when you see your father?"

Marilyn nodded, her glassy eyes brightening. "Yes. You're absolutely right. We must take our little road trip. Yes, we must."

I turned toward the door. "What about Mr. DiMaggio?"

Marilyn laughed. "Joe? Don't worry. He can't stay here. He has to get back to San Francisco for Christmas. His family would never forgive him."

"But won't he want you to go with him?"

"I already told him. I already told him that I want to be alone this Christmas. I told him I have to be by myself. I reminded him that I filed for divorce back in October. So, as soon as I feel just a little bit stronger, we are going to go on our Christmas road trip, and we'll remember it for the rest of our lives."

Marilyn finger-combed her hair. "I don't even know what day this is."

"It's Tuesday, December 21."

She grew alarmed. "Christmas is Saturday, isn't it?"

"Yes..."

She sat up straight, braced by her hands. "Then we have to get going, Darla. I have to get myself together. We have to pack."

"It's okay," I said. "I found an atlas in the magazine rack near the bookshelf. It won't take more than three or four hours to drive to Rhode Island. We have plenty of time. You should rest today."

Marilyn sank back into the pillows and closed her eyes. "We can't just go directly to Rhode Island, we must take the long, round-about way. The out-of-the-way way. Never go the short way, when the long way is more fun."

Marilyn's breathing grew shallow, her eyes twitched, and she drifted off to sleep. I watched her sleep for a while, thinking about our little trip, pushing away worry. Was she really up to it?

And first, I had to face Joe DiMaggio.

CHAPTER 20

"She's not going anywhere," Joe snapped.

He was pacing the living room. I sat stiffly on the couch, feeling like a bad girl who'd been sent to the principal's office.

When Marilyn awoke at 2 o'clock, Joe entered her bedroom and closed the door. Within minutes, I heard his voice thundering, and Marilyn answering in a surprisingly strong voice. The quarrel went on for about five minutes, and then Joe came storming out of her room, slamming the door behind him.

He paced the hallway outside Marilyn's room, fuming and ignoring me, which was fine. Eventually, he wandered into the living room and paced more, lost in his own irritation.

Joe was a big man, impressive and intimidating, with good shoulders, martial energy and a clear, direct gaze that could pierce right through you.

He stopped, pointing that direct gaze at me, giving me his considered attention. "The problem with Marilyn is she doesn't have any damned idea of how to take care of herself. Half the time, I don't know what world she lives in. I never have."

I wanted to say, *Well, that's why she wants to be alone now, because she is trying to take care of herself.* But, of course, I didn't utter a word.

Joe grumbled on, glancing at his watch. "I have to catch the next plane out of Idlewild tonight, and one way or the other, Marilyn's going to be on that plane with me. She needs someone to look after her, separation or no separation."

He faced me with frank curiosity. "Now, who are you and how do you know Marilyn?"

I literally gulped. "We just met. I mean, Marilyn and me. I… I live around here."

"Then why aren't you home where you belong?"

I shrugged.

"What does that mean? Why does Marilyn want you hanging around? I don't understand it. She uses people as crutches, you know. Well, of course you don't know, because you're a kid. Have you ever heard of Natasha Lytess?"

I had, of course, because I'd read about her in old magazines. Natasha Lytess was an acting coach Marilyn relied upon for some of her movies. But I shook my head, playing dumb.

"No, of course you don't know. Well, Natasha Lytess was another one of Marilyn's crutches. On *The River of No Return,* that woman drove everyone crazy, including the director, Otto Preminger, who fought with Marilyn during most of the shoot. Natasha was Marilyn's acting coach, and Marilyn consulted her after every damned take. If Natasha didn't like it, they'd have to shoot the scene again, and again. Do you know what Mitchum called that movie? *The Picture of No Return.* And if that wasn't enough, Marilyn sprained her ankle, and I stopped everything and hurried to the set with my own doctor and spent several days with her while she recuperated. I told her then she should get rid of that nuisance of an acting coach. But she wouldn't."

I stared down at the floor, knees shaking.

"So, young lady, you're just another one of Marilyn's crutches, and I don't like it."

The icy silence seemed to last forever. I finally mustered enough courage to lift my eyes. Joe's face changed as a new thought struck. He pointed toward Marilyn's room, pinning me with another one of his piercing stares.

"Okay, then. Do something useful. Go in there and help Marilyn pack. Tell her she has to get on that airplane with me this evening, and she can't be late, like she always is. She seems to listen to you. Why, I don't know, but go in there and help her, so we can get out of here and you can go back home where you belong."

I ducked my head, obedient, but I couldn't move. Fear of him stuck me to the couch.

I cringed when he barked, "Go on, tell her."

I shot up and went slinking over to Marilyn's door, avoiding Joe's burning eyes, feeling like a scared dog. Sonny saw me, sensed trouble, and sprang from the couch, scampering off to my bedroom. Not being one of the most courageous of dogs, he was off to hide under the bed.

I lightly knocked on Marilyn's door. "Marilyn… It's Darla."

Her voice was breathy. "… Come in…"

I opened the door and entered, closing it behind me. I was surprised to see that she was out of bed and sitting at the vanity, wearing a skimpy satin gown, brushing the tangles out of her glossy hair.

She leaned forward, examining her face. "My eyes are puffy. I've got to put on some makeup."

I folded my hands, searching for words. "He..., I mean Mr. DiMaggio, asked me to tell you to go with him," I said, apologetically.

Marilyn winked at me, then said at a whisper, "Stay in here, honey. We'll wait him out."

She was quiet as she brushed her hair, her expression wistful.

"I love Joe, Darla, even after everything; after all the arguments and the separation, I still love him. But right now, I am trying to find myself. That's not easy. Joe will understand. Maybe not today, but he will. Deep down, Joe's a swell guy and he's a lot more sensitive than most people know."

Marilyn glanced at the door, with its splintered door-frame and broken lock. She whispered. "Well, we can't lock the door, since Joe busted the thing, so we'll just have to wait and see."

My temples throbbed with tension. She smiled at me through the mirror, and it was a little girl's smile, filled with delightful mischief.

She continued in a whisper. "Here's what's going to happen. When Joe knocks on the door, I'm going to get up, jump into bed and pretend I'm too sick to move or travel. I'll tell him I've got to rest. I'll plead with him to go without me. I'll tell him that the Greenes will be returning any day now, so I won't be alone. And then I'll tell Joe that I still have the pearl necklace he gave me on our honeymoon in Hawaii. It's such a lovely necklace, 44 Akoya pearls, and a gold clasp with diamonds. Joe bought it in Japan directly from Mikimoto, so the quality is excellent. I'll tell him I'll put it on and think of him."

Just then, Joe knocked on the door, and the whole scene played out just as Marilyn said it would. Joe wasn't happy about Marilyn staying behind, and he shouted, fretted, turned in a circle and fumed. Finally, he shoved his hands into his pockets and gradually softened.

He returned to Marilyn's side and whispered, "I love you."

I'd been hovering in the corner of the room like a scared mouse. He glanced over and told me to leave the room, and I did.

When he left Marilyn's room, he ignored me, hunching into his cashmere overcoat and pulling on his leather gloves. At the front door, he passed me one last disagreeable glance, opened the door and left.

When I heard the car engine fade into silence, I released a trapped breath and returned to Marilyn's room. She was already packing.

"Should we leave now?" she asked, excited.

"It's going to be dark soon," I said. "Maybe we should wait until morning."

She considered it. "Well, maybe you're right. I wasn't really lying all that much. My head is still all fuzzy and I'm so hungry. Okay, let's leave first thing in the morning. Tonight, we'll eat left-over turkey and open our Christmas presents."

"Presents?" I asked.

"Of course. I bought you a Christmas present."

I blushed with shame. "... But I... I didn't..."

She came to me, giving me a little hug. "Don't worry about it, honey. *You* are your present to me. You are my perfect Christmas present."

I stepped back, looking at her with misty eyes. "On our trip, I'm going to find you a Christmas present. I'm going to take a lot of pictures and I'm going to give you something no one has ever given you, and never will."

Marilyn said, "I don't need a thing, except you by my side when I walk up to that house, knock on that door, and ask to see my father. That's when I'm going to need you."

Later that night, while we ate dinner, Marilyn said something that made me laugh.

"When I'm making a movie, I love to do things the censors won't pass."

"Like in *Niagara*?" I asked.

Marilyn dropped her voice into a naughty whisper as if people might be listening in.

"I'll tell you a little secret, Darla. I liked the character Rose Loomis. She's a tramp, yes, and she conspires to kill her crazy husband, but she has guts."

"So you liked playing the bad girl?" I asked.

Marilyn gave me a delicious smile. "I loved it. It was a good dramatic role. It was my first Technicolor film and since I *was* playing a tramp, a bad girl, I wanted to get it right."

Marilyn grew animated. "Here's another secret. I was naked under the bed sheets at the beginning of the movie, when Joseph Cotton comes in. I knew that Rose, as the bad girl, would be naked, and I wanted it to be real and I wanted to feel it real. We got that past the censors. But while we were filming the shower scene, the director, Henry Hathaway, kept shouting at me to stay away from the shower curtain and away from the lights, because I insisted on being naked then, too. I told him that Rose would never take a shower wearing a flesh-colored suit. But to pass the censors, they had to darken the shower scene in post-production. Oh, well, we got the first scene past the censors, and the studio made money on that movie. I heard that a lot of men went to see it just because of the bedroom scene."

"How does it feel to make all that money?" I said, dreamily.

Marilyn laughed. "Honey, let me tell you another little secret about that picture. Even though I had a starring role, I was still under contract to 20th Century Fox as a stock actor at a fixed salary. I actually made less money on that picture than my makeup man did."

I stared in disbelief, and Marilyn threw her head back and laughed. "Darla, Hollywood is all about illusion and busted dreams. It's a magic show."

And then she stopped eating, looking lost in an old regret. She stared somberly out the window, as if she were seeing things happening out there, beyond that window, into the endless darkness.

After we'd washed the dishes, Marilyn seized my hand and led me into the living room, where she'd already started a roaring fire. I sat on the floor and she hurried off, barefoot as usual, to a nearby closet. She soon returned with a small, square box, wrapped with shiny red paper and a lovely white bow. Anxious and excited, she eased down beside me, sitting cross-legged, and handed me the little box.

"Open it, honey. I had so much fun picking it out when you were in the lady's room at the department store."

Silently, with a full heart, I carefully plucked off the bow and unwrapped the little box. I knew it was jewelry, but I couldn't imagine what it could be.

I held the velvety black jewelry box for a few seconds before carefully lifting the lid and parting the silver tissue paper. Marilyn must have seen my captivated eyes expanding on the glossy pearl earrings.

"Do you like them?" Marilyn asked.

I couldn't speak. I'd never seen anything so beautiful.

"They're not from Tiffany's, but I thought they would be perfect for you."

I could only stare through blurry eyes, as tears of gratitude formed.

"They're South Sea pearls and diamond drop earrings," Marilyn said. "Wear them on your next date and no boy will be able to resist you."

I wiped tears, wishing my mother were there, sitting with Marilyn and me.

Marilyn pushed up, excited. "All right, put on the earrings. Where is your camera? I want to take lots of pictures of you wearing them."

And she did. And then I snapped photos of Marilyn in various poses, each one better than the last. We danced, sang and snapped photos until exhilaration fell into exhaustion.

Later, in bed, I was worried. I loved being in this time. I loved being with Marilyn. But after the holidays were over, where would I go? What would I do?

CHAPTER 21

That night I was plagued by nightmares; of dark men with glowing yellow cat eyes coming for me, their big hands reaching, fingers curled, teeth sharp and gleaming.

I fumbled awake in darkness, grateful to be awake, wherever awake was. I tossed back the quilt, got up and left my room to check on Marilyn. Her lights weren't on. I exhaled an audible sigh through my nose. Thankfully, she couldn't lock the door because of Joe's attack, and I gingerly nudged it open and peered in. I saw the shadow of Marilyn's body and crept in a few feet to get a closer look. When I heard her gentle breathing, I relaxed, left her room and silently closed the door.

Back in my bedroom, Sonny slept soundly. Before climbing back into bed, I stole a glance at the window. Pale moonlight leaked in and made the world seemed magical. Well, wasn't it? Wasn't the world a magical place?

Marilyn spent most of the next day, Wednesday, resting, packing and talking on the phone. I was anxious to leave, but I knew I couldn't push her, so I read part of a novel, packed and took Sonny for a walk. Returning to the house, I was surprised when I saw Eddie's minty Ford parked in the driveway. I wasn't sure if I liked it that he'd come, or didn't like it. I started for the door with a little grin on my face.

Inside, Eddie was in the living room standing stiffly, like a piece of carved stone. Marilyn was talking to him. When I entered, she turned with an affectionate smile.

"Darla, look who's here. It's Eddie, your friend. The young man who was at the Busy Bee."

I slowly closed the door behind me and bent to unclip Sonny's leash. He made for Eddie, who managed to bend his trembling knees enough to pat Sonny on his head.

Eddie faced me with a strained, sheepish smile. "Hello, Darla. I thought maybe we could, you know, take a drive and go get a burger and a milk shake or something."

Marilyn beamed. "Doesn't that sound like fun, Darla?"

So Eddie had screwed up his courage to meet Marilyn and ask me out. His newfound courage brought expanded attraction. He had courage after all. But I put on a remote, bland face.

"I don't know... Maybe."

Marilyn came toward me with an encouraging wink. "Maybe? You should go, Darla. Get out of here with your friend and have some lunch. We can leave this evening. We have lots of time."

Fifteen minutes later I was sitting next to Eddie in the front seat of his immaculately clean car, sniffing his Aqua Velva aftershave and wearing my South Sea pearls and diamond drop earrings.

The two-lane road unraveled through dips and turns, past trees and ponds and distant hidden homes nestled behind groves of trees.

"I'm glad you came out with me. I wasn't sure you would," Eddie said, anxiously.

I searched for any topic of conversation. "I like your car. It really is impressive, and it's so clean."

"I like things to be neat and clean."

I thought, *he would run for the trees if he saw my room*. Instead, I said, "So you got all brave and daring and you met Marilyn."

He shifted nervously. "Yeah, well, I saw her at the restaurant, you know, so I felt like I'd kind of already met her. She's nice," he said, smiling. "Yeah, so down-to-earth and nice. And I think she's even prettier in person than on the screen. She sparkles, doesn't she?"

"Yeah. So where's Blondie?" I asked, wanting to provoke.

His smile was instantly erased. "Blondie? Oh, you mean Pam?"

"Yes, Pam. Whatever."

"I didn't want to go out with her. We had broken up."

"Obviously not."

"Don't be so sassy. You're real sassy and, I don't know... well, sassy."

I grinned a little, liking the insult. "Well, I'm sure you know that in the dictionary redundant means, re-dundant."

I was being a smartass and enjoying it.

"So what does that mean?"

"Never mind. Are you going to college?"

"Yes."

"What year?"

"Sophomore."

"Majoring in?"

"Business. My father wants me to run the business someday."

"Is Blondie in college?"

He glanced over. "Sassy, Darla. Okay? Sassy. Her name is Pam, and she's a nice girl, but we just don't have that much in common."

"Well, she shouldn't have gone up to Marilyn like that. She shouldn't have made a scene. That was stu-pid."

"I tried to stop her."

"But you didn't stop her."

"You don't have to be jealous of her."

"I'm not jealous of her," I said, feeling jealous. "I mean, she's all bouncy, flouncy and perky. I'm not jealous of that."

"Well, you're definitely not bouncy or perky."

"Oh yeah?" I said, jutting my jaw out and folding my arms. "What am I, then?"

"Sassy," he said, jerking a confirming nod.

I faced forward. "Whatever."

"Are you a senior in high school?"

Of course I lied. "Yeah."

"Are you going to college next year?"

"Yeah."

"Where?"

"Who knows?"

"You better start looking into it. It's almost January."

"Why aren't you majoring in science, or stargazing, or astrophysics?" I asked.

Eddie dismissed me with a slight wag of his chin. "Because my father wants me to go into the business."

"Seems a shame not to do what you love."

"Don't worry about it," he said, snappishly, obviously not happy about his major.

"Do you like the construction business?"

"Yeah, it's okay." He changed the subject. "Look, do you want to go somewhere fancy or somewhere more casual?"

"Definitely casual."

Twenty minutes later, we sat on opposite sides of a booth at an A&W Root Beer Restaurant, staring at menus.

"I'm going to get a chili dog," I said, excited. "And a root beer. Oh, no, wait a minute. Make that two chili dogs, with extra cheese, and a root beer float, with extra ice cream. That girl over there just finished her float and it looks sooo good."

Eddie looked up, studying me. "You certainly have a good appetite."

"Yeah, well, I've read that these places had really good food, and the ice cream was always fresh."

"What do you mean, 'had good food?"

I kept my eyes glued to the menu. "Forget it."

Eddie's eyes lingered on me. "See, that's what I mean. You say and do things that I just don't get. You're different somehow."

"Anything wrong with that?"

"No, no, there's nothing wrong with that. It's just… well, different, that's all."

His eyes kept exploring, making me uncomfortable.

I stared back at him and shrugged, palms up. "What? Why are you staring at me?"

"You've changed your hair, and your face looks different. I noticed it at the Busy Bee. And I like those earrings."

That pleased me. "Do you like the change?" I said in a small voice, blushing a bit.

Eddie's voice softened. "Yeah, I like it."

"Marilyn helped me with it."

"Oh, well, Marilyn… Yes, well, all I can say is that she did a good job and the change is good. You look a little older and a little sophisticated."

Eddie had said all the right words and I began to feel hot attraction for him. He was angling his gaze out the window, suddenly taken by some idea and I was sure it had something to do with the stars. For some reason, I found that attractive, a guy who had his head in the stars. I glimpsed his handsome profile and thought, *This is a guy I could hang out with, and kiss, and hug, and maybe even love someday.*

When he faced me again, I stared boldly at him, taking in his moody, honest eyes, his hard set jaw. I sensed a soft, erotic energy, but maybe that was projection, or maybe I saw something in him he had not yet discovered in himself.

When he'd spoken about his business major, I'd seen frustration and restlessness. When I called Pam "Blondie," I'd seen amusement and conflict. Eddie was a white-hat guy. I thought, *What kind of man will you become, Eddie?*

I liked Eddie. I liked Eddie too much and way too fast, a first for me. No other guy I'd met had intrigued me like Eddie. I wanted to kiss him, like Marilyn had kissed Tony Curtis in the movie *Some Like It Hot*.

"Why are you looking at me like that?" he asked.

Fortunately, the waitress drifted over and we ordered.

We didn't talk much as we ate, and I ate like a girl who'd been marooned on a desert island for weeks and hadn't had a good meal.

Eddie was amused and pleased and, as I watched him eat in a precise, calm and measured way, he became ever more attractive. My heart began to hurt a little, another first. What was it? Well, of course, it was an awakening—it was the first blooming of love for a man.

Eddie asked if I wanted to see an afternoon movie, and I asked which one. He said, Frank Sinatra in *Young at Heart*. I'd seen it two or three times in the future and it wasn't one of my favorite movies. I thought Frank whined too much about his bad luck. He should have gotten off his ass and taken some action.

But I wanted to be with Eddie, so I called Marilyn and asked her if it would be okay.

Her voice seemed to sing with happiness. "Oh, yes, Darla. Go. I haven't seen it yet, but Frank says he likes it. You can tell me all about it."

The theater was nearly full. What ruined the experience were the clouds of cigarette smoke that floated across the screen as if the fog were rolling in. I thought, *What is it with these people*? Obviously, smoking hadn't been banned in movie theaters yet.

It was dark outside when we left the theater. As we drove back to the house, Eddie shared his movie evaluation, and it was close to mine.

"Not Sinatra's best movie," Eddie said. "I liked Doris Day, though, and the song."

"Yeah, me too," I said, feeling uncharacteristically comfortable with Eddie. I'd never been relaxed around other guys.

As the silence stretched out and we came to the final bend in the road, Eddie glanced over. "Are you going to be around in the next few days?"

"No… Marilyn and I are going on a little trip."

When he spoke, I heard disappointment in his voice, and that pleased me. "Oh? Where to?"

"Rhode Island."

"Relatives?"

I didn't want to explain. "Yeah… relatives."

"When will you be back?"

"I don't know."

Eddie turned into the driveway and drove up toward the house, parking behind the station wagon. He shut off the lights but kept the engine running.

We sat still, me searching for a subject to expand the moment. I couldn't think of anything. I wanted Eddie to kiss me.

Eddie heaved out a nervous breath. "Well, okay then…"

And neither of us moved.

Eddie breathed out again. I waited, my hands folded, feeling vulnerable and humbled by a torrent of brand new and confusing emotions.

"Well… okay then. I guess… Well…" he stammered, his voice shaky. "You know, I was thinking, Darla, that I'd like to come by again. We could go out again. Do something. We could look through my telescope. Well, I guess that doesn't sound all that fun to you, does it?"

I turned sharply. "Yes, it does. I love looking through your telescope."

He brightened. "Really? Truly?"

"Yes."

"See, that's another reason I like you, Darla. You're up for things. You get enthusiastic about things. So can I see you again, soon? Can we go out?"

I stared at him, remembering something I'd read in one of my mother's old poetry books. *Time is fragile… each moment connected to the other… each fleeting.*

"I'd like to, Eddie, when I get back. I'd like to go out."

Eddie nodded, more confident and assured. "Good. That's good. Okay. Marilyn gave me the number to the house. When will you be back?"

I shrugged. "Maybe after Christmas."

"Good. I'll call you."

He walked me to the door and, when he didn't kiss me, my heart felt the rejection. It ached. I wondered if I'd ever see him again.

Before he climbed into the car, I wiggled my fingers goodbye, like I'd seen Marilyn do in a movie. It was time for THE END to roll across the screen, the swift and possible end to this love affair.

I stayed outside, watching the car's red taillights melt away; waiting until Marilyn opened the front door.

"Darla, honey. Is everything all right? It's cold out here. We should leave soon. It's after six o'clock."

I turned to her with a smile, seeing her lovely face, framed in the door light.

I gazed at her, thinking, *Am I making ripples in time that will affect the future?*

CHAPTER 22

Our journey finally began about an hour later. While I was out with Eddie, Marilyn had packed her bag and made ham and cheese sandwiches. We grabbed a six-pack of 6-ounce Cokes and loaded everything into the station wagon. I carried a confused Sonny in my arms while Marilyn fed him doggie treats and kissed his ears.

Although Marilyn had said we should wait until morning, I knew that was a delay tactic, so I said, "If we don't leave now, we'll never make it. And we've got to make it. This time, Marilyn, you've got to go."

We started off into the risky night, traveling along winding, two-lane roads, skirted on both sides by black, snowy trees and spreading meadows, where distant houses were silhouetted, their windows blinking like tiny fires.

"Did you plan our trip?" I asked.

Marilyn nodded. "Yes. First, we're going to Binghamton, then to Syracuse, then to Montpellier, Vermont. Then we're off to Springfield, Mass., and Boston and, finally, Providence."

"Wow, we really *are* taking the long way around."

"Are you in a hurry?"

"No. But are you sure we'll make it to Rhode Island by Christmas?"

"Oh, sure. Anyway, I'll need all that time to build my courage. And besides that, I want to see some of New England. I've only seen New York City, Niagara Falls and Connecticut. If we're going on a Christmas journey, then I say, let's really have an adventure."

"So... Your father is in Providence?"

Marilyn inhaled a breath, as if she needed strength to verbalize it. "It's about 20 minutes from Providence, in a little town called Collier. Have you ever been to Rhode Island?"

"No. Never."

And then we were quiet, as Marilyn's eyes clouded over and her pretty mouth sagged a little into worry. She began to hum a tuneless song. I wondered if we'd make it to Rhode Island. I wasn't sure Marilyn was really up to it. I wasn't even sure if *I* was up to it.

"Did I tell you what I thought about my father when I was a little girl?"

I looked over.

"I was just a little girl when I saw a photo of a man I didn't know. It was hanging in the hallway. He was quite handsome, and he had a pencil-thin mustache, much like the one Clark Gable wore in some of his pictures. I asked my mother who he was, and she said, 'That's your father.' I was so happy, and for a long time after, I fantasized that my father *was* Clark Gable. For a while I even slept with his picture under my pillow, and I proudly told my classmates that I was the daughter of the great Clark Gable. Of course they laughed at me, and it always made me a little sad and a little mad."

Marilyn tried to laugh off the memory. "And here I am, all these years later. Sometimes I think I've been living a nightmare, and I don't tell many people that, not that it matters all that much. All of us have our problems, don't we? It's not that I'm the only one. But do you know what makes me so very sad and I can't shake it? Only two weeks ago I had to fill out an official form in front of my secretary, who had to witness it. I was so embarrassed when I came to the line marked 'Father'. I had to write 'Unknown.'"

I sat up. "Soon, you'll never have to write 'unknown' again."

"Yes... And maybe then the nightmares will stop."

I began to have second thoughts about joining Marilyn when she met her father. Even if she did summon the courage to find the house and stroll up and knock on the door, the possibilities of what might happen were daunting. Marilyn Monroe was fragile and emotionally vulnerable. If her father wasn't there, how would Marilyn respond? If he welcomed her with open arms, how would she respond? If he didn't welcome her, how would she respond? Whatever the outcome, I would be a third party, tangled up in an emotional moment; a once-in-a lifetime event, packed with uncertainty and volatile passions.

I turned around to see Sonny curled up, sound asleep in the back seat, the long walks and a full belly of food having made him sleepy.

The radio played Christmas carols and radio jingles; they broke my somber mood and brought a smile. Years later, I watched them again on *YouTube*.

*"You'll wonder where the yellow went, when you brush your teeth with **Pepsodent**."* The deep-voiced announcer spoke with authority when he said, *"New formula **Pepsodent** contains IMP. There's nothing as good for getting teeth white."*

After Phil Harris and The Sportsmen Quartet sang *Jingle Bells*, the peppy ad for *Alka Seltzer* played, *"Plop, plop, fizz, fizz, oh what a relief it is."* The singer sounded like an irritating seven-year-old kid with a whiny voice, although surely everyone in 1954 must have known the kid was actually some voice-over artist, imitating a kid.

The old jingles, the Christmas carols and the hypnotic hum of the engine soon lulled me to sleep, and I nodded off. I hadn't slept much the night before, and I was light-headed, still feeling emotionally hungover from Marilyn and Joe and all the drama.

I shook awake when Marilyn tapped the brakes and we slowly came to a stop. I yawned, peering ahead, seeing the sweeping red dome lights of two police cars, one car parked diagonally across the road, the other parked at the sloping shoulder.

"What's all this about?" I asked.

Marilyn snatched the headscarf beside her, adroitly pulled it over her head and tied it snuggly under her chin.

"I don't want the cops to know who I am," she said, also slipping on her black-rimmed glasses, allowing her mouth to sag, eyes to droop. It was a startling transformation.

"It will be in the papers tomorrow. What happens if my father reads about it, figures out that I'm coming to see him and runs back to California?"

She grew edgy. "I'm going to pretend I have laryngitis, so you do all the talking, okay?"

I nodded, feeling the heavy responsibility. I cleared my throat, thinking I'd imitate that irritating seven-year-old kid in the *Alka Seltzer* commercial.

A policeman with a flashlight approached, the beam pointed down at the road. When he drew near, I leaned toward Marilyn and the window she was cranking down.

The policeman was young, with a mild face and bored eyes. Marilyn angled her head down and away, as he stooped toward the window.

"Hello, ladies, sorry to bother you, but we're looking for an escaped convict."

I presented a pleasant smile and pitched up my voice, hearing it squeak and crack, sounding more like a sick parrot than the voice in the commercial.

"We're just passing through," I said. "My friend here has a bad cold, and she's lost her voice."

"Have you seen anything suspicious?" the policeman asked.

"No... Nothing."

"Have you seen a big guy walking along the road, maybe hitchhiking?"

"No..."

"Where are you headed?"

"Binghamton, for Christmas."

He shined his beam into the backseat, the shaft of light striking Sonny. He lifted his head and barked, a little snappy bark that said something like, "*Get that stupid light out of my face, you bum. Don't bother me.*"

The policeman said, "Cute dog."

Marilyn's chin was resting on her chest. I grinned brightly. "Yeah, he's a good dog."

"All right, ladies. Drive safely now and Merry Christmas. Hope your friend feels better real soon."

"Thank you," I said, as Marilyn rolled up the window.

After we passed through the roadblock, Marilyn removed her glasses and pulled off the headscarf.

"He was handsome, wasn't he?" Marilyn said.

"I don't know. I guess."

"That was some voice you had back there," Marilyn said. "I almost laughed out loud."

"Me too. I guess I won't be doing voiceovers."

Marilyn laughed. "You could do cartoon characters. I thought it was funny."

"I'll stick to writing and taking photos."

Thinking about the escaped convict made me uncomfortable and I gazed out the window, my eyes searching the night, seeing my faintly mirrored image. The road ahead suddenly looked unfriendly, as it curved, steepened, fell and darkened.

Marilyn saw the hitchhiker before I did. "Look, Darla, a hitchhiker."

I sat up, squinting, as she put a foot to the brake. Ahead, on the shoulder of the road, I glimpsed the silhouette of a tall man. My heart seized up. I couldn't believe Marilyn was slowing down.

"You're not going to pick him up, are you?"

"There's nothing around here, and it's so cold and dark out there. He's probably tired and hungry."

"But Marilyn," I sputtered. "What about the roadblock? The convict?"

"Oh, honey, don't you worry about that."

Marilyn pulled the car onto the shoulder of the road and stopped. I stared at her, incredulous, powerless. Framed in the headlights, with a hand shading his eyes from the sharp light, I saw he was big, wearing a long, heavy coat and a black cowboy hat, pulled low over his forehead. He didn't look like the kind of man you'd want to pick up on a cold, dark night in December—or any other month of the year.

CHAPTER 23

Marilyn had replaced her scarf and glasses. "Roll your window down, Darla, so the man can talk to us."

The man was just outside my window, one hand pushed deep into his long, black coat pocket, and the other clutching a small worn suitcase. He lingered above me like a big, dark shadow. Sonny was trembling. I was trembling.

"Marilyn...?" I pleaded.

"We're just going to talk to him. It's okay. Really."

It took all my nerve to roll the window down halfway.

Marilyn leaned toward me and the passenger window, so she could speak to him.

"Where are you going?"

The man stooped down, and I got a quick look at his face. My first, immediate impression? The man favored a young Johnny Cash, the country singer, only I wasn't sure if Johnny Cash was known or popular in 1954. He spoke in a smooth bass-baritone, like Johnny Cash.

"As far as you can take me," he said.

"We're going to Binghamton, New York," Marilyn said. "And then further north, to Rhode Island."

If he recognized Marilyn, he didn't show it.

I leaned back in the seat, as if expecting an attack, and my restless, scared eyes squinched up.

"If you'd be so kind, I'd love to travel with you for a spell. I'm a bit cold and used up from travel."

His manner was mild, and his voice calm, with the sing-song cadence of a southern accent. He didn't seem threatening.

To my horror, Marilyn said, "Climb into the backseat, if you don't mind riding with Sonny, our dog."

The man touched two fingers to his hat. "Much obliged, ma'am," he said, sounding like a cowboy.

He opened the back door and, before climbing in, he removed his hat, ducked his head, and slid his suitcase onto the seat. He sat, closed the door, and let out a weary sigh.

"The heat feels good," he said. "The cold has seeped into my bones."

Sonny's pitiful, frightened eyes watched the man, his body quivering.

The man turned to Sonny with a soft smile. "Now there's no need to be afraid of me, Sonny. I love dogs, and they've never had a cause not to love me. I've always had dogs hanging around. But it's okay, I know it takes dogs time to get used to folks, so you just go ahead and sniff me out for a while."

I smelled booze on the man's breath, and I was sure we were all done for. No doubt this was the convict the cops were looking for, and this guy was going to shoot us, strangle us, or beat our heads in and take the car. Every single nerve in my body was alive with fright.

Marilyn nudged the car into gear, and we started off into the blackest night I can remember.

No one spoke for a time, as we drove along a serpentine road that I was certain would eventually drop us off the end of the world. Marilyn glanced into the rearview mirror and smiled at the man. I had to see what had prompted that smile, so I slowly turned.

The man had crossed his arms, and his chin was resting on his chest. He was asleep, and Sonny had inched closer to him, studying him, his chin resting on his paws.

"He must be exhausted," Marilyn said softly.

I still didn't trust him. "He's been drinking," I whispered.

Marilyn twisted up her lips. "So what? Who wouldn't? It's cold out there."

I was amazed by Marilyn's *laissez-faire* attitude; her utter lack of fear. How could a person be so courageous in one sphere and so frightened in another?

"What are we going to do with him when we stop at a motel for the night?" I asked.

"I'll pay for his room. From the looks of him, he needs a good night's sleep."

Our headlights pierced the night and I grew more edgy and confused, feeling a bleak anxiety, as if I were trapped in a nightmare.

Marilyn hummed along with the radio, and I tried to sleep, but couldn't. About an hour later, Marilyn checked the rearview mirror, smiling into it. "Feeling better?" she asked.

I twisted around halfway. The man was awake. He interlaced his fingers and stretched his arms, his palms facing ahead.

"Oh yes, ma'am, I am feeling much better, thank you. I didn't mean to drop off like that."

"That's okay," Marilyn said. "Have you traveled a long way?"

"Yes, ma'am, I have."

"You have a southern accent."

"Yes, I do. I'm originally from Arkansas. Pardon me for not introducing myself. My name is John. John R. Cash."

I shut my eyes against impossibility. *No way*, I thought. *There is no way this man is **the** Johnny Cash, or would be Johnny Cash.*

"I'm Norma Jeane and this is Darla."

"Please to meet you both, ladies. Again, I'm much obliged that you picked me up back there, and forgive me for saying, but maybe you two ladies shouldn't have. I only mean that... well, you never know who you're picking up, especially on a dark road at night."

There was plenty I wanted to say in agreement, but I kept my mouth shut.

"Sonny could protect us," Marilyn said, with a little laugh.

When I swiveled my head around, Sonny's head was resting comfortably on John's leg and he was stroking him. John had a craggy and hard, but handsome, face. From the dim glow of the front dashboard lights, I saw that his raven black hair was mussed, and a little curl hung like an inverted question mark over his forehead. The man was a dead ringer for Johnny Cash, no doubt about it.

"Sonny is good people," John said. "I knew so right away."

I spoke up, hoping John was close to his destination. "Where'd you say you were going?"

"Well, darlin', I'm headed for Texas, that's home."

Marilyn stared at him, baffled. "Texas? But you're going the wrong way, John."

His laugh was low and mild. "Yes, I know. But I've got something to do I should have done a while back. Now, I've got to finish it."

Marilyn waited for his answer. I stared hard, nearly certain that this was the real, the great, the future legend, Johnny Cash. My father had been a Johnny Cash fan for years, and I had played Cash's album *Hello, I'm Johnny Cash* repeatedly, until my stepmother screamed at me to stop. I especially loved the song *Route 1, Box 144*, a sad and haunting story, and *If I Were a Carpenter*. Cash's mellow singing voice was warm and personal, filled with longing and wisdom. I'd often listen to one of his songs when I couldn't sleep, or when my father and Carol had one of their fire and gasoline arguments.

Before I could stop my mouth, I heard myself say, in a startled wonder, "You're Johnny Cash."

He offered an easy, wrinkled smile. "Well... I go by John. You can just call me John. But I like the sound of Johnny, Darla."

Words caught in my throat. "Yeah... Johnny," was all I could force out.

"Are you all right, honey?" Marilyn asked, sensing my unease.

"I'm good," I said, swinging my gaze from Marilyn back to Johnny, and then from Johnny to Marilyn, then back to Johnny. I felt drunk, or loopy, as if the world were spinning around like a merry-go-round.

"So, how far are you going?" Marilyn asked.

Johnny turned his eyes toward the rearview mirror and Marilyn. "I'm sure it's out of your way. I'm headed for a little town in Vermont, just south of Burlington."

"We were planning to go to Montpellier," Marilyn said. "We can take you to Burlington."

John scratched his head. "That would be very kind of you, but I don't want to put you out, especially since it's almost Christmas."

Marilyn's eyes were warm in the rearview mirror. "Don't worry about putting us out, John. Darla and I are on a Christmas adventure. As long as we get to Rhode Island by Christmas Day, we'll be just fine."

"And who is in Rhode Island, Norma Jeane?"

Marilyn's voice rose a bit, as if forced. "My father."

"That's a real nice thing to do; going to see your father on Christmas."

Marilyn changed the subject. "Are you close to your father, John?"

"Norma Jeane, my father is a man of love. He always loved me to death. He worked hard during the depression, in sawmills, on the railroad and in the cotton fields, and he never hit me. Never. I don't ever remember a really cross or unkind word from him."

Marilyn's smile failed. Her eyes returned to the road. She seemed both touched and envious at the same time, at least that's how I translated her sudden melancholy expression.

"And who's in Burlington, John?" Marilyn asked. "Your father?"

"No... not my father. The wife of an old Air Force buddy who was killed over in Germany. It wasn't any kind of combat that got him; it was a silly jeep accident. Just one of those senseless deaths that God sends to test the people left behind, I suspect. Billy and I were good friends. We did our basic training at Lackland and technical training at Brooks Air Force Base, both in San Antonio. Then we were assigned to the 12th Radio Squadron Mobile Security Service at Landsberg, Germany."

He paused before continuing, twisting his hands, and I sensed he wanted to get it all out, and what better way to do it than with strangers.

"I hope I'm not being a burden on you two, but I suppose sometimes it does a person good to talk about things, especially when feelings get all bunched up inside. Anyway, a few days ago I was sitting in some bar in town, and I got to drinkin' too much because Vivian and me—Vivian's my wife... we got into a little argument and I don't even remember what it was over now."

"Isn't it funny how that is?" Marilyn said. "We get into arguments with somebody we love and later we can't remember what it was all about."

"Ain't that the truth, Norma Jeane. But like all those old songs go, I was drinkin', feelin' low and lost and ugly about myself, and I thought that Christmastime was the time to do it. To do what Billy had asked me to do. I visited Billy in the hospital after the jeep accident, and the last thing he asked me to do for him was to go see his wife, Doris, and tell her how much he loved her. So I left that neon bar in Texas and started off, and somewhere along the way, I lost most of my money."

I asked, "Is your wife still in Texas?"

"Yes, she is, Darla. She was about your age when I met her, only 17-years old when we met at a roller-skating rink in San Antonio. Pretty little girl she was, and she still is."

He paused, turning to look out into the night. "We dated for three weeks and then, as life would have it, I was deployed to Germany for a three-year tour."

"Will you get back home for Christmas?" Marilyn asked.

"I have to, Norma Jeane. After I see Doris, I'll have to hop a freight or some cargo plane or something and get back to Vivian. I called her the day I left and told her what I had to do. I told her how I'd got to thinking about Billy and was feelin' real bad that I hadn't gone to see Doris, like he'd asked me to."

"I think it's a good thing to do, John," Marilyn said. "It's a kind thing and a thoughtful one. I'm sure your wife understands. It's a promise you have to keep."

"Yes, Norma Jeane. It's a promise I should have kept when I got discharged in July. I should have traveled to Vermont right then, instead of going home to Texas. But... sometimes I'm two people. John is the nice one and Cash causes all the trouble. They fight."

And then John got quiet and so did Marilyn. I watched the night fly by, as the crazy reality of time, place and company got all jumbled in my head. It was part dream, part daydream and part hallucination. At least, that's how it felt.

"Look! There's a diner. Is anybody hungry?" Marilyn said. "Let's stop and eat."

"But we have ham and cheese sandwiches," I said.

"We'll save them. The diner will be more fun, don't you think so, John?"

John lowered his head. "You two ladies go ahead. I'm not the least bit hungry. Sonny and me will wait for you in the car and we'll both catch us a little nap."

"No, sir, John," Marilyn said. "You come in and keep us girls company. We might need you to protect us," Marilyn said, with a laugh and a toss of her head.

Marilyn drove into the half-filled lot of a traditional diner, under a green neon sign that said The Victory Diner. She shut-off the engine, tugged her scarf snuggly over her head, and then adjusted her eyeglasses. They helped hide some of her famous face, but not all of it. She pulled a tissue from her purse, blotted off the rest of her red lipstick, and then turned to me.

"A day or so ago, Darla, you mentioned something about a movie titled the *Misfits*."

Surprised, I nodded. "Yeah... But I meant *Niagara*."

Marilyn nodded, smiling contemplatively. "Look at the three of us. We couldn't be more different, kind of like misfits, and we're each off on our own adventure. We could be called the misfits, couldn't we?"

CHAPTER 24

As we passed through the double glass doors, Marilyn ducked her head, letting me lead the way to the hostess stand. John was behind Marilyn, tall, ruggedly handsome and distinctive, and Marilyn was... well, Marilyn. The square diner featured a long, triangular formica countertop with swivel stools, and ten-to-twelve yellow upholstered booths scattered about the room, each with a tabletop jukebox. Near the entrance, a tall, spruce Christmas tree displayed kitschy plastic ornaments and glowing red and green tree lights through layers of sparkling tinsel.

Sleepy and bored eyes lifted and found us, awakening a little, settling on Marilyn and John.

I stood ramrod straight, feeling snotty and special. After all, I was with a world-renowned actress, whether this crowd knew it or not, and I was being escorted by a soon-to-be music legend. I wanted to say, *Eat your hearts out, you nobodies* but, of course, I let my arrogant demeanor speak for itself. I was a princess, passing through a town inhabited by lowly serfs. I was floating, exalted and royal. In short, I was all puffed up at being a nobody, lucky to be with two somebodies, who were modest, friendly and kind.

A hostess with lazy eyes and a protruding lower lip glanced at Marilyn, her eyes suddenly awake, aware, exploring and unsure. But Marilyn slouched, placed a hand to her mouth and faked a hacking cough. Put off, the hostess glanced away, sure that this could not possibly be *the* sexy Marilyn from the movies *Niagara* and *The River of No Return*. And, anyway, why would Marilyn be away from Hollywood, making an appearance in that little diner out in the middle of nowhere?

Satisfied her observation was correct, our hostess dropped a mint into her mouth as she escorted us to a rear booth that looked out on the parking lot, and Marilyn sat with her back to the dining room.

Being a gentleman, John let me slide in first and, to my nervous delight, he sat next to me, both of us facing Marilyn.

The dining crowd had returned to their conversations, and we were close enough to the triangular counter to pick up some conversation. Marilyn reached for the paper menus, propped between the sugar dispenser and the salt and pepper shakers, and handed one to John and one to me. John didn't even glance at it. He shifted uncomfortably.

"I'm just going to have coffee," he said.

"Oh, John, at least have a donut or a hamburger deluxe with it," Marilyn said. "I'm going to have a cheeseburger deluxe, so we might as well have two."

"Make it three," I said, delighted to be a joiner, and shocked to see that a cheeseburger deluxe cost only 45 cents. Coffee was 10 cents and milk shakes were 30 cents.

"Then three it is," Marilyn said. "And why don't we have three chocolate milk shakes."

"Just coffee," John insisted.

A thin, attractive waitress with pointed breasts and plenty of makeup wandered over, pad and pencil at the ready. She wore a tan and white nylon uniform and her dishwater blonde hair was styled in a flip. She was all business until her lusterless eyes found John. Instantly, they lit up with sexy pleasure, and she turned her full attention on him.

"And what will you have, sir?" she asked, with a quick batting of her long lashes.

"Now don't you go calling me sir, darlin'," John said with a friendly grin. "It makes me feel like I'm back in the Air Force."

"Oh, you were in the Air Force?" the waitress asked, delighted they had something in common. "My little brother was in the Air Force. Where were you stationed?"

"I was in the 12th Radio Squadron Mobile of the U.S. Air Force Security Service at Landsberg, West Germany. Where was your brother?"

"Oh, he wound up out at Edward's Air Force Base in California fixing airplane engines. Then he got out, married an Ohio girl, and they moved somewhere in Ohio, and he bought himself a farm. Now he raises hogs and corn and kids."

"Well, God love him, darlin'. My family farmed twenty acres of cotton and other crops, and I worked right alongside my parents and siblings in the fields. It's good being close to the earth."

"And what are you raising now?" the waitress asked, stepping closer to John.

"I'm afraid I've been raising lots of trouble for myself. Darlin', the beast in me is caged by frail and fragile bars."

The waitress's face colored with heated attraction, and her eyes went all dreamy.

"Are you gonna be in town long?"

"No, ma'am, I'm just passing through. Now, I'd better order something before you close up the place."

"Oh, we don't never close. We're open twenty-four hours, so you just sit there and relax. Now what can I get for you?"

"These women think I should order a deluxe cheeseburger. What do you think?"

The waitress's eyes fluttered, offering him a flirtatious invitation. "I think you should order whatever you want. Aren't you the man? Shouldn't a man your size choose for himself?"

John flashed his winning smile—a smile that someday, in the not-too-distant future, would charm millions. "You just said a cotton-pickin' mouthful, darlin'. Just bring me a donut and a cup of coffee."

The waitress lingered a moment, not wanting to leave John's aura, but she finally left, glancing back over her shoulder at him with a coy smile.

Marilyn placed her chin in her palm, grinning at John. "John, honey, that woman just fell in love with you."

John kept his lopsided grin. "Well, Norma Jeane, the woman has a pretty set of blue eyes and a heart of goodness. That I can see. You know what else I can see," he continued, studying Marilyn for the first time. "You show a remarkable resemblance to Miss Marilyn Monroe. I'm sure you must hear that all the time."

Marilyn's grin vanished. She straightened, lowered her chin and turned her head from him. "Yeah, I do hear that sometimes."

"You ought to be flattered, Norma Jeane. I think Marilyn Monroe is one of the prettiest women on the movie screen today. Vivian and I saw her in *The River of No Return,* and she said Marilyn was her favorite actress. Vivian said she's got that somethin' that all real movie stars have, except she has more of it."

Marilyn tried not to look pleased.

I said, "Do you sing, John?"

John turned to me. "Now what makes you think that, Darla?"

"It's your voice. You have a good speaking voice. It's easy and nice to listen to. I bet you're a great singer."

John gave me a warm smile. "Well, yes, Darla, I do sing, and I love singing. In the Air Force I started a band called *The Landsberg Barbarians.* We had a lot of fun."

In a booth to our left, two young men sat eating, a guitar case propped conspicuously next to one of the boys. I wanted to hear Johnny Cash sing, and I wanted everybody else to hear him sing.

"Would you sing for us?" I asked.

John folded his hands on the tabletop, searching my face. "Well, Darla, I don't have my guitar and I'm not so sure these folks want me to interrupt their supper."

"Will you excuse me?" I asked.

Reluctantly, John pushed up and stepped aside. I slid out and went over to the two 20-something boys who were munching on hamburgers and fries. One boy was broad and handsome; the other boy was skinny,

with small restless eyes, a weak chin and a goofy grin.
The black guitar case was propped next to him.

When I stepped over, they glanced up, mildly curious. My earrings, new makeup and nifty hairdo helped
bolster my courage. "Hello... I was wondering if I
could borrow your guitar for a few minutes. Do you
see that man over there? He's a great singer and I want
him to sing a song for me."

The handsome boy looked me over and seemed
pleased, and that pleased me. His smile was fetching.
The boy with the goofy grin held that grin while his
chilly eyes met mine. He didn't seem impressed by me.
He swung his eyes to John. I looked at John, who
seemed amused by my chutzpah.

"What's he going to sing?" Goofy Grin asked.

I shrugged. "I don't know."

"Do you sing?"

"Only for my dog, but he doesn't like it. He howls."

"How old are you?" the handsome boy asked, interest in me building in his eyes.

I straightened my shoulders. Now I was having my
own little flirtation, and it was fun.

"I'm eighteen," I lied, once again.

"You live around here?"

"No..."

"You gonna be around for a while?"

I almost said yes, because the boy had the most gorgeous almond eyes, auburn hair and wicked little mouth
I'd ever seen. I would have kissed him right then and
there if I'd been a little crazier.

"Maybe... I don't know," I said, not wanting to slam
the door on this sudden and hot moment.

"What do you mean, maybe? You either know if you're going to be around or you don't. Unless you're a tease. I don't like teases."

That chilled me down. I didn't like his manner or his snotty tone. But I couldn't take my eyes off his lips. "I just mean, I don't know. We might stay around here for the night or something. I mean, I don't know because we might leave. When I said, I don't know, that's what I meant. It's simple to understand, isn't it?" I said, with a force that surprised me. Why was I getting huffy about it?

The interest in his eyes faded, like dark clouds covering a bright sun, and my 16-year-old soul was devastated. He'd written me off.

"I don't loan my guitar out to anybody," Goofy Grin said.

And just like that, I was ready for a fight. My hands formed fists. "Why are you two such assholes?"

Both stiffened in hot offense. Maybe girls weren't so profane in 1954, but I didn't care.

"Beat it," the handsome boy said. "Go sing to your dog and leave us alone. No guitar for you, okay, baby?"

Angry and humiliated, I turned to leave, feeling like Sonny when he crept off with his tail between his legs.

Suddenly, Marilyn was beside me, beaming, still wearing the scarf and glasses. She placed a five-dollar bill on the table between the two boys.

"Hello, boys… Can we please rent the guitar for just one or two songs? Is five dollars enough?"

Five dollars was a lot of money in 1954. I later learned it was the equivalent of about 30 dollars in 1998.

Neither boy looked at the money. They gawked at Marilyn, looking her up and down, their eyes nearly bulging. They'd had no problem recognizing her. Goofy Grin dropped his grin, and Handsome with the Wicked Mouth looked stupid.

Goofy pointed at Marilyn. "But you're... You're Marilyn..."

Marilyn cut him off with a smile and a flick of her hand. "No, I'm not Marilyn Monroe. I get that all the time. I'm Norma Jeane, a nobody. Is it a deal? Can we rent your guitar?" she asked, sweetly, placing a second five-dollar bill on top of the first.

Goofy Grin scrambled to his feet, snatched up his guitar case and swung it onto the booth seat. He fumbled about, snapping the latches open. With care, he lifted the guitar from the case and presented it to Marilyn as if it were an award, his hands shaky.

The guitar had a beautiful, cherry sunburst finish and a rosewood fingerboard, inlaid with mother-of-pearl parallelograms.

Marilyn accepted it. "Thank you, gentlemen. My friend over there, John, is going to play one or two songs and then we'll bring it right back. Promise."

With that, Marilyn turned about and carried the guitar to John.

"Now, John, honey, please play us a song."

John looked at Marilyn, at me, and at the two boys, and then he shook his head, grinning.

"After that performance, how can I say no?"

He took the guitar, appraising it with appreciation, then glanced at the boys, nodding to them in approval. "It's a pretty one," he said. "A fine instrument. Thank you, boys."

The boys had their hands in their pockets, eyes still focused on Marilyn. It was clear they didn't believe her denial of being Marilyn.

I had returned to the booth, feeling defeated and wilted like an old flower. I was irritated at myself and, for the first time, I was irritated at Marilyn. She'd charmed them, as she always charmed everyone and, next to her, I looked like a silly, teenage bitch.

She must have felt it. Her eyes found mine, and she smiled tenderly at me and mouthed the words, "I love you."

How could I stay mad at her, or envy her, and not love her back?

John pulled a guitar pick from his pocket and strummed a few chords, producing rich, deep tones. Curious and skeptical heads swiveled around, watchful. He tuned a string or two, then swept his dark eyes out over the diner, while looping the guitar strap over his shoulder.

"Ladies and gentlemen... Folks, please pardon me for interrupting your suppers. I'm just going to sing a song or two for Darla here, and then I'll be on my way and you'll never hear from me again."

I nearly burst out laughing. Within a few years, Johnny Cash would be a household name.

CHAPTER 25

"My name is John R. Cash, and I'm going to sing a song I wrote while I was serving in the Air Force in Germany. The song is called *Folsom Prison Blues*."

He began the song, standing tall and austere, plucking the bass string, imitating the sound of a boxcar's clickety-clack along a railroad track. Goose bumps crawled up my spine. I'd heard that song hundreds of times in the future, and the hard lyrics and driving beat always thrilled me. But these people were hearing it for the first time, and they were meeting the incomparable Johnny Cash for the first time.

Johnny sang in a deep, resonate baritone, not as gravelly as it would become in later years, but just as honest and true, alive with originality and darkness.

"… I hear that train a comin'…"

I observed the guests in the diner, at first showing only mild interest; they were polite but more interested in food and conversation than music. But as Johnny leaned into the guitar, and his voice took on strength, and his eyes filled with a lively, warm light, the faces were gradually transformed. Smiles appeared; there was finger tapping, toe tapping.

Slowly, inevitably, the room awakened to Johnny, who flashed with lightning, who unlocked dull prison brains, who aroused emotions, stirred hearts and gave birth to a new sound and throbbing excitement.

I grabbed my camera and clicked off shot after shot—of Johnny and the diners, who were now mostly standing, some clapping, some whistling.

Marilyn stood by our booth, content to be out of the limelight. I snapped photos of her enthusiastic clapping; her eyes bright with happiness.

I was drugged with ecstasy, my camera snapping away. When Johnny struck the last chord, the room erupted into raucous applause, crying out "More! More!"

He looked out over the audience, his eyes glistening with gratitude.

"Thank you, folks. I thank you for that. You're all very kind. I'm gonna finish up now, with the first song I ever sang with my mother down in the cotton fields in Arkansas. It's a simple song called *What Would You Give in Exchange for Your Soul.*"

He sang it simply, with honest emotional feeling that stirred everyone. I lowered my camera and, having never heard the song, I was nearly moved to tears. The room fell into silence: the jukebox was silent, the cooks and waitresses were silent, and the customers were silent, all caught up by the unpretentious reverence of the song and the gifted man in black who was singing it.

When the applause finally died away, it would be another moment I'd never forget: John R. Cash signing autographs on napkins, business cards, menus, and postcards snatched from the postcard carousel at the front entrance. It was obvious to anyone present that night that John R. Cash would one day be a big star.

Marilyn returned the guitar to the two speechless boys, turning back to us with a little wink.

When we finally sat to eat, our waitress, who was lost in hypnotic love over John, told him that the crowd had chipped in and paid for our dinner, including the tip.

"They insisted that you have the cheeseburger deluxe with extra fries and a large vanilla milk shake."

With true humility, John thanked her. Then standing up, he waved, thanking the crowd, who cheered him again.

Before our waitress reluctantly left our booth, she refilled John's coffee cup and slipped him a folded piece of paper, certainly her telephone number and address. Other women in the diner would have done the same, but they were with husbands or boyfriends, so all they could do was flash him kittenish eyes.

John thanked the waitress, politely, and she finally wandered away like a lovesick teenager, absently refilling coffee cups, staring off into space. Surely her mind was alive with images of romantic nights and warm summer days, locked in kisses with John.

We ate in silence for a time, John eating voraciously, and Marilyn amused by the entire event. Once again, I was amazed that no one other than Goofy and Handsome had recognized Marilyn Monroe. Even with the scarf and glasses and her frumpy sweater, I'm sure I would have known her. But that night, all eyes had been focused on the future Johnny Cash and away from the mystery woman beside him.

"I'm glad to see you're eating, John," Marilyn said, with an endearing smile.

He looked sheepish. "I guess all that singin' made me hungry."

I asked a kind-looking man nearby if he'd take a picture of the three of us, and he snapped several. I imagined how we looked. There we were, eating in a diner, Johnny Cash, Marilyn Monroe and me. Surely we could have fit into the 1942 painting by Edward Hopper, *The Nighthawks*, one of the best-known images of twentieth-century art. The painting depicts an all-night diner in which three customers, all lost in their own thoughts, have gathered. It is viewed from outside, through the diner's large glass window.

In 1985, Gottfried Helnwein painted a parody of that Hopper painting, using the same setting but featuring Marilyn Monroe, Humphrey Bogart, James Dean and Elvis Presley. He titled it *Boulevard of Broken Dreams*. Years later, I would study both paintings, recalling that wonderful and perfect night, keenly aware of the impossibility of ever convincing anyone in the world (and sometimes even myself) that it had ever happened.

Before we left the diner, I asked Johnny if he'd take a photo of Marilyn and me, using my camera. I suggested to Marilyn that we pose, as she and Jane Russell had posed, for a still publicity photo for the movie *Gentlemen Prefer Blondes*. She loved the idea and really got into it. We stood back-to-back, hipshot, heads up, facing the camera and flashing sexy smiles.

John enjoyed himself tremendously, aiming the camera, adjusting his posture, directing us with hand waves and gestures, finally snapping two or three shots. It was great fun and I couldn't wait to see the result.

We drove off into what seemed to me the dark waters of the night. It was so very dark, and we were often the only car on the road for miles. In 1954, there were few streetlights, and only an occasional billboard sign advertising a motel, or a leaning sign recessed from the road, announcing a gas station.

John and Sonny napped, I stared blankly, still lost in the diner's magic, and Marilyn hummed, appearing contented and happy. I lost track of the time and the miles. Before I knew it, we were past Albany and on our way to Montpellier.

John awoke and stretched, glancing about sleepily. "Where are we?"

"On our way to Montpellier," I said.

He ran a hand through his hair. "I suspect it isn't far to Shelburne. That's where Billy was from, Shelburne."

I flicked on the overhead dome light and studied the map. "We should be there in about an hour."

Marilyn yawned and glanced at her watch. "It's nearly midnight. Let's stop at a motel for the night. Then you can look your best tomorrow, John, when you meet Doris."

John squirmed. "If you don't mind, Norma Jeane, I'll just stay in the car till dawn and then I'll hitch another ride into Shelburne come first light."

Marilyn glanced at him through the rearview mirror. "But John, don't you want to make a good appearance for your friend's wife? You can shower and shave and get a good night's sleep."

John leaned forward with grateful eyes. "Norma Jeane, you've been as kind as an angel, but I cannot impose on your generosity any further."

Marilyn swerved into the Parkway Motel parking lot, a quiet little place set back about thirty yards from the highway, with separate little cottages, each placed snuggly under the cover of snowy trees. Near the motel office stood a blinking red sign that read VACANCY. The motel office window displayed a hanging Christmas wreath with a lavish red bow, and a standing, three-foot, waving Santa Claus.

The office was lit by a night-light, casting an eerie blue glow. No one was visible, and the cottages were dark, all guests fast asleep. The message displayed above, on the motel marquis, read MERY CHRISTMAS!, with one R from MERRY missing.

Marilyn pulled up under a green, overhead awning and stopped near the office's glass door.

She reached for her purse and removed her wallet. Our eyes met when she retrieved some bills and handed them to me. "Darla... go in and register the three of us. You and me in one cottage, and John in the other."

Again, John inclined forward in protest. "Now, Norma Jeane..."

She looked at him, resolute, interrupting. "... John, you must look your best tomorrow. It's an important visit, isn't it? Isn't that what your friend, Billy, would want? Would he want you showing up at his wife's doorstep looking tired and worn out, like a tramp? You've come all this way, and I wouldn't sleep knowing you were out here in the cold. So please accept this kindness from a stranger who loved your singing tonight. John, I just know that someday you're going to be a great singing star. So tonight, you must get a shower and some sleep."

John hung his head as I left the car. The temperature had dropped, and it was bitterly cold. I was glad Marilyn had insisted that John stay the night in one of the cottages. As we left the diner, I'd noticed the fatigue in his eyes and the growth of beard that added a world-weariness to him.

I rang the bell. The woman who appeared at the glass door in a pink housecoat and white slippers was accompanied by a large, black-and-white mutt with watchful eyes and a bobbed tail. She ordered him back as she unlocked the door and looked up at me.

She was a diminutive woman in her 60s, with soft, sleepy eyes, a round face and a friendly manner.

"I'm sorry to get you up," I said. "Do you have two cottages for the night?"

She smiled broadly, obviously happy for the business. Her voice was high and small, almost like a child's. "I do have two, and only two. I knew I'd rent them tonight," she said, touching the side of her nose, her little eyes gleaming.

"Duke here..." she said, pointing to the dog, who stood his ground, his wary eyes not leaving me for a second, "... would not settle into his bed. When he doesn't settle into his soft, Scottish dog bed, I know we're going to have guests. It never fails. Duke has never been wrong. Now, my husband, who is sound asleep in that back room, doesn't believe me. But do you know what I tell him? I say, 'If you talked to Duke like I do, if you watched him like a good detective, then you'd see for yourself.'"

My eyes shifted about and I smiled, thinking, *Is this woman a little crazy or have I stumbled even deeper into the* **Twilight Zone**?

"Well, that's nice," I said.

The woman stepped back, opening the door so I could enter. The dog watched me as if I'd offended him.

"Come in, child," she said. "It is Christmas cold out there, and the radio said we are going to get some more snow."

I entered the office warily, aware of the dog and, as I did so, the little woman cupped her hands around her eyes and peered out the glass door, smiling, then waving at Marilyn. Marilyn waved back.

I said, "That's my older sister, and the man is our friend, who'll be sleeping in the other cottage."

After I registered and paid for the night, I gathered up the two keys, returned to the car and told Marilyn where to park.

Our cottage and John's were next to each other, joined by a flat, steppingstone path, cleared of snow and ice. When I handed John his key, he looked at Marilyn with gratitude and said, "You're a good soul, Norma Jeane. I'm sure the good Lord will always bless you and keep you in his loving arms."

John touched the brim of his hat. "Good night, ladies. Sleep happy dreams."

Inside, the cottage had knotty pine walls and smelled like an old cedar closet. Marilyn cranked up the wall heater and let me have the first shower, while she snatched up the phone to call Milton Greene and Joe DiMaggio.

The shower stream was weak, the pipes rattled, and the water sputtered first with cold water, then hot, then shocking cold. I cursed it, darting away from the icy spray, my face covered with soap.

When Marilyn took her shower, she hummed away as if everything were just fine.

We shared a squeaky, lumpy double bed, and when the lights were out, Marilyn laid on her back. I heard her soft breathing and I sensed her eyes were open.

"John has something special, doesn't he, Darla?"

"Yes... I bet he will be a big star someday."

"Yeah, honey, I think you're right. I hope when it comes, he doesn't lose his way like so many of us do. He is such a good man. I feel it. He's honest and true, and that's so hard to find in the entertainment business."

"I'll be sorry to see him go," I said.

"Me too. I hope it all turns out well for him."

My head settled into the puffy pillow. "What a day," I said with a sigh.

A silent breath of laughter escaped Marilyn's lips. "Yeah, it was a real beaut. I'm loving our adventure, Darla. What would I have done if you hadn't come along?"

An inexplicable pang of longing swelled within me. I had grown so close to Marilyn in just a few days, and yet it seemed like months. Where would our journey end?

I dropped my arm toward the floor and rested my hand on Sonny's sleeping body. He was warm to the touch and his breathing was easy. I had nearly succeeded in mentally erasing my future in 1998—that far-off dreamworld which, as of now, hadn't even happened. This world, and this time, were definitively my reality now, and I was having the time of my life.

"I feel so far away from everything," Marilyn said, wistfully. "So far from my mother, my past, from Hollywood. It feels so good to be away. It feels so good to be Norma Jeane again, a shy girl working in a military factory, spraying down aircraft with fire retardant. That funny girl who modeled and made up different names for herself, like Mona Monroe and Jeane Norman. Those were fun days, Darla, just like this adventure with you is so much fun."

"I want to stay, Marilyn," I blurted out, my voice shaky and emotional. "No matter what, I want to stay."

Marilyn lifted on elbows, and I could see her dim silhouette. "You can stay, honey. Of course you can stay. We'll work everything out, don't worry."

She eased down, and we lay in the dark, my ears ringing in the quiet.

Marilyn said, "Darla, if things don't go well with my father, will you travel back to Weston with me? Will you come live with me in New York? Next month, I'm going to start acting lessons at the Actors Studio. Will you come with me? You can go to a private school in New York and finish high school. How does that sound?"

When I spoke, it was a pleading whisper.

"I want to stay."

CHAPTER 26

The next morning, it took us until 10 o'clock to get back on the road. Johnny knocked on the door a little before 8 and woke me, but not Marilyn. Through a closed door, I told Johnny we wouldn't be ready for at least an hour, then I gently nudged Marilyn. She mumbled something but barely stirred. I was pretty sure she'd taken some sleeping pills the night before and, sure enough, when I went into the bathroom, I found one of her pill bottles toppled over on the sink, with the cap lying next to it.

After I'd finally succeeded in waking Marilyn, I escorted her to the shower, where she fully awakened under the erratic hot and cold water. She came back into the bedroom and carefully applied her skin and eye makeup, omitting the signature red lipstick. Then she fussed with her hair and took a long time deciding what clothes to wear. She didn't say much, and I had the feeling that she was getting cold feet now that we were closer to our destination. I wondered if she would go through with it.

It was lightly snowing when we finally climbed into the car and motored off. John was clean-shaven and looked rested, clearly excited to be fulfilling his friend's dying wish at long last. We found a coffee shop just off the road, and I dashed in to buy donuts, coffee for Marilyn and John, and a Pepsi for me. Back on the road, none of us talked much as we nibbled on the donuts. I drank the Pepsi and blew on the bottle top, producing a foghorn which made the other two chuckle.

Johnny had chosen a sugar donut, and his black shirt was dusted with confectioner's sugar. He laughed at himself as he slapped it clean, and Marilyn said he reminded her of a Christmas ornament. Then we all laughed and fell into elaborate conversation, each sharing memories of our happiest Christmases.

Since snow was falling across the picturesque Vermont countryside, blanketing the two-lane road, Marilyn decreased the car's speed. Our mood shifted as we approached the town of Shelburne, and the quality of the silence changed. Our parting was imminent, and we all felt a little sad.

We entered the city limits and John viewed the town, his face falling into quiet sorrow.

"I've never been here," he said, "but Billy told me so much about it that I feel like I have. There's the movie theater he took his wife to. And the tower clock where he said he first kissed his wife while they stood under it in the rain. There's the car lot where he bought his last car. He said this little town was the prettiest place during Christmas, and now I see he was right. Darla, look at the colored lights strung on the streetlights and in the shop windows. Makes you want to sing *Jingle Bells*, doesn't it?"

"That's a lovely Christmas tree in front of the court-house," Marilyn said. "And look, kids have already built a snowman."

"We don't get snow like this down in Arkansas at Christmas," John said. "If it comes at all, it's only a light mix and short-lived once it's on the ground. This is a nice little Christmas present for me. I wonder if Vivian's ever even seen snow."

"Do you know where the house is, John?" Marilyn asked.

"Straight down Main Street, past the courthouse four blocks until you come to Maple Street. Turn right. Two streets later, turn left onto Sycamore. It's the third house on the right, number 5107."

We finished the drive in silence, and when Marilyn pulled up to the curb, John peered out to appraise it, letting out a long, audible sigh.

"It's a pretty little place, isn't it? White house, with gray shutters. Two stories, all just like Billy said. Front porch swing for warm summer nights. Did I tell you he had a two-year-old boy?"

"Do you want us to wait for you, John?" Marilyn asked.

"No, Norma Jeane. I hope to sit with Doris for a spell. Maybe we'll pray together. Billy said she was a God-fearing, praying woman. Billy wasn't so much a Bible-reading man himself, but he had a good heart and he was kind to his fellow man. I'm sure God welcomed him home with open arms."

Marilyn twisted around and extended her hand. "John, I wish you everything happy. I'm so glad you joined Darla and me on our Christmas adventure."

John looked back at her, his gaze acute and sharp. "Marilyn, whenever I settle into one of those theater seats, and when the lights go down and that projector flickers on, and your pretty image appears on that screen, I will sit back and smile to myself. No matter what part you play up there on that silver screen, I will know you as the good and kind woman who did as Matthew said, 'For I was hungry, and you gave me food. I was thirsty, and you gave me drink. I was a stranger, and you welcomed me.' Marilyn Monroe, as my good mother used to say, 'May the good Lord bless you and keep you. May the Lord make His face to shine upon you and give you peace.'"

John and Marilyn shook hands, she with tears in her eyes. "Thank you, John. You knew all the time, didn't you?" Marilyn asked.

"Miss Monroe, you just naturally stand out as the brightest star in the sky. How could I not know you?"

"I would get out and give you a big hug, John, but I don't want it to look bad for you. I don't want your friend's wife, or her neighbors, to get any wrong ideas."

"Thank you, Marilyn. I appreciate that."

He turned to me, smiling warmly, wearing his black coat and black hat.

"Darla," he said, "all God's blessings on you. You have a certain mysterious sparkle about you that makes me want to ask you a hundred questions, but we're out of time. Perhaps someday in the future, we'll meet again."

Just before he exited the car, he turned back to me. "By the way, I love those earrings. They look real nice on you."

I grinned. "They're a Christmas present from Marilyn."

He replaced his hat and touched it with two fingers, in a final goodbye. "Merry Christmas to you both."

And then John R. Cash left the car, suitcase in hand. Marilyn and I watched *The Man in Black* lean into the wind and make his way slowly up the stairs to the porch, snowflakes dancing about him.

I thought... *There he goes, the man who will soon be singing with Elvis Presley and Jerry Lee Lewis; who will become friends with Bob Dylan and so many other music legends. He will be inducted into the Rock & Roll Hall of Fame in 1992, and I will watch it on TV with my father when I'm ten years old.*

Once he was inside, we drove away and didn't speak for a long time. We were soon in New Hampshire, driving south, passing winter lakes and tree-stubbled hills heavy with new snow. Every once in a while, we saw a squadron of snowy geese glide across the winter sky.

"What are we going to do tonight?" I asked, finally, wanting to break the silence. "It's Christmas Eve."

Marilyn slowly came out of her elegant melancholy, leaned forward and squinted at the thickening snow on the road. Trees extended down both sides of the highway and there were little drop-offs into unseen ravines, which made us both jittery.

"I want to get as close as we can to Rhode Island and then we'll find a little town that has a motor inn, and a church with one of those white church spires. We'll go to church, sing Christmas carols and then find a home-style restaurant that serves good and hearty food. Does that sound like fun?"

I nodded, growing uneasy as the wind picked up, rippling the snow and pushing at the car. The power lines leaned silver in the distance and a deer, alert in a snowy field, leaped away toward the cover of trees, a beautiful thing blessed with agile majesty.

I turned on the radio for distracting Christmas music and to get the latest weather report. More snow was forecasted by some chirping falsetto announcer imitating a speaking Rudolph the Red-Nosed Reindeer.

"Hello, all you kiddies out there. I'm Rudolph the Red-Nosed Reindeer and I'm forecasting more snow tonight, so you can bet that we're going to have a white Christmas. Santa is going to be so happy with all this snow," Rudolph said. "It's so much easier to land in a lot of snow than to land on dry land. Don't you worry, kiddies, I'll be leading Santa's sleigh tonight, so each and every one of you will receive your presents from Santa on time. Merry Christmas!"

And then Bing Crosby began crooning *Rudolph the Red-Nosed Reindeer.*

I made a sour face. "Wow, that was stupid and silly."

Marilyn laughed. "Where's your Christmas spirit?"

Minutes later, clouds of foggy snow seemed to isolate us. I glanced over to see the strain of indecision on Marilyn's face.

On the bending country road, the car's back tires fought for traction. The taillights ahead were blurry, blinking on and off, as the driver tapped the brakes, forging ahead with caution.

It happened in an instant. On a right curve, the back tires slid away, and Marilyn was helpless to control the car, the steering wheel spinning like a roulette wheel.

Neither of us screamed, the way women often do in the movies. We watched in stunned silence as the car went sliding off the road, rear first, plunging down into a ravine and landing with a hard thud.

My head struck the window, but Marilyn managed to grab hold of the steering wheel and stay mostly upright. For seconds the shock held us in a kind of tableau, neither speaking nor moving.

Finally, Marilyn found a breathless voice. "Honey, Darla, are you all right?"

My hand examined and explored my head. "Yeah, I think so."

"Oh, my, that happened so fast. I'm so sorry."

"It's okay. I'm okay, really."

The rear end had plowed into a mound of snow and, when I glanced about, I saw trees quaking in the wind, showering us with whirling flakes.

"Okay, honey. You stay put. I'm going to get out of here and go find help."

"Let me go," I said. "I have better shoes than you. And my coat's heavier."

As I worked to wriggle myself into a position to open the door, I saw it was hopeless. The door was wedged deeply into the snow, and when I put my shoulder to it, it wouldn't budge.

"Okay, Darla, I can get out. I'll go."

"Maybe you should shut off the engine," I said, "… Just in case something got broken and gasoline is leaking."

Marilyn did so. She glanced out her window, staring into the blowing, snowy world.

"Okay, honey, here I go. I'll be back as soon as I can find someone."

Her door was also jammed shut. She pushed and nudged, bounced her shoulder off it and cursed, but the door wouldn't open.

She blew out a sigh. "Well, if this isn't a silly mess."

"Somebody must have seen us slide off the road," I said, my voice shaky with nerves. I wasn't so sure about that but I'd said it to comfort Marilyn, and to comfort me. If we were straining to see the cars ahead and behind us, then other drivers were experiencing the same conditions, and it was possible no one saw us spin away and fly off the road.

Marilyn folded her arms, more perturbed than frightened. "Well, we can't just sit here until the snow covers us up. Come over. Maybe if both of us push on the door, it will give way."

I had my doubts, but what did we have to lose?

We pushed, grunted and shoved. The door didn't budge. Sonny barked, glancing about with spooked eyes as if to say, "Get me out of here!"

CHAPTER 27

A screaming police siren never sounded so good. Minutes later, three men skidded down the embankment, two wearing police caps and heavy coats. The other, a broad man with a square face, black ski cap, and reassuring smile, pressed his face to Marilyn's window and assured us he'd have us out in no time.

Ten minutes later, we scrabbled up the hill toward the road, assisted by the two patrolmen, me clutching a petrified Sonny and Marilyn struggling to avoid the deep drifts. She had removed her glasses, and her scarf was flung away by the surging wind; her hair was whipping about her face, a free hand swiping it from her eyes. She laughed, surrendering playfully to the moment, and I think she was actually enjoying herself.

At the crest of the hill, when the policemen helped haul us up to the shoulder of the road, they recognized Marilyn, and it was just as I'd expected. Their faces registered shock, astonishment and worshipful disbelief.

"Hello, boys," she said, as they gaped at her, spellbound. "Thanks for the rescue."

They ignored me, of course, at least for a time.

One cop brought woolen blankets and covered our shoulders, shy about standing close to Marilyn.

Marilyn wrapped herself, posing and smiling as if in a photoshoot. "I am so glad you boys came along when you did. We thought we were going to freeze to death."

A few minutes later, we were sitting in the back seat of a police car, the red dome light sweeping. Marilyn sipped a paper cup of hot coffee that one of the cops had poured from his thermos, while I tipped back a 6-ounce bottle of Coke.

Despite our accident, we laughed and joked, mostly from nerves and adrenalin. The two patrolmen who'd help free us sat in the front seat, thrilled to be living the true dream of rescuing Marilyn Monroe, and having her seated in the back seat of their patrol car.

The patrolman seated behind the wheel turned about to face us. He had a hang-dog kind of face, with slow-moving eyes and a little pencil mustache. His voice had a lilting quality to it, and the hint of a Boston accent. "I'm patrolman Medcaff, Miss Monroe, and my partner here is patrolman Withers. Now, first of all, how is the dog?"

I spoke up. "He's cold and scared, but he'll be okay."

Marilyn stroked his head. "Sonny has had quite an adventure, haven't you, pretty boy?"

Medcaff continued. "There's a nice hotel about three miles from here. I'd suggest you stay there tonight. Harry will haul your car up and tow it to his garage to check it over. He said he'd have it ready for you by morning and drive it over first thing."

"But it's Christmas Eve," Marilyn said. "Doesn't Harry have a family? Shouldn't he be with them?"

"Don't you worry about that, Miss Monroe. Harry's got two sons who are on their way to help him. All Harry asks is that you autograph a couple of calendars that have you posing on the cover. He has them hanging in his garage. If I recall, one of them has been hanging in that office since 1951. I know for certain that it's one of his prized possessions. Now I hope that doesn't offend you, Miss Monroe."

Marilyn sniggered. "Of course not. I'll give Harry a little Christmas kiss, too, and kiss his sons for all they're doing for us. And, yes, I'd be honored to sign the calendars. It's the least I can do."

Medcaff said, "That will be the best Christmas gift old Harry has ever received, right, Ralph?"

Ralph nodded enthusiastically. "You can bet on that."

Marilyn put a thoughtful finger to her lips. "Boys, instead of the hotel, is there a charming little bed-and-breakfast where Darla and I could stay tonight?"

The two patrolmen exchanged a quick glance. Patrolman Withers removed his hat and scratched his blonde, flat-top head, thinking about that. He had a kind, baby face and a sharp, pointed nose. He cleared his throat and lowered his tenor voice into authority.

"Miss Monroe, the only bed-and-breakfast close to here is run by... well... by an older woman who's a little different. Her name is Miss Bernice Blodgett."

"What makes her different?" Marilyn asked, her interest piqued.

Patrolman Withers tugged on his right ear, searching for the right words. "Well, she's nice and all that... It's just that..."

Patrolman Medcaff cut in. "… What Ralph is trying to say is that Mrs. Blodgett does horoscopes and reads cards, and things like that. Now, some people don't take to that kind of thing. They find it evil or wrong or just plain weird. Some guests just up and leave, or they complain to the Chamber of Commerce, and sometimes they complain to us. Of course nothing she does is against the law, it's just that there are those who believe things like that are not proper or godly."

"Is the place clean?" Marilyn asked.

"Oh, yes, ma'am. Mrs. Blodgett's house is as clean as you'll find," Patrolman Withers said.

Patrolman Medcaff continued, struggling for words. "Miss Monroe, Mrs. Blodgett was my high school English teacher, and she was as strict a teacher as there ever was. Now, I'll not speak bad about her because I respect her. She made me read *Moby Dick*, and I don't believe there is a teacher alive who could have got me to read that big ole book except her, because she believed in me and I didn't want to disappoint her."

He lowered both his head and his voice, and he spoke in a conspiratorial tone. "If all the truth be told, Mrs. Blodgett just plain scared me into reading that thing. I think she scared all of us into making better grades than we were capable of. But I'm getting off the point here. All I'm tryin' to say is; well, a person like yourself may not be comfortable in a place with all that occult business flyin' around. And it is Christmas Eve and all. Do you know what I'm tryin' to say, Miss Monroe?"

"Boys, if it's clean, and it has a nice warm bed and a fireplace…" Marilyn stopped for a moment. "Do the rooms have fireplaces?"

"Oh, yes, ma'am," Patrolman Withers said.

Marilyn smiled with contentment. "Then I'm sure that Darla and I will be just fine. I guess it would be too much to ask if Mrs. Blodgett would have any champagne available?"

The patrolmen traded another quick glance.

Medcaff said, "Well, I don't know about that, Miss Monroe. There is a shop in town that sells wine and beer. Some snacks too, if you want them, but Mrs. Blodgett is known for her good cooking. Now, no one has ever, as far as I know, ever complained about the food she gives her guests. We could drive you over to the wine shop before we take you to Mrs. Blodgett's place, if you like."

Marilyn beamed. "Darla and I will toast you with our first glass."

The patrolmen's smiles expanded into pure pleasure.

As we drove up to Mrs. Blodgett's Bed and Breakfast, and I got my first look at the place, I couldn't help but think of the house in the iconic novel *Anne of Green Gables*, by Lucy Maud Montgomery. Even partially covered in snow, it possessed a remarkable resemblance to the white, two-story home with green shutters and roof. It was surrounded by abundant hedges and trees, and the yard was enclosed by a white picket fence. From the red brick chimney, a thin trail of gray smoke curled up into the wind, and a wreath with a red bow, hanging on the front door, added a Christmas welcome. The house seemed to say, "I am cozy and warm. Come on in!"

A signpost on the front lawn held a green, hinged, rectangular sign that creaked in the wind and, as the wind moaned and the sign creaked, they sang a kind of haunting duet. The sign read **Mrs. Blodgett's Bed & Breakfast.**

I easily imagined a scene from the novel: Marilla standing on the porch with a black shawl, and Anne standing next to her in a brown dress with puffed sleeves.

"I love it," I said.

Marilyn peered out. "It is a pretty little house, isn't it? And all sugar-coated with snow."

"We'll help you with your bags and the champagne," Withers said, as he left the car.

We entered through the gate and hurried up onto the porch, as waves of snow curled over us. Patrolman Medcaff had called Mrs. Blodgett from the wine shop to tell her we were coming, and to make sure she had a room. Standing there by the front door, shivering, I noticed a frosty-haired, wintery-looking woman wearing granny glasses, peering out at us through the square glass window, which was covered by a white lace curtain and a Christmas wreath. She didn't open the door.

I blinked a look at Marilyn, who was staring back at me, as if to say, "*Is she going to let us in?*"

Taking charge, Medcaff stepped up to the door and squared his shoulders. He spoke to Mrs. Blodgett through the door.

"Mrs. Blodgett, everything is all right. These are the two women I called you about. They're the ones who need a room for the night."

Mrs. Blodgett squinted at us, her little eyes looking us up and down. Finally, she unfastened the lock, removed the chain and opened the door, giving Medcaff the once over. He stepped back, like a high school kid expecting a good dressing down.

"You scare me when you come around like this, looking all official and proud. I was expecting two women, not you, Mr. Medcaff," Mrs. Blodgett brusquely explained.

Medcaff removed his cap and held it tightly in his hand. "These ladies' car slid off the road. Harry had to come. He's hauling the car out of a snowbank right now and taking it to his garage. So Ralph and me drove the ladies over here as a courtesy, that's all."

Mrs. Blodgett made a face of irritation. "What you mean to say, Mr. Medcaff, is Ralph and I, not Ralph and me. How many times did I try to hammer that, and more, into your impervious head? Have you intentionally forgotten everything I taught you?"

Patrolman Medcaff looked down at his shoes. "No, ma'am. Pardon me."

Mrs. Blodgett had twinkling, perceptive eyes, a smart, determined face and a small twist of a mouth that suggested she could give out as good as she got. I could readily understand why Patrolman Medcaff gave this woman a wide berth. Although she was thin and clearly in her 70s, she appeared formidable. One would never call this woman by her first name. She was, and I suspected she would always remain, Mrs. Blodgett. Period!

"What is the matter with that scared dog?" Mrs. Blodgett said, frowning. "I don't take dogs into my house," she said, firmly. She folded her arms and jerked a nod to Sonny, who was cowering in my arms, his pitiful eyes filled with fright.

Mrs. Blodgett continued. "When a dog is scared like that, there is a good chance he will defecate all over my house. I don't take to cowardly animals."

Marilyn spoke up. "Oh, Sonny is no trouble. Really, he's not. And he's not so cowardly once he gets to know you. He's better behaved than most people, and he will not soil any carpet or floor. Guaranteed. Promise. We can pay extra for him, if you want, but he's no trouble at all."

Mrs. Blodgett studied Sonny's scared, twitching eyes. "When was he born?"

I leaned forward, not sure I understood. "I'm sorry. Did you ask when was he born?"

"Yes, when is the dog's birthday? What day?"

I recalled the month. Dad had given Sonny to me on my fifteenth birthday, along with his birth papers and puppy photo. "I'm not positive about the day, but I know he was born sometime in the middle of July."

Mrs. Blodgett threw up her hands. "Oh my Lord, he's a Cancer, just like my late husband, Wilfred."

Patrolman Medcaff cast a knowing glance toward Marilyn, as if to say, "See what I mean?"

"Well, all right then, bring him in, but you watch after him."

"I will," I said, politely. "He's not destructive."

"From the looks of him, he's as terrified as a trapped rabbit."

I got defensive. "It's just that he's not used to being away from home, and he's been through a lot."

"All right, come in then, ladies, before this wicked winter wind blows you way over to Keene, New Hampshire."

We stepped onto a doormat in a small foyer and stomped the snow from our boots, then stepped aside as Patrolman Withers deposited our suitcases and the bag holding the two bottles of champagne.

"You've got to remove your shoes," Mrs. Blodgett demanded. "I keep a clean house and I don't want all of New Hampshire traipsing about, scattering mud and snow on my carpets. And close that door, Mr. Medcaff. You're letting all my heat out."

Medcaff shut the door, while Marilyn and I tugged off our boots. Marilyn was amused. She leaned toward my ear and whispered, "What a character, huh?"

I nodded, flashing a hint of a smile. I figured Mrs. Blodgett was in her middle seventies, but you wouldn't know it from her crackling energy, direct, focused gaze and efficient manner.

A heavenly aroma filled the house. "It smells so good in here," I said.

"I have a turkey in the oven, with walnut/apple stuffing. It's a good thing you two happened by. Two guests canceled because of the snow, and two others are snowed-in in Boston and probably won't get here until sometime tomorrow."

Marilyn scribbled down Patrolmen Medcaff's and Wither's addresses, promising to send them autographed photos. After Marilyn kissed them each on the cheek, with thanks, they drifted away, lost in a misty trance, looking younger, healthier and happier.

Mrs. Blodgett promptly gave us the one-dollar tour of the place. It was a warm and welcoming house, with a polished mahogany staircase leading upstairs, and a shining dining room with embroidered place mats on the antique cherry table and six upholstered chairs surrounding it. The antique corner cabinets exhibited fine bone china and crystal glassware.

The living room held early American furniture, a thick royal blue carpet with an old upright piano, a humpback radio, and a warm, gleaming fire in a stone fireplace. A small Christmas tree stood before the front picture window, beautifully decorated with Victorian ornaments.

On the mantel were figurines and two framed black and white photos, one of a serious, balding, bespeckled man, and the other, of a younger, handsome man, wearing a retro military cap and uniform.

If Mrs. Blodgett recognized Marilyn, she didn't show it, and being honest and forthright, she surely would have said something. I suspected she'd never seen a Marilyn Monroe movie, and she didn't seem the type to read fashion or movie magazines.

"All right now, ladies. I've got work to do in the kitchen. Your room is upstairs to the right. The other two rooms are empty, so you've got the entire place to yourselves. You have two twin beds, classic novels to read, many by Charles Dickens and Jane Austen, and a clean, private bathroom. No need for sharing down the hall. Dinner will be promptly at six, so be on time."

I tensed up. True to everything I'd ever read about her, Marilyn was never on time for anything. If we were late, I wondered what the drill sergeant, Mrs. Blodgett, would do. Refuse to feed us? From the delectable smells permeating the house, I hoped not. I was already hungry.

Mrs. Blodgett said, "We'll have turkey and dressing, cranberry sauce, sweet yams, string beans, corn and, for dessert, an apple pie. I hope that is satisfactory. Oh, yes, and let us conclude our business right now and get it over with. For the two of you, the bill is sixteen dollars, one dollar for the dog."

Mrs. Blodgett ushered Marilyn to a small parlor, just off the living room, to an antique rolltop desk. Marilyn signed her name on the registration card, Norma Jeane Baker, and paid the nightly rate.

Our room was decorated in a muted blue and white trim, with two four-poster canopy beds and lovely, matching pleated draperies. The two windows looked out into a snowy world of trees, a nearby Queen Anne house, and a rambling meadow.

I lowered Sonny to the floor, and he quick-pawed it into the bathroom to hide. I couldn't deal with him. I was exhausted, my ankle was throbbing from climbing up the snowy hill, and my head ached. I dropped down onto the white and blue patterned quilt, sighing deeply.

"Oh, honey, that looks so good. I'm going to take a bath and then join you."

Marilyn was shedding her clothes as I closed my eyes, seeing white dots swim across my inner vision. I was bone-tired from the stress of the day. What a trip it had been! As I drifted off to sleep, my body twitched and jerked, releasing anxiety I'd suppressed when the car spun out of control and landed us in the ditch.

I kept my eyes tightly closed, suddenly longing for my father's comforting presence. I wanted to hear his scratchy, deep voice and smell that funky aftershave he wore, even though Carol and I despised the smell, and we told him so several times.

With a grin, he'd say, "Can't a man splash on the aftershave he likes without two females yappin' at him?"

I saw his sad face and warm smile and heard him calling for me to come home.

CHAPTER 28

When I awoke, I glanced over at Marilyn's bed. She was lying under the covers, staring at the ceiling. I could almost hear her brain working. A half-drunk glass of champagne sat on the night table to her right.

Sensing I was awake, she rolled her head toward me with a smile. "Good nap?"

"Yeah... I feel better."

"You still have your cap on."

I lifted up and peeled off my blue ski cap. When I gazed into the mirror opposite the bed, I saw my hair was spiked from static electricity. "Wow, I look like Einstein," I said, finger-combing it.

"I love Einstein," Marilyn said. "I'd marry him in a half minute."

"Einstein?"

"Yes... He's so nice and smart."

"Yeah, but... I mean, he's Einstein," I said, not even sure myself what that meant. But I couldn't imagine Marilyn Monroe and Einstein together. "He must be really old now... How old is he?"

"I don't know, maybe he's in his seventies. Maybe seventy-three or seventy-four."

"Isn't that old?"

"His age has nothing to do with it. I hear he's very healthy, and I've always been attracted to smart men, and who is smarter than Einstein? I hope I can meet him someday."

Marilyn was always surprising me.

"Where's Sonny?" I asked, changing the subject.

"He's asleep in the bathroom. I made him a little doggy bed with a towel. We won't tell Mrs. Blodgett. I gave him some dry food, but he wouldn't touch it. I hope he's all right. He's sleeping a lot, and he's not as playful as he was when you both first came to the house."

"I'll go check on him."

Sonny was curled up in a little ball, sleeping soundly. He barely responded when I pet him. I leaned in closer, suddenly worried, listening to his breathing. I would feel lost in 1954 without Sonny. And what if I wanted to go back home to my father? Dr. Miles hadn't been able to find the path home after her dog died.

I suddenly got scared. I touched his nose. It was moist, so he probably didn't have a fever, and he hadn't seemed hurt after the car accident.

"You have to stay healthy, Sonny," I whispered near his ear. "I need you." He lifted his head, stared uncomprehendingly, sighed, and then tucked his head back into his paws.

I went back into the bedroom. "I think he's okay. Maybe he's just tired. Maybe he's homesick or something... or maybe he's just not a good traveler."

"Homesick for the orphanage?" Marilyn asked, in a doubtful tone. "On second thought, never mind. I don't want to know."

I had the urge to tell Marilyn the truth, but I didn't, afraid it would complicate everything, and the last thing she needed was more complications. Instead, I fished for a topic. "Mrs. Blodgett is kind of strange, isn't she?"

Marilyn reached for her glass of champagne and toasted me. "Yes, but I like her. As you can see, I started without you. Hope that's okay... Do you want one?"

"No, thanks."

Marilyn took a sip. "Mrs. Blodgett is her own woman. I like that. It takes energy and intelligence to run a place like this, with no man around to help. I suppose some people think she's ridiculous, but what do they know? So many people come up to me and say, 'Miss Monroe, you're perfect.' They don't know how imperfect I really am."

She adjusted herself, lying on her side facing me, her expression serious, her eyes holding that faraway look that I'd often seen. "Do you know what I say to them, Darla? I say, imperfection is beauty, madness is genius, and it's better to be absolutely ridiculous than absolutely boring."

I considered her words then laughed a little, my laugh sounding like Marilyn's. Was I imitating her? I certainly hoped so. There was no one better to imitate than Marilyn Monroe. So I got up, poured myself a glass of champagne and refilled Marilyn's glass.

After we'd both had a few sips, to my delight, Marilyn began telling stories about the movie *How to Marry a Millionaire.*

"Betty Grable is such a kind person. Once in between takes, she actually painted my toenails. Now, how many Hollywood stars would do that?"

I didn't know much about Betty Grable, except that she'd starred in *The Farmer Takes a Wife,* a movie I'd watched on the *Late Show* with my father when I was a preteen.

"And speaking of older men," Marilyn said, waving her champagne glass in the air. "Lauren Bacall had a line in *Millionaire* that always just broke me up, and we had to do take after take. I'll never forget it. Lauren Bacall's character says, 'I've always liked older men... Look at that old fellow, what's-his-name in the *African Queen.* Absolutely crazy about him.' Of course, Lauren was referring to her real-life husband, Humphrey Bogart."

We laughed foolishly, much too hard. It was champagne laughter, but it was one snowy Christmas Eve that I will never forget.

To my amazement, Marilyn and I were seated in the dining room at precisely six o'clock. Marilyn wore dark slacks and a red and white festive blouse with a matching red jacket. Her lipstick was muted, her eyes shined, and her gold earrings dazzled.

I wore one of my new outfits, blue slacks, an emerald green blouse and the pearl earrings Marilyn had given me. Marilyn had styled my hair up in a twist and then applied my makeup, including soft, pink lipstick. I felt fashionable and quite fetching, and I wished there were a boy or two around to appreciate me. Eddie popped into my head and I recalled our date with a secret smile. Was he thinking of me, too?

Beatrice Blodgett's Christmas Eve table held a centerpiece of two tapered red candles surrounded by evergreen, and there were sprigs of holly artfully arranged around the three place settings.

The golden-brown turkey gave off a blissful aroma that lifted our noses, making me salivate. It was accompanied by baked yams, cranberry sauce, fresh butter rolls and string beans topped with bacon bits and onions.

Marilyn and I swelled with excitement.

"I am so hungry," Marilyn said.

After Mrs. Blodgett entered with an apple pie and placed it on the side table, Marilyn rose from her chair, approached Mrs. Blodgett and, to the woman's stiff surprise, kissed her on the cheek.

"Thank you, Mrs. Blodgett, for making our Christmas Eve so special and memorable."

Mrs. Blodgett stepped back, recovering, fussing with her white apron. "Well... Well, I mean to say... well, it's nice of you to say so."

Before she sat, Mrs. Blodgett reached for a cut-glass decanter of red wine, removed the top and poured Marilyn a small glass full.

"This is elderberry wine, not the best and not the worst."

Her laser gaze studied me. "How old are you, young lady?"

"Sixteen," I said with regret.

She shook her head. "Too young."

After pouring herself a glass, we toasted, me with water and Marilyn and Mrs. Blodgett with wine. In unison we said, "Merry Christmas."

We passed the food, scooped, imagined and tasted. Marilyn sat at one end of the table, I sat to her left, and Mrs. Blodgett sat opposite me, not at the end of the table, as I'd expected.

We savored the food, gushing at the flavors, the freshness and the presentation. Truly, it was some of the best food I'd ever eaten. The turkey was juicy and tender and the string beans, which I'd always considered an enemy, were oozing with flavor. The butter rolls melted in my mouth, and the yams were sweet and tasty.

"Where did you learn to cook like this?" Marilyn asked.

"From my mother. She was the only girl raised on a farm with six brothers. She did all the cooking, cleaning and laundry, plus she nursed her own mother who suffered from consumption. We call it tuberculosis now. She told me that a woman who can't cook shouldn't even call herself a woman. She was a hardy woman, and a good woman, who finally married a horse doctor and had children of her own."

We fell into a delicious silence while we devoured our food, and it was Mrs. Blodgett who broke our eating silence, startling Marilyn with a question.

"All right, now," she said, matter-of-factly. "Mike Medcaff said you're famous. That's Patrolman Medcaff to you. He was one of my students in high school, when I was still a teacher. Anyway, what is it that you do? What makes you famous?"

Marilyn was lost in the magic of the food. She chewed slowly, finally swallowing and taking a drink of water.

"I act in films."

"Films? I haven't been to see a movie since… Well, let me see now, I don't know when." She scratched the back of her head. "I saw Rita Hayworth in a movie in the 1940s, but I don't remember what it was. I used to love Charlie Chaplin. Now *he* was funny and talented, not like some of these silly movie people today I sometimes read about in the newspaper or hear on the radio. I suspect most actors today sing a bit, dance a bit, speak a few ungrammatical phrases and jiggle around."

Marilyn looked at her apologetically and swallowed some food. "I'm afraid I'm one of those movie people who sings a bit, not so good; dances a bit, but not so great either; speaks some lines, and jiggles around."

"What's your movie name? Mr. Medcaff told me, but I was busy when he called, and it didn't stick."

Marilyn hesitated. "Marilyn Monroe."

"But on the register, you signed your name Norma Jeane Baker."

"That's my baptism name."

Mrs. Blodgett gazed up at the ceiling, pensive. "Oh, yes, I've heard the name. I thought you looked familiar. I've never seen any of your movies, but I'm sure I've seen you on magazine covers at the drugstore and at the beauty shop."

Mrs. Blodgett pointed at me. "And what about you, young lady? Are you and Marilyn Monroe related?"

I swallowed down two string beans. "No, ma'am. We're just…"

Marilyn cut in. "We're friends having a Christmas adventure together. Darla lives not too far from where I'm staying in Connecticut."

"When is your birthday, Darla?" Mrs. Blodgett abruptly asked.

I stared. "Birthday?"

"Yes. What day of the month were you born? If I had to guess your astrological sign, I'd say you were a Sagittarius, born in December. Am I right?"

I cast my surprised gaze at Marilyn and then at Mrs. Blodgett. "Yes, I was born on December eighteenth."

Mrs. Blodgett sat back, self-satisfied, blotting her mouth with a napkin. "Yes… I can see that."

Her eyes landed on Marilyn with confidence. "And you, Miss Monroe, are a challenge. I suspect that you are not as you appear. With that mane of hair I would say Leo, but I'd wager you were not born in August. I would say Leo is the sign on your ascendant, that is, how you project yourself to the outer world. How people see you.

"The fact that you are driving alone with Darla, without a man, suggests that you like independence. Therefore, I'd say you've got some Aquarius in you, a lover of independence. Also, you're kind. I can see that by the way you hugged me back there and the way you defended your dog. Kind and sensitive, that's Pisces."

Marilyn and I stared stupidly, having little idea what the woman was talking about.

Marilyn said, "I don't really know all that much about astrology."

Mrs. Blodgett didn't seem to hear her. "The way you speak is unusual, and you speak lines in the movies, and I bet you read books, and I'd wager that you like smart men more than muscle men. All right, I'm going to say that you, Miss Monroe, were born in June, which makes you a Gemini."

Marilyn lit up with surprise, laying her fork aside and applauding. "That's remarkable. You're right, Mrs. Blodgett. I was born on June first."

Mrs. Blodgett appeared a bit smug as she sipped her elderberry wine, as if to reward herself for her astute analysis.

"All right, enough for now. After dessert, and after we sing some Christmas carols by the piano, we'll put on our warm coats and attend the Christmas Eve service at the Methodist Church. Do you have any objection to that?"

We both shook our heads.

Marilyn smiled warmly. "This is the first white Christmas I've ever had, and I am loving it."

Mrs. Blodgett offered a pleased nod. "Good. Now, when we return home, we'll have coffee, and then I'll take out the cards and read your futures."

I stopped eating, alarm rising in my chest. This woman was perceptive and skilled, that was obvious. What would those cards reveal? That Marilyn was going to die in 1962? That I was a time traveler from 1998?

CHAPTER 29

The apple pie was scrumptious, the crust light, the apples a touch crunchy and not too sweet. Marilyn mooned over her piece, delighting in every bite, oohing and aahing, until a pleased Mrs. Blodgett cut another portion and delivered it onto Marilyn's plate.

"You two ladies are a boost to an old woman's ego. I'm so pleased you have enjoyed yourselves, and I am pleased you came by. Otherwise, as you can see, I would have been eating alone, sitting here listening to Christmas carols on the radio."

Marilyn and I insisted on helping with the clean-up. Mrs. Blodgett allowed us to clear the table and stack the dishes on the kitchen counter, while she stored the leftovers in glass bowls, covered with colorful lids, sliding the bowls neatly into the refrigerator.

"All right now, no more work for you two, or you'll be demanding your money back. I'll finish these later tonight," she said.

We left the kitchen, following Mrs. Blodgett through the dining room to the piano. She sat down commandingly on a swivel wooden stool, and picked through sheet music, her glasses perched on the end of her nose.

She began to play with sure, heavy hands, her head stooped toward the music. Marilyn and I gathered round and we all sang *Oh Come All Ye Faithful, Oh, Little Town of Bethlehem, Jingle Bells* and *Silent Night.*

After the singing, I took a reluctant Sonny outside for a short walk around the yard. He relieved himself and then trotted back inside and up the stairs to the room, making a beeline for the bathroom. He gobbled up a few bites of food, drank some water, and flopped down into his towel bed, letting out a contented sigh. I stroked his head and was just about to go downstairs when Marilyn came into the room to get her coat and scarf.

"Sonny's better," I said. "He ate a little."

"That's good, honey. But if he's not his old self soon, we'll take him to the vet right after Christmas."

Marilyn studied herself in the mirror as she put on her scarf and glasses.

"Marilyn," I said, "are you comfortable having Mrs. Blodgett read your future?"

She turned to me with a cheery expression. "I can't wait. I think it will be so much fun. That woman is amazing, isn't she? I wish we could stay a little longer so I could learn some of her recipes. She is simply a magician in the kitchen. Have you ever tasted food that good?"

"No," I said honestly.

She buttoned her coat. "We'd better go. Mrs. Blodgett is waiting."

After she left the room, I ran back into the bathroom to say goodbye to Sonny. I kneeled beside him and caressed his ears.

"I love you, Sonny. Don't worry. You'll get used to living in this time." He barely lifted his head, looking at me with sad eyes that nearly broke my heart. Maybe he missed my Dad. They'd been good friends and walking buddies, and Dad was always bringing home toys and snacks for him.

He squinted me a look. I said, "Who knows, maybe I'll take you back to the woods and you'll find the path home," I said.

But will I go with him if he does? I thought.

I stood, conflicted, slowly moving into the bedroom, glancing out the window into the darkness outside; at the light snowfall that glistened as it drifted past the muted streetlamp below. Was my father out there somewhere, wandering in future shadows, searching for me?

I missed him. I wanted to call and wish him a Merry Christmas. I wanted to buy him a Christmas present. I wanted to hear his voice, and go to a movie with him, and hear him laugh. I wanted to watch him descend to the family room after a long day at work, sag into a chair, give me his contagious, lopsided smile, drop his head and then drift into a snoring nap.

I stopped the gnawing need to see him. I just shut it down. But as I left the room, I paused, certain I heard him call to me—sure I heard his voice riding the outside wind as it moaned around the house.

Inside the small, charming Methodist church, we sat in a back pew, as per Marilyn's request. It had a central aisle with two rows of wooden pews on either side, and beautiful old stained-glass windows. The church was subdued in candlelight and adorned with poinsettias and evergreen branches; a lovely little manger scene was arranged near the altar.

Christmas hymns from a muted organ filled the church, while eight choir members, dressed in blue pleated robes and cradling hymnals, filed into the choir loft behind the pulpit and stood reverently. By nine o'clock the church was nearly full.

A tall, taciturn minister, dressed in a black suit and black tie, held a Bible aloft, but his worshipful eyes were fixed heavenward, as if Christmas angels hovered in the surrounding air. I followed his eyes and searched the quivering shadows, finally lowering my eyes and focusing on the profile of a man a row ahead of us. He was about the same age as my father. Dad was born in May 1954, in a little town in New Jersey. Maybe Dad and my stepmother were at church right now, in 1998.

My mind drifted as I gazed at the flickering candles on the altar, and I wondered, if I died in 1954, would I be reborn to my same parents in 1982? When I reached sixteen, would Sonny and I leave for that walk in the snow, blunder down the same path and enter 1954 again? Would I be stuck in a loop?

More thoughts elbowed in until my brain locked up. I closed my eyes, listening to the congregation sing the last verse of *Angels We Have Heard on High*.

I gave Marilyn a coy side glance. She sat perfectly still, rapt by the sacred atmosphere, lost in the peace and hypnotic Christmas magic. Despite her scarf and glasses and attempts to remain inconspicuous, I noticed an occasional eye steal a glance at her. It soon became apparent that at least one of the patrolmen had spread the word that Marilyn Monroe was staying at Mrs. Blodgett's Bed and Breakfast.

Mrs. Blodgett sang at the top of her voice, and it was a good strong voice, a pretty soprano, even though her speaking voice was low and raspy.

We left the church quickly to avoid any crowds, and we walked home leisurely, as light snow drifted and shimmered in lamplight. It was a beautiful Christmas Eve—a Christmas card spectacle, with a loveliness all its own. It was a quiet and attractive little town, tucked away from the chaos of the world.

Marilyn must have felt it too. She didn't say a word as we walked. Once, with a girlish smile, she extended her hand to catch melting flakes, her eyes lit with playful wonder. As we arrived back at the house and before we passed through the gate, she stopped, tilted her head back and opened her mouth, letting the flakes land on her tongue.

After we had shed our coats, the moment I'd been dreading arrived. Mrs. Blodgett pointed to a card table in the parlor and asked us to carry it a few feet from the fireplace, and to place three parlor chairs around it.

"I'm going to the kitchen to pour three glasses of eggnog. When I return, I'll take out the cards and we'll glimpse your futures."

Marilyn was excited. I was worried.

As the three of us gathered around the table, I sipped the delicious eggnog, but was disappointed there wasn't any booze in it, no rum, brandy or whiskey. My father always spiked ours with one of the three.

Marilyn sat opposite Mrs. Blodgett, and I to her left. The fire hissed and popped as Mrs. Blodgett opened a chic yellow scarf and removed a set of ordinary playing cards.

"You don't use Tarot cards?" I asked.

"I don't need Tarot cards, Darla. Everything I need to know is contained in these. They speak to me," she said, beginning expertly to shuffle the cards, cut and repeat the shuffle.

"When did you start reading cards?" Marilyn asked.

"At sixteen, Darla's age."

"How did you learn?" I asked.

"I didn't learn. I just picked up the cards one day and they just seemed to speak to me in a kind of poetic language. Not words exactly; more like feelings and impressions. Sometimes I see images and sometimes not. Sometimes faces appear, or I see a series of scenes, like in a movie."

"You must have a real gift," Marilyn said. "Do you ever do readings for yourself?"

"I can't read my own life, and I don't know why. Nothing arises, no images or faces or feelings. I could read my husband, though, quite well."

I said, "Was he... well, did he want you to do readings for him?"

Mrs. Blodgett narrowed her eyes wisely. "Wilfred was a practical, placid man, and not a curious one. He worked as an accountant and never took much stock in what the cards said. He mostly laughed at me and called me his..." Mrs. Blodgett stopped, with a bit of a blush. "Well, I don't need to tell you that. I'll just say that he thought I was part witch. For my birthday one year, he even bought me a broom as a joke. I thought it was hilarious, and I galloped all over the house with him laughing his head off at me. Of course, I was much younger then."

I shot Marilyn an anxious glance, but her eyes were glued to Mrs. Blodgett in fascination.

"That is so amazing. I can't wait," Marilyn said.

Mrs. Blodgett finished the shuffle, adjusted her glasses and focused her eyes, first on me, and then on Marilyn.

"All right, who would like to go first?"

Marilyn looked at me. "You can go first, Darla."

"No, no. You, Marilyn. You go ahead."

Marilyn lifted her chin, ready. "Okay then, I'll go first."

"Very well," Mrs. Blodgett said, inhaling a deep breath, pursing her lips and shutting her eyes, as if going into a trance.

CHAPTER 30

Mrs. Blodgett's eyes flicked open and fell on Marilyn. Without looking at them, she reached into the deck and drew out four cards, all face down, and spread them out in a single row before her. Her eyes focused on the first card as she turned it over. It was the Jack of Spades.

Marilyn and I waited, she nibbling on a fingernail.

Mrs. Blodgett studied it before turning over the next card. It was the Ace of Hearts.

Again we waited, hardly breathing. Mrs. Blodgett seemed to be roaming in her own inner regions. The next card was the Nine of Diamonds, and the last, the Queen of Hearts.

Her eyes studied Marilyn for a moment before traveling the room, finally resting again on the cards. When they lifted, I saw a blank emptiness that unnerved me. It was as if someone else was prowling behind those eyes.

"What do you see?" Marilyn asked in her movie star, breathy voice, her brows raised in query.

Mrs. Blodgett eased back in her chair, making a pyramid of her fingers, placing them below her mouth, as if she were in prayer.

When she spoke she didn't look at Marilyn or me. She didn't seem to be looking at anything.

"Marilyn... your fame will increase. It will increase past what I can see, far into the future."

Marilyn was hanging on every word, sitting bolt upright.

"Do you see marriage? Will I marry again?"

Mrs. Blodgett didn't hesitate. "Yes, you will marry again, and he will be an older man."

"Will our marriage be a happy one?"

"I can't see that. Often, when I can't see, it means I'm not being allowed to see."

"Who's stopping you?" Marilyn asked.

"My guide."

"Your guide?" Marilyn asked, not understanding. "Who is your guide?"

Mrs. Blodgett's eyes settled softly on Marilyn. "My guide's name is Liliana."

Marilyn's eyes explored that as she stared into the middle distance. "Wow... what a pretty name. She sounds female."

"More female than male, but a little of both, I think," Mrs. Blodgett said.

I didn't know what to think. I didn't know if I believed Mrs. Blodgett. I didn't know if the woman was a gifted psychic or just plain nuts. But then I had to tell myself that I was a time-traveler from 1998. Maybe I was the one who was nuts?

"Will I have kids?" Marilyn asked.

"I don't see that," Mrs. Blodgett said. "I see great fame, and I see confusion. I'm finding it difficult to penetrate that confusion."

"Boy, that's been the story of my life since I was a little girl," Marilyn said. "Do you see a father? Do you see my father anywhere in those cards?"

Mrs. Blodgett lowered her head. "I see an absent father, Marilyn. I see a father in the shadows."

Marilyn's face fell in disappointment.

"Don't despair, Marilyn. You will have many wonderful experiences, and you will be adored by the world for many years into the future."

Marilyn propped herself up on one elbow, her chin resting in her palm, suddenly looking glum. "So, Darla, maybe we should leave tomorrow morning and drive back to Connecticut. Maybe there's no reason to go on."

I straightened my back. "No. I say we keep going and stick to our plan. Maybe you can bring him out of the shadows. Maybe he's been waiting in the shadows for you to come and pull him out into the light? Anyway, how will you know unless you try?"

Marilyn looked at me with warm appraisal. "You're a sweet kid, do you know that? Your mother would have been so proud of you."

Mrs. Blodgett directed her attention to the cards. "Marilyn, you can ask me a question and then select any card from the deck."

Marilyn grew thoughtful, a finger tracing her lips. "It's all make-believe, isn't it?"

Mrs. Blodgett waited. I waited, not sure what Marilyn meant.

Marilyn continued. "Millions of people live their entire lives without finding themselves, don't they? But it is something I must do. My question is, will I ever find myself?"

Marilyn touched her neck, staring hard at the cards. At last, her hand snaked toward the waiting deck, and she selected a card.

"Turn it over," Mrs. Blodgett said.

Marilyn did, and it was the Queen of Spades.

I jerked a glance at Mrs. Blodgett to get her immediate first impression. Her eyes went frosty and then flat. I saw no light in them.

At first, Marilyn waited in mounting anticipation. Then a lovely courage changed her face and she sat stoically, ready to meet her fate.

Mrs. Blodgett cleared her throat and, for the first time since I'd met the woman, I saw anxiety in those flat eyes. I saw gloom, as if I were staring into a foggy, dark cave. When her eyes cleared, I saw an aching grief—but only briefly—for seconds. She blinked again, and all the stormy clouds were swept away and her eyes brightened as she put on a mask of mild reassurance.

"Well, Marilyn, you will continue on your quest to find yourself. It will be a journey into the unknown, like most things in life. It will be a worthy and necessary journey."

In that searing moment, I knew that Beatrice Blodgett had seen Marilyn's death. I could also tell that it shook the woman to her very core, and she was having difficulty managing the truth of it.

Marilyn turned her attention to me again, with an easy smile, a hint of sadness in her eyes. "I guess I've had enough. Can you please read Darla's cards now, Mrs. Blodgett?"

"Maybe she shouldn't," I said, in full dread mode.

Mrs. Blodgett looked me over. "If you would rather I not, Darla, then I won't."

"No, please, Darla," Marilyn said, in protest. "It's all for fun anyway, isn't it, Mrs. Blodgett?"

Mrs. Blodgett didn't answer. She kept her steady eyes on me. "It's up to you. I can put the cards away if you wish."

I looked at Marilyn for support and she nodded. "Go ahead. I did it and it didn't hurt a bit."

I nodded. "Okay..."

I had to admit, part of me *was* extremely curious to see what Mrs. Blodgett would find.

Mrs. Blodgett went to work, shuffling and re-shuffling, her eyes screwing into the cards as she sliced, sifted and cut.

As she laid the four cards before her, a chill leaped up my spine. The first card she turned over was the Ten of Clubs. The second card was the King of Spades; the third, the Ten of Hearts; and the last, the Jack of Diamonds.

Mrs. Blodgett studied the cards for a time, her eyes cool and distant. Then she shut them, lifted her chin slightly, and rocked her head gently from side to side, as if she were hearing inner voices. When a puff of wind whooshed down from the chimney, I half expected a ghost to sweep in and blow out the twitching candle flames.

When Mrs. Blodgett finally opened her eyes, she stared beyond me at nothing. And then her forehead knotted into a frown. I grew worried and worked to maintain a placid dignity.

It was Marilyn who broke the silence, speaking at a near whisper, as if not to disturb our card reader's thoughts.

"What do you see, Mrs. Blodgett?"

To my surprise, Mrs. Blodgett looked at me with an expression of puzzled inquiry.

"I can't find you in the cards, Darla. I see doorways and long, dimly lighted hallways. Those doors are partially open, only an inch or so with light leaking out, but I can't open them fully to enter the room. I can't see inside. Those doors won't budge. This has never happened to me before. It's as if you're hiding somewhere and I can't find you."

Marilyn gave a grimace of disappointment. "Do you mean you can't see anything about Darla?"

"I see vast distances and snowy pathways. I see a pink moon, and I sense a loss of a parent or maybe both parents, but that's as far as I can go. As I said, I can't get inside those rooms, and I find it quite disconcerting. Even my guide can't enter through those doors."

"Can you see anything in her future?" Marilyn asked.

Mrs. Blodgett shook her head. "Darla's future is locked up, so to speak and, to put it in a way you can understand, I don't have the key, and neither does my guide. I really don't understand it."

Both women appraised me with new eyes, as if searching for a doorway into my mystery.

Marilyn said, "Well, Darla, we are going to be spending a lot of time together. Perhaps some of your mystery will come to light."

I gave her a timid smile and shrugged, playing the fool. "Who would have ever thought that I was such an enigma? I thought I was just plain old, boring Darla Gallagher."

Mrs. Blodgett gathered up the cards and replaced them in the yellow silk scarf, folding the four corners over it and resting her hands on top. "You are hardly boring, my dear Darla, and I suspect your life will be anything *but* boring."

Mrs. Blodgett arose, concluding the readings. "Ladies, it's time for me to finish up in the kitchen, say my prayers, and then go to bed."

"Are you sure we can't help?" Marilyn asked, rising to her feet. "Three can work faster than one."

"No. You and Darla enjoy your Christmas Eve. I'd suggest you go upstairs and take that dog out for a walk. When was the last time you walked him?"

"Just before church," Marilyn said.

Mrs. Blodgett passed me a final, bewildered glance. "Darla... when I look at you, a poem by William Wordsworth comes to mind. It's one I taught my students, insisting that they memorize it, to their infinite revulsion. The poem is entitled *A Night Thought*. I'll give you a taste of it. You can read the rest on your own.

> Lo! where the Moon along the sky
> Sails with her happy destiny;
> Oft is she hid from mortal eye
> Or dimly seen,
> But when the clouds asunder fly
> How bright her mien!

"I love that," Marilyn said. "What does the word 'mien' mean?"

Mrs. Blodgett nodded, with an arched eyebrow. "Ah, yes, Marilyn, ever the curious Gemini. The word 'mien' means appearance, look, expression or countenance."

Marilyn turned around to face me. "Yes, it fits Darla. Yes, it fits her very well."

Later, Marilyn and I were on her bed, sipping champagne, my first glass, and her second. I was in a twitchy, moody funk and Marilyn was subdued and reflective.

"I wish I could sing a song like John Cash or recite a poem like Mrs. Blodgett, Darla. I wish I could be the moon that sails along the sky in a happy destiny, like you."

I set my half-drunk glass aside on the night table. I'd lost my enthusiasm for it, as I recalled the deep sorrow I had seen in Mrs. Blodgett's eyes during Marilyn's reading. I couldn't push away my sudden blues. I couldn't push away the dark thought that Marilyn was on the road to self-destruction and she should, at least, stop drinking.

I turned my head aside as I said, "Marilyn, maybe you should stop drinking so much champagne. Maybe you should stop taking barbiturates and amphetamines, too."

Marilyn reached for my arm, touching it gently. "Oh, honey, I don't take so much, really."

I turned to her; my voice filled with conviction. We were face to face. I had to say what I was feeling. I couldn't have stopped the words if I tried.

"But you will, Marilyn. You'll start taking more and more of them. Do you know what they'll be? I do, because I memorized them. All of them."

Marilyn looked at me strangely.

I continued. "You'll take Amytal, Sodium Pentothal, Seconal and Phenobarbital. And more, you'll get prescriptions for morphine, codeine, Percodan and Librium. And you'll drink vodka, too. Don't you see what taking all of these will do to you? They're not good. You have so much talent, and you're so pretty and kind, and funny, and you are so good; so you need to stop taking so many things now. If you cut back now on the champagne and the sleeping pills and all that other stuff, you'll be healthier and happier. You'll live a long and happy life. Don't you see?"

Marilyn's eyes opened fully, staring, not with anger or malice; not with consternation or defensiveness. Tears sprang to her eyes, and she gripped my arm in a tender, fragile way that nearly broke my heart. She started to speak and then stopped, overcome with emotion.

I said, "I want you to live a long life, Marilyn. Don't you see? That's why I came here. That was my purpose for coming to be with you. I know that now. I came to help you... To help you live a long and good life. You know how Hollywood is full of wrecked souls and broken dreams... broken people and broken lives. Yours doesn't have to be."

Marilyn let the tears flow down her cheeks, not wiping them away. She tried to speak again, but faltered, shaking her head in frustration. Finally, after the emotion had run out, she took me into her misty eyes.

"Do you know, dear Darla, that after my performance in *Clash by Night*, Darryl Zanuck said, 'She's a sexpot who wiggles and walks and breathes sex, and each picture she's in, she'll earn her keep, but no more dramatic roles.'"

I waited for her to continue, seeing anger flare in her eyes. Was she purposely deflecting the conversation?

Marilyn angrily rolled over onto her back and stared hard at the ceiling. "'No more dramatic roles' is what he said. Well, do you know what? I know how third-rate I am. I can actually feel my lack of talent as if it were cheap clothes I was wearing inside. But, my god, Darla, how I want to learn. To change, to improve. I don't want anything else. Not men, not money, not love, but just the ability to act."

She rolled her head toward me and I searched her eyes, waiting to link the connection from drugs and champagne to acting.

Her voice softened and became breathy. "I have to confess that I get the blues sometimes so bad I think I'm going to bust, and then I think of my mother in that mental institution diagnosed with schizophrenia, and it just makes me crazy. All right then, so the blues come at me in all directions and so I crack open a Nembutal capsule and add a Chloral Hydrate tablet, the old 'Mickey Finn,' and then I sleep, and it all goes away for a while: my mother's face, my third-rate acting, my divorces and those sneering studio bosses. Without a little help, Darla, I can't sleep, and to be a good actress, the kind of actress I want to be and must be, I have to sleep. Don't you see?"

She gave me a pained look, willing me to understand and approve. "Don't you see, Darla? Do you understand now?"

The fight drained out of me. I had no more words. I knew my eyes were restless and turbulent. I knew they held fear and disappointment.

I swung off Marilyn's bed and went to my own, jerking back the quilt and sliding under it, tugging it up to my chin. My emotions and thoughts were strangling me and I fought tears. I shut my eyes, wanting to escape.

"Yes, Marilyn, I see," I said flatly. "I'm really sleepy. Good night."

A moment later, Marilyn switched off the light.

"Merry Christmas, Darla."

"Merry Christmas, Marilyn. I love you."

"And I love you, honey." And then she quoted from the poem Mrs. Blodgett had recited. "'Lo! where the Moon along the sky, sails with her happy destiny.' I want that for you, Darla."

"Thanks... Big day tomorrow," I said.

Marilyn's voice was barely audible.

"Yes, a big day."

CHAPTER 31

The next morning, Marilyn again struggled out of sleep. She finally appeared in the dining room, patting down a yawn around 9:30, a half-hour past the breakfast limit, which ran from 7:30 to 9 a.m.

Mrs. Blodgett and I were finishing our pancakes at the dining room table and, surprisingly, Mrs. Blodgett didn't mention Marilyn's tardiness. As Marilyn sat, Mrs. Blodgett arose, stepped to the side table, reached for the percolated coffee pot and poured Marilyn a cup.

"Thank you, Mrs. Blodgett," Marilyn said. "You may have just saved my life. I really need this coffee."

"Merry Christmas, Marilyn," Mrs. Blodgett said pleasantly, standing by.

Marilyn smiled through bleary eyes. "Yes... Merry Christmas to you both and good morning. Sorry I'm late. It's silly, isn't it? I've been on the front page of so many calendars, but I'm never on time, and I often don't know what day it is."

I grinned. "Funny."

Marilyn stretched her arms up. "Gosh, have you looked outside? It's a winter wonderland. So beautiful, just like a Christmas card. Sorry I was such a sleepyhead this morning. The bed felt so soft and warm, and the blue sky and the sun coming in through the window were so cheerful, I just wanted to be lazy and indulgent."

"And you should be lazy and indulgent on Christmas morning," Mrs. Blodgett said, again to my surprise. "Would you like some pancakes, Marilyn?"

Marilyn thrust a shoulder forward and glanced up sleepily at Mrs. Blodgett. "Just some toast will be fine."

Mrs. Blodgett made a face. "Pshaw, Marilyn! I am not going to send you off on the road with just toast and coffee. I can fry you some eggs, if you like."

Marilyn seemed pleased to be cared for. "Okay, you win. Eggs sound good. Scrambled."

"And toast?"

"Yes, thank you. I feel so pampered and relaxed. This place is better than a five-star hotel. I don't know when I have felt so relaxed."

"All right, then, you just sit and drink your coffee and orange juice—the pitcher is to your right, and I'll be back in a minute."

She started for the kitchen, then remembered something and turned back. "Oh, by the way, Harry Conklin called, and he's bringing your car over around ten o'clock."

"I'm so sorry he's working on Christmas Day," Marilyn said.

"Don't you worry about Harry. He's always been a worker, even as a kid. And, anyway, I suspect he is quite excited and pleased to be seeing you again."

Marilyn smiled affectionately. "This town is so nice. Hey, wait a minute. I don't even know the name of this town."

"This little town is just a comma in the novel of the country, Marilyn. It's called Hastings. Now let me go scramble those eggs."

After she slipped into the kitchen, Marilyn turned to me. "I heard you take Sonny out for his walk this morning. He seems happier today. He slept with me for a while. How did you sleep?"

"Not bad."

"You snored a little," Marilyn said, with a little giggle.

Of course, I was horrified. "No... No. Really?"

Marilyn held up her thumb and index finger, a tiny space apart. "Just a little. It was cute."

"Not so cute," I said, dropping my chin. "Snoring is not cute. No way that's cute."

"How do you feel, honey? You talked a lot in your sleep."

I lifted my eyes. "What did I say?"

"I could only make out a few words. I remember you said something like 'The path is over there.' And you said, 'Dad, where are you?' You said other things, but I couldn't understand. You tossed and turned a lot. Do you feel okay?"

I swallowed the last of the pancakes, masking my surprise at having mentioned my father. "Yeah, I feel fine."

Marilyn rearranged herself in the chair, reached for the pitcher of orange juice and poured her juice glass full. She took a couple of sips and held the glass up. "This would be so perfect with a little champagne in it."

I looked directly into her eyes, drained empty from lack of sleep, and I wished she wouldn't talk about champagne.

"So I guess you didn't sleep all that good?"

Marilyn gave a little shake of her head. "Not so good and not so long."

"What time do you want to leave?"

She was silent for a time as she sipped the orange juice. Her eyes glazed over, and she was picking absently at the white tablecloth. The kitchen radio played *I Saw Mommy Kissing Santa Claus*, sung by some kid, a song I'd always loathed.

"It shouldn't take long to get there," I said. "I studied a map. Even on snowy roads I think we can be there in about three hours, maybe less."

In a small voice Marilyn said, "I don't know..."

I leaned toward her, studying her sleepy face, feeling some of her vague anxiety. I knew what was going on behind that face: she was seriously thinking about canceling our trip and returning home to Connecticut. She was scared, and I was feeling circumspect.

Oddly, I felt older than I had only a few days before, feeling I was on the cusp of adulthood. Maybe it was because of hope, or because some of that hope had receded after my talk with Marilyn the night before. After our talk about drugs and booze.

I'd seen what booze had done to my father, often making him irritable, sad and erratic. I'd watched him age and cry because he couldn't stop, even when he knew it made things worse.

And I'd been blessed with foresight. I knew that Johnny Cash would begin drinking heavily when his star began to rise, and that he'd become addicted to

amphetamines and barbiturates, often using stimulates
to stay awake during tours.

Booze and drugs were not romantic or cool. I saw,
firsthand, their destructive power, and I vowed never to
fall under their spell.

"Marilyn, if you don't go see your father, you'll always wonder, 'What if?' You'll always wish you had.
It will be one more thing that will bring the demons and
the night blues. One more reason to reach for the pills
and the booze."

Marilyn averted her eyes, her voice softening. "Darla, when I first saw you lying there in the snow by the
side of the road, I thought you were so young. So helpless."

Marilyn smiled sweetly, still not looking at me.
"Now I look at you, and you seem all grown up and
wise. Can you give me some of that?"

"I'm not so wise. I don't even know what grown up
is. Is anybody grown up? I just know that you have to
go through with this."

Marilyn's eyes opened fully. "Well, you know
what? He probably won't even be there. Maybe that
gumshoe detective got it all wrong and my father won't
be there, and our road trip adventure will be over.
We'll drive off laughing, and I'll say, 'What a schmuck
I was for trying to find him.'"

Marilyn had nearly finished her breakfast when Harry and his two stocky sons arrived with the station wagon. It had been cleaned and polished, the engine tuned,
the oil changed, the tires rotated, and the gas tank filled.

The three stood on Mrs. Blodgett's porch, looking
proud, excited and entranced when Mrs. Blodgett final-

ly let them in to meet the world-famous Marilyn Monroe.

Mrs. Blodgett ordered them to wipe their feet on the door mat and not to enter the house any further than the hallway.

"As hardworking a man as you are, Harry Conklin, you always seem to have a way of bringing the dust and oil of that garage with you, God love you."

While the men snapped photos using box cameras, Marilyn once again switched on the power of her beauty, as she always did when she posed for photos; the unforgettable smile, the half-open lips, the one bent knee to make her appear a little curvy—the way she'd taught me to stand just a few days before.

She thanked the men profusely, offering to pay them for their work. When they refused, their hands pushed deeply into their pockets, their heads lowered and shaking, she pulled a 20-dollar bill from her jean's back pocket and forced it into Harry's hand.

As promised, she autographed five calendars and six movie magazines, and then also promised to mail autographed photos of herself when she returned to New York.

Again, I witnessed Marilyn's ability to make people happy. She was energetically eager to please, never artificial, never arrogant, and never mean. In those shining moments, it was hard to believe that this beautiful, authentic soul was also confused and lost, always in search of something that seemed just beyond her reach. I could only hope that after meeting her father, she would choose a healthier, more positive and contented life.

We finally left Mrs. Blodgett's B&B a little after noon. Before Marilyn left the porch, Mrs. Blodgett placed both hands on her shoulders, peering deeply and earnestly into her eyes.

"It has been a pleasure to have you stay here, Marilyn. I hope you will come back and visit. As soon as your next movie comes to town, I'm going to march down to the theater and watch it."

"You may not like it," Marilyn said, apologetically. "The title is *The Seven Year Itch*, and it's a silly picture, really. It will be out sometime next year."

"If you're in it, I'm sure I'll like it. You drive safely now. Harry said that most of the main roads have been cleared, so you shouldn't have any difficulty getting along."

Marilyn kissed Mrs. Blodgett on both cheeks, her eyes soft, her voice emotional.

"Do you have children, Mrs. Blodgett?"

"Wilfred and I had a son. Richard was a career Army officer, and he was killed in World War II."

Marilyn's face fell into sorrow. "I am so sorry."

Mrs. Blodgett removed her hands from Marilyn's shoulders, patting her gloved hand. "It's all right, my dear. The good Lord is taking care of him, as indeed he is taking care of all of us at this very moment."

We drove away, Marilyn wiping tears and tooting her horn. Mrs. Blodgett waved, shading her eyes from the snow's glare.

As I watched the good woman diminish and fade from view, I thought, *What a brave, strong and amazing woman. I hope I'm like that when I'm old.* And then I thought, *Mrs. Blodgett should have had many daughters.*

CHAPTER 32

We drove under a serene blue sky on a quiet, two-lane highway, the shoulders of the road piled high with plowed snow. We passed farmhouses and barns, icy ponds, and tall snowy pines that sprayed white dust into the air when the wind stirred their crests.

The radio filled the silence, already hawking local after-Christmas sales and playing carols sung by singers I'd never heard of. Marilyn didn't hum along as she had before. I sensed that she missed Mrs. Blodgett and felt uneasy leaving that comfortable and nurturing space for the uncertainty of what was to come. I wanted to offer comforting words, but I'd already said enough, and probably too much.

I fell into my own thoughts, preoccupied with what I'd do if things went badly with her father. I had no idea, and the more I thought about it, the more I got a blurry headache.

And then, out of the blue, Marilyn said, "Did I tell you that my first husband, Jimmie, is a Los Angeles police detective?"

"No..."

"I thought about him when the patrolmen helped us after the car went off the road. I thought about Jimmie most of the night. After we were married, we settled into a four-room house in Van Nuys and, boy, was I ever happy. I chose every furnishing in the house, from the kitchen cutlery right down to the doormat. Do you know what else I remember? I didn't think about it until lately, but I sometimes called Jimmie 'Daddy'. Why did I do that? Marilyn would never do that."

"Marilyn?" I asked, confused about the third-person reference.

"Yes, Marilyn Monroe would have never called Jimmie 'Daddy'."

I let it go. "Did he remind you of your father?"

"No, not at all, and that's what's so strange about it. He was five years older, just twenty-one. But Jimmie was so good to me, and we had fun. On sunny afternoons, we would often drive down to Santa Monica Beach and eat cold hot dogs and potato salad. It sounds so simple now, but it was fun. I laughed with Jimmie."

She grew quiet again, staring out at the road as if she were watching the movie of her life unfold before her. "I never wanted to be Marilyn—it just happened. Marilyn's like a veil I wear over Norma Jeane, and sometimes things get blurry, and sometimes when people call me Marilyn, I wish they'd just call me Norma Jeane, like John Cash did."

I thought about that, and I wondered if I had an alternate persona. I didn't think so.

The road was winding and bumpy. Marilyn jerked the steering wheel right, taking a hair-pin curve that squealed the tires. I gripped the edge of the seat with both hands, observing that Marilyn seemed to be driving on autopilot.

"Things changed in 1943, when Jimmie enlisted in the Merchant Marine. And then he got called up for duty overseas. I wrote to him a lot, several times a week, and he wrote back. They were good letters. Jimmie wrote good letters. But then I got lonely and restless, I think. The house was quiet, and the war was going on, and I felt like I should be doing something, too. So I got a job at the Radioplane factory."

She laughed, raked a strand of hair from her eye and glanced over at me. "Imagine me, Darla, Norma Jeane, inspecting parachutes and preparing planes for flight. But I did work hard at it. I really wanted to help those boys who were fighting all over the world."

"Did you like it?"

"I liked being out of the house and being useful. I think all girls want to feel useful, and not just useful around the house. Don't you think?"

"Yeah, I think so. I'm not sure I'm cut out to be a wife."

"You'd be a wonderful wife, Darla. You're so smart and sensitive."

"But I don't want to be stuck in the house all the time. I want to travel and take pictures and write stories about all the people I meet."

Marilyn grew animated. "You know what? I'll help you. You can start writing about me, and I'll make sure your stories get published and distributed to all the major magazines."

A jolt of excitement gushed through me. "Would you? Really?"

"Of course."

Then she turned serious. "But you can't write about us, here and now. You can't write about our journey. This has to be a secret. I don't want anyone to know about this. You can understand that, can't you?"

I nodded, disappointed, but not showing it. "Sure. Of course."

"We'll have so many other journeys together. There'll be a lot of other things for you to write about. And you can use some of the photos you've already taken."

I shut my eyes, imagining it all. John had snapped several photos of us in the diner and, of course, I'd taken many photos of Marilyn and him. They were on a roll of film I'd have developed as soon as I returned to 1998—that is, if I returned to 1998.

What should I do? The longing to see my father was growing inside me more every day. Was I feeling pity? Did I pity him for the clumsy way he'd lived his life; for the mistakes he'd made and was still making?

Now that I'd lived with Marilyn and met Joe Di-Maggio and John Cash, I'd seen how all human beings are fallible and make mistakes. I'd been humbled. I saw my own mistakes much clearer, and in closeup. Perhaps I'd made a mistake in coming to this time or in not telling Marilyn the truth of who I was and where I came from? Life was a lot more complicated than I had ever realized.

Had I abandoned my father and somehow broken our natural link? That thought terrified me. Dad had always been my solid foundation—my pole star—the one sure thing I could always count on. I knew, without any doubt, that my father loved me and would protect me, and he would die for me if it ever came to that. So what should I do?

If I did find a way to return home, what would I do with the finished photos? I could prove to the world that I had time traveled back to 1954 and met Marilyn Monroe and Johnny Cash, before he *was* Johnny Cash. That would be the beginning of my photojournalism career. I glanced at the backseat. Two rolls of film were stored safely in metal film canisters in my camera case, which sat next to a dozing Sonny.

As we approached Providence, Rhode Island, we were forced to take a detour on a narrow side road that hadn't been completely plowed. Marilyn coaxed the car along, saying she wasn't about to wind up stuck in another ravine.

And then we got lost. I shook out the map and, with my index finger, searched our location. I couldn't find it anywhere on the map. Next, I reached into the glove compartment for the *New England Guidebook*. I still couldn't find the road we were traveling on.

"We can't be more than a few miles from Collier," I said.

"Maybe we're not supposed to get there. Maybe God is stopping us."

"I don't believe that," I said, narrowing my eyes on the guidebook. "According to this, there are a lot of textile mills around here. And there's a haunted house called the Walcott House, built in 1720."

"Let's avoid that one," Marilyn said. "I've been haunted enough."

We crossed a bridge over a rushing stream, hearing boards rattle under the tires. I was back to studying the map when Marilyn shouted out, "There it is! The sign for Collier!"

I looked up as we approached the white rectangular sign, printed in bold black letters.

City of Collier, RI, Pop., 14, 481.

I saw Marilyn swallow, and then I swallowed. We were here, at last. Our journey was about to come to an end.

We were finally deposited back to the main road, and Marilyn eased back on the accelerator, the car traveling at about 20 miles per hour. Fortunately, no one was behind us. We passed a variety of homes, from colonial to Cape Cod style.

"Do you have the address?"

Marilyn's voice was barely audible. "I have it on a piece of paper in that guidebook. It's the book marker."

I cracked the book, removed the folded page, opened it, and read. "264 Ash Street."

"Yeah, that's it," Marilyn said, her jaw tightening. "Which way?"

I found the street on the map. "It's... just up a bit, maybe three or four blocks. It will be on the right."

Marilyn's hands trembled on the steering wheel. She looked over uneasily. Stress lines had formed around her mouth and eyes. "So, do you know what I've been thinking? A girl doesn't need anyone who doesn't need her."

"Do you want me to go with you... I mean up to the door?"

"No, honey, thanks. Sometimes a girl has to go at it alone. This is one of those times. Anyway, my mother told me never to tell anyone who he is, so I guess that should include you too, Darla. I think it's for the best."

Marilyn turned left onto a side street with square lawns, bare trees and modest homes, some Tudor style, some Victorian. We both squinted looks out the windows, searching for the address.

I pointed. "There it is! 264. It's that dark green house with the big tree in front of it."

Marilyn eased the car to the curb and jiggled the gear into neutral. She applied the parking brake. Seconds ticked by before she shut off the engine. We waited in an infinite, throbbing silence.

And so, by unpredictable and circuitous routes, we had finally arrived at our perilous destination. I felt as if sunlight should come breaking through the moving clouds and bathe us in a golden blessing. It didn't.

So much was riding on the next few minutes.

CHAPTER 33

When Marilyn left the car, softly shutting the door behind her, Sonny stood on hind legs, front paws on the window, wet nose against the glass, eyes alert, tail moving. I watched Marilyn's unsteady stride as she crossed the sidewalk and stepped onto the front walkway. She mounted the four steps to the porch, pausing at the door, standing tall, shoulders back.

I'll never forget those four porch steps. Perhaps they were the most difficult four steps Marilyn ever took, and she took them with pride, dignity and courage.

After that, I looked away. I didn't want to see the rest. If she was rejected, I didn't want to see it. If she was welcomed in, I didn't want to speculate. She'd tell me all about it when she returned.

I glanced at the dashboard clock. It was 3:12 p.m., and the sun was at the top of a band of trees, the sky turning gray and orange—a wounded winter sky.

I waited in agitation with my back to the house, facing the oncoming sunset. Sonny had left the window and was curled on the backseat, waiting.

I let my mind drift. I began to recall old articles and biographies I'd devoured about Marilyn's life in 1955, as well as documentaries I'd repeatedly watched. I wondered how this encounter with her father might change things—might change the future.

In 1955, Marilyn would live in New York at the Waldorf-Astoria and begin acting classes with Lee Strasberg at the Actors Studios, right in the middle of the theater district. She would always be late for class, arriving just as the door was closing. Marilyn would try to creep in inconspicuously, without makeup, her luminous hair hidden under a scarf but, of course, the other students knew that the most famous movie star in the world was in their acting class.

After all, only a few blocks away, above Loew's State Theater, at 45th and Broadway, there appeared yet another Marilyn, with makeup, shining hair and a daz- zling dress—the Marilyn everyone knew. She was 52 feet tall on that infamous billboard advertising *The Sev- en Year Itch*, the first movie that Mrs. Beatrice Blodgett would see in years at her local theater in Hastings, New Hampshire. And what would she see?

A hot blast from the subway grating would cause Marilyn's white dress to billow up around her thighs, her face an explosion of delight.

But Mrs. Blodgett would know the real Marilyn Monroe: the insecure, shy, 28-year-old woman who was, at the very core of herself, kind and sensitive.

Marilyn greatly impressed Lee Strasberg. Years lat- er, Strasberg stated that the two greatest acting talents he'd worked with were Marlon Brando and Marilyn Monroe. It was a quote that startled me the first time I read it, especially considering the other talented actors who'd studied with him, including James Dean, Paul

Newman, Montgomery Clift, Robert De Niro, Jane Fonda, and Al Pacino.

When I heard footsteps approach, my thoughts stalled, my stomach churned, my ribs tightened. I faced forward, just in time to see Marilyn circle the front of the car, open the door, slip in behind the wheel, and gently close the door. I was desperate to read her face, but I couldn't. Calmly, she rested her hands atop the steering wheel and gazed ahead, her eyes vague and large, as if she were in mild shock.

I waited, breath deepening, afraid that if I uttered a word, Marilyn might shatter.

Vast time seemed to pass before she mechanically inserted the key into the ignition, cranked the engine and shifted the three-speed into first gear. As we drove away, I glanced back at the house, not seeing anyone standing on the porch or peering out from behind a curtained window.

When Marilyn turned off on a side road, there was still plenty of daylight, but the sun had descended into pillows of violet and white clouds. We bumped along a rutted dirt road, to where, I had no idea.

Moments later, near a cluster of trees, Marilyn stopped and keyed-off the engine. She shoved the door open and got out, found a nearby, foot-worn, snowy path, and started toward it, leaving the car door open. A sharp, icy breeze blew in, and I saw Marilyn hadn't taken her gloves or hat. I buttoned my coat, grabbed her gloves and hat, and left the car.

Sonny was on hind legs at his window, whining, wanting out. I snatched his leash and opened the back door. He lumbered out, giving his body a weary shake. I clipped the leash to the ring on his collar, shut the car doors, and started after Marilyn down a path that narrowed under the spreading, bare branches of heavy trees.

By the time I caught up with her, she was standing on the edge of a frozen pond, watching two teenagers, a boy and a girl, ice skating across it. The girl wore blue, with a white ski cap, and the boy wore black, with a red cap. The boy was obviously a beginner. He skated clumsily, hands jutting out, body in spasm about to fall, while the girl, skilled and gliding, used laughter and wiggling fingers to coax him on.

Marilyn was hatless, with her hands on her head, watching the duo, her eyes following the couple's ice ballet, both comic and entertaining.

I drew up silently beside her and we watched the skaters for a time. The boy finally lost his balance, spilling to the ice, sliding on his butt. The girl bent over laughing. She circled him while he sat, arms folded, making a playful, ugly face and sticking his tongue out at her. Their play was fun to watch; a grateful distraction that also brought a pang of envy. I thought, *That could be me and Eddie.*

Marilyn smiled. "They're having such fun. Do you know how to ice skate?"

From necessity, Sonny found a spot and hiked his leg.

"Yes... I learned when I was a girl. My father taught me."

As soon as the words left my mouth and hit the cold air, I wanted to yank them back.

Marilyn kept her smile. "Yes, your father. How nice," she said, with genuine sentiment. "Maybe I'll learn someday. I could skate in Rockefeller Center in New York."

"It's not so hard."

"That girl is about your age," she said.

"Yeah, I guess so."

"Do you think the boy is handsome?"

"I don't know. I can't see him all that well."

The girl extended her arms and helped him up. Holding his hand, she skillfully and patiently guided him along and, over the next few minutes, he improved.

"Aren't you cold?" I asked. "I brought your hat and gloves."

"I'm all right."

I decided to ask the question. "So, I guess it didn't go all that well?"

Marilyn turned to me, her eyes open wide, staring blindly, as if she weren't really seeing me. "No, honey, it didn't go so well. Not well at all."

She turned her attention back to the skaters and compressed her lips.

"Was he there? Was your father at the house?"

Her eyes dropped, then came back up. "Yes, he was there." She made a small laugh, but there wasn't any joy in it. "And guess what? He didn't look so much like Clark Gable. He didn't even have a mustache."

The air was cold and silvery, the lake flat and gray. I wiped my red, runny nose with a balled tissue and shivered. Sonny shivered.

"It's cold out here, Marilyn. Maybe we should go back to the car."

She was silent for a long time. When she spoke, her voice sounded strange and far away, as if the words were private thoughts that had escaped her lips.

"They were having Christmas dinner. I guess I crashed it. The woman who answered the door was nice. She recognized me right off. I saw the surprise in her eyes. She was young, maybe in her early 20s. She let me in. When she closed the front door behind me, I felt like a trapped animal. I knew I shouldn't have come. I could just feel it."

The wind rattled the limbs of trees around the pond and cut into us sharply. Marilyn didn't seem to feel the cold.

"I told the girl I'd come to see my father. I told her I was Norma Jeane. I heard the words leave my mouth, but I felt detached from them as if I was watching myself say them, and I couldn't believe I'd even spoken his name, a name that had lived in my head as fiction for so many years."

Marilyn looked at me. "Boy, you should have seen her face. She turned white, like paper, and I could read her thoughts. I really could, Darla. She was thinking, *This is Marilyn Monroe, and she is completely out of her mind.*"

Marilyn glanced away again, folding her arms tightly across her chest. "Well... then he just appeared. I guess the dinner was in the dining room and he heard me. Anyway, he walked in, not as tall as I had imagined, and not as handsome as I had believed, and not as pleased to see me as I had wished. He stared at me in a frosty silence and I just stared back at him in disbelief. For a moment I thought maybe I'm doing a scene in some bad picture; maybe the cameras are rolling, and I have a line. But I can't remember my line. Not one single word. And then I want to say, Cut! Can we do this again? I hate this scene. I hate this script and I hate this awful movie. Can we do this scene again and get it over with, so we can wrap this picture, so I can finally get on with my life?"

I kept my eyes on her.

"But it wasn't a movie. It was as real as real has ever been, cold, fierce, private and terrible. I looked at him, my father, and I think, is this the guy who's responsible for helping to bring me into this world? This guy, who looks at me with such accusing eyes, as if I'm threatening him?"

Marilyn inhaled a breath and blew it out into the sky. "And then it was all over in just a few, short words."

She began to shiver. "… Words I'll never forget. His words that I'll never be able to get out of my head, for as long as I live."

She kicked at the ground. "My father… He was my mother's shift foreman at Consolidated Film Industries where she worked as a film cutter. Did I already tell you that? Who remembers? Anyway, that's where they met. That was the beginning of my movie, Darla, and it just won't end. There is no end to my movie."

Marilyn faced me, our eyes level. "I couldn't remember my lines, but he certainly remembered his. He said, 'Miss Monroe, I don't know why you are here. I am having Christmas dinner with my family. I don't have anything to say to you. If you must talk to somebody, then call my lawyer.'"

Tears swelled in her eyes. One broke free and ran down her cheek.

Marilyn struggled to speak, emotion squeezing her chest. "And then it was over, not the movie, just the scene. That lousy scene, and I couldn't remember any of my lines."

Marilyn swiped the tear and struggled to smile. "Well, Darla, I guess our Christmas journey is over."

Then tears pumped out of her and she bent over, sobbing. I dropped Sonny's leash and reached for her, drawing her into my arms, feeling her body convulse, as darkness crept in around us.

CHAPTER 34

Marilyn lay curled in a fetal position, having finally fallen asleep in a motel bed after three glasses of champagne and a sleeping capsule.

It had taken all my strength and will to tug her away from that pond and help her back to the car. She was lethargic and defeated, and in no condition to drive. The shock had finally struck, and she couldn't speak or think. So I eased her down into the passenger seat, shut the door and loaded Sonny into the backseat.

I slithered in behind the wheel and automatically reached for my seatbelt, remembering Dad's instructions. Of course there was no seat belt. Since I'd just turned 16, I didn't have a temporary driver's license, but Dad had taken me for driving lessons several times, mostly at the mall and on side roads. He said I was a natural-born driver, and I enjoyed driving, feeling in control of a car.

But I'd never driven a standard shift and, even though I'd watched Marilyn and thought it wasn't that difficult, as I started the car and rammed the gear into First, I was damp from nerves and sadness. Fighting the clutch, we ramped and jerked our way back to the main road.

I drove slowly, arms rigid, sitting up straight and stiff, no doubt looking like a stick girl driving. When I found the first, low rambling motel, I muscled the car into the parking lot, grateful I hadn't killed us all or destroyed the clutch and the engine.

I booked us a room for the night, ushered Marilyn inside and turned up the heat. As I helped her into the double bed, she was cold to the touch. I covered her with the sheet and blanket and went outside to the office to get her a cup of hot coffee. When I returned with it, she was asleep, or maybe in a trance, mumbling incoherent words. So I sat across from her on the second bed, sipping the coffee, feeling it warm my chest, while Sonny laid flat on the brown, fuzzy carpet at my feet.

"What now, Sonny?" I asked.

His eyes were closed. He, too, was asleep. Then came a dark, swelling loneliness. A loneliness that was rapid and biting. I slumped my shoulders, rested my head on the pillows and nodded off.

I awoke suddenly when I heard Marilyn leave the room, quietly closing the door. I jumped up to follow her, finding her at the car, tugging on her suitcase and sliding it out of the cargo space.

She heard me and turned, closing the lid. "I need some champagne, honey. We've got one bottle left."

Back inside, she peeled the foil, released the wire cage and boosted the cork. It released in a sigh of gas, popped and sailed, bouncing off a wall. She splashed some in a water glass, the bubbles belching up. Looking at me, she shrugged loosely and tossed the bubbles back, taking the champagne down in one swallow. I turned down the offer to join her, as she tipped the bottle and poured the glass full.

Her mood was dark, her eyes swollen, and her spirit damaged. That was easy to see.

I dropped down on the bed as she paced, glass in hand.

There were things I wanted to say but didn't. I felt angry, too, and I hurt for her. I blurted out, "You've lived without your father this long, so who needs him? Look at all the things you've done, and you've done them all without him. You're one of the greatest movie stars of all time and he's just a nothing. An insecure, jerk of a man. A scared man. You're better off without him."

I was surprised by my fuming, belligerent tone.

Images of my own father flooded in; memories of him and me at Coney Island when I was a little girl. Even though the place had lost much of its luster from the old days, Dad had brought it to life for me, turning it into a wonderland. He'd hoisted me up on his meaty shoulders and we'd explored, Mom at our side. We saw the iconic Wonder Wheel Thrills neon sign behind the "Spook A Rama" sign. We went to Jazz's amusement arcade and, although Mom and I were too scared, Dad rode the Coney Island Cyclone, arms up, a big kid's grin on his face.

The day was bright and warm, Mom and Dad laughed easily and often, and Dad was not drinking so much. We ate hotdogs at Nathan's and strolled the boardwalk at sunset, me licking a big orange and yellow sucker.

It was one of the happiest days of my life. I felt safe, exalted and loved, and all was right and good with the world. I thought my Dad was the best man, the best father, the best husband in the world, and my mother the prettiest wife and mother. Now, here with Marilyn, I ached for her, and I ached for me. I suddenly ached for the whole world. Did that mean I was all grown up?

Standing in that motel room watching Marilyn's wounded eyes, I realized that I missed my father like crazy. I suddenly felt out of place—out of time and place—as if marooned on a deserted island with no hope of ever being rescued.

An inner thunderclap of panic startled me. What if I never saw my father again? If I couldn't get home, who would I be? I was homeless, nameless and rudderless. I stared at Marilyn. As much as I loved and cared for her, I was also terrified for her. In a sense, she was homeless, nameless and rudderless. She had no true home, her name was not her own, and she was as lost as a child in the dark woods at night.

A slow, boiling fear crawled up my spine. Could I find that doorway back home?

Marilyn stopped pacing, leveling her eyes on me. "I'll tell you this, Darla. I'm going to become the best damned actress you ever saw. I'm going to be an artist, not just a celluloid aphrodisiac."

Her words brought me back to the present. "I'm sorry, what did you say?"

Marilyn placed a hand on her hip, the glass of champagne in her other hand. "I said, I'm going to be an artist, not just a celluloid aphrodisiac."

I was distracted, my flitting thoughts already tracing my steps back to where Sonny and I had pierced that time travel doorway.

The longer Marilyn stared at me, the softer her eyes became. "Darla... my sweet, Darla. My true friend, Darla. We have had quite a time of it, haven't we?"

I nodded, surprised by confusion and emotion. I wanted to leave this time and return to my own, and yet I didn't want to leave Marilyn. Where was my true, authentic life? I wanted to jump back and forth between the two worlds. Was that possible?

"I hate to see it come to an end," Marilyn said.

"Come to an end?" I echoed.

Marilyn's dark mood suddenly lifted, and the sun returned to her eyes. She came toward me, energized.

"Darla, I just had a new thought. Here's what I think we should do. In the new year, we'll move to New York. I'll start acting lessons, you'll enroll in a private school and begin photography lessons. We'll both be in school and improving. Doesn't that sound like fun? Then, whenever I'm not making a picture, you and I will pile into a car and start off on another journey, just like this one. Maybe we'll go on a Valentine adventure and meet a couple of guys and fall in love for a while. Why not? We'll make ourselves up to be the most gorgeous broads those men have ever seen. Then we'll have an Easter and a Fourth of July journey. You'll take pictures, and I'll start my own production company and make the kind of movies I want and then..."

Marilyn boosted her glass toward the ceiling as if it were a trophy. "You'll win photography awards and writing awards, and I'll win an academy award. And then... Well, what else is there? We'll live happily ever after, just like the people do in the movies. How do my crazy and fun plans for the future sound?"

She was on a high again and, as always, her high moods were contagious. "It sounds perfect. As Humphrey Bogart's said in *The Maltese Falcon*, his last line: 'The stuff that dreams are made of.'"

Marilyn gave me a kiss on the cheek. "Merry Christmas, Darla."

And then I remembered. I pulled back. "Hey, wait a minute. I have *your* Christmas present. Remember when I told you I was going to give you something that no one else could give?"

Marilyn nodded, vigorously, excited. "Yes..."

I held up a finger. "Well... I have it."

I went to my camera case, retrieved one of the two metal film canisters and walked it over, both hands behind my back, with my right hand closed around it. Playfully, I held out both closed hands. "Guess? Oh, and you have to pretend that my hands are the wrapping paper."

Marilyn laughed, playing along, a finger tapping her lower lip. "Okay, let me see. Right hand or left hand? What could it be?"

She reached and tapped my right fist. "That one."

"Right!"

I opened my hand and held it up to her. She leaned her head back. "Blank film?"

"No. A complete roll of film I took on our journey."

Marilyn's eyes filled with joy. "Oh, Darla. How wonderful! How perfect!"

"Of course, the film has to be developed, but I figured that part of the present is the surprise of seeing them for the first time."

She hugged me again. "Oh, I can't wait. Do you know what I'm going to do? Send them to Paul Morgan in New York. He is one of the greatest photographers in the world. He'll make sure they come out perfect, so I can keep them always."

She laughed gleefully. "It's my favorite Christmas present. My absolute favorite."

And just like that, she was Marilyn again, or Norma Jeane again, or just her own fun, authentic self again.

"I'm suddenly starving. Are you hungry? Mrs. Blodgett packed us some turkey sandwiches."

I wasn't hungry, but I didn't want to dampen Marilyn's mood, so I said yes.

After we ate the sandwiches, Marilyn grew drowsy, and she wandered off into the bathroom. I knew why. I knew she was reaching for sleeping capsules. What could I do?

Later, she called me in. She was throat-deep in the tub with mountains of foam covering her. She was all giggles and pleasure, lifting a hand to blow bubbles with one hand and sipping a glass of champagne with the other. This was the Marilyn I loved the most; the playing, girlish Marilyn, who didn't seem to have a trouble in the world.

"Whenever you're depressed, Darla, take a bubble bath. It will always cheer you up."

After I left the bathroom, I felt a strange shift of mood, a slow, on-coming depression. I looked around the room. Everything seemed foreign, as if it were in the wrong place; as if I were out of place; as if I were an intruder.

There was a gnawing in my gut; a hard twist of emotion. My father's face passed across the inner screen of my mind, his expression downcast, his eyes pleading. He reached out for me. I blinked, trying to clear my vision, but his image stuck to my eyes.

Was he calling for me, way out in the future? His only daughter who was yet to be born?

By the time Marilyn had finished her bath and her third glass of champagne, she was rambling and exhausted, yawning with every second breath, her eyes glazed and fatigued. She was asleep as soon as her head hit the pillow, and I stepped over and covered her.

For a while, I stared down at her, my arms folded as I listened to her long, purring snore. Had the accident of time and place—my time traveling and spending time with Marilyn—changed her script? Had it changed the script of the world? Would she now survive past her 36th birthday?

I heard my father's voice in my head. "*I love you, Darla. You know that, don't you? You know that you've always been the light of my life; the best thing in my life.*"

I cocked my head right, surprised by a flashing thought, like a blinking red light. I crossed to the opposite side of the room, parted the drapes and gazed out into the wall of darkness.

It was a thought I'd had before, after Joe DiMaggio had left; after we drove away from Mrs. Blodgett's. In the final analysis, could I save Marilyn from herself, or would she have to save herself, as we all must do? That thought had come to me around the same time I felt, intuitively, that I was in the last act of my time travel adventure. It had much to do with my father and our last conversation.

"Dad, maybe you shouldn't drink so much. Maybe you should cut back some... just a little."

He held me at arm's length. "Yes, Darla, you're right. I should do that. Yes... I should."

But he didn't say, "I **will** do that."

I closed the draperies, thinking, *Why stay with Marilyn Monroe when my own father needs me? If I could return to my own time, maybe I could help save him from his drinking addiction. As his only child, didn't I have the responsibility to love him, be with him, and try to help him? Wouldn't my mother want me to do this? If she knew the truth, wouldn't Marilyn want me to return to my 1998 life, and to my father?*

Marilyn mumbled something in her sleep. I turned toward the bed and watched her. She said something I couldn't understand, her voice feathery soft, her feminine fingers wiggling, curling, resting gently next to her scattered hair. I would miss her. I would miss her because I now knew, for certain, I had to leave. My father needed me, and I needed his love. We were a family. Even if he'd married someone I didn't like, we were still a family.

I could hear and feel the fragile finality of the moment, like the soft ringing of a bell or the fluttering away of a lovely bird as it sails off into a flaming sunset.

All day, I had felt but ignored this pressing sensation—a growing insistent voice that seemed to say, *"Time is running out."*

Marilyn had no father, at least not one who loved her; who cared about her; who missed her. But I did have a father, and I belonged with him and he with me. The love we shared was strong, even if it had been strained by death and remarriage and adolescent growth. Our love was secure, a bond that would never fade or die, just as my love for my mother would never die.

Being far from my Dad and witnessing the despair and pain that kept Marilyn emotionally imprisoned by her father's absence and neglect, only amplified the love I had for my father. He was alive here and now—and alive in the future. I felt his presence all around me. He needed me, and he was calling for me.

It was time. I had to find that doorway to 1998 and return home to my father.

I dimmed the lights and sat down at the desk. In the drawer I found some motel post cards, stationery and a pen. I switched on the desk lamp and began to write.

Dear Norma Jeane:

> *Dreams really do come true. I met you and I had the time of my life. I will never forget our journey and the people I met: Joe Di-Maggio, John R. Cash and Mrs. Blodgett.*

> *This is not an easy letter to write, but I must write it. I hope that roll of film that you will send off to New York will reveal to you how much I care about you; how much I want for you, and how much I have grown to love you. Whenever you look at the photos, I hope you'll remember me with fondness, and recall our Christmas adventure, 1954.*

> *I'm sorry to have to say that I won't be able to join you in New York in 1955. I must go*

back to my life. I was running away. I can't run anymore. Someone needs me and now I know that I need him. You see, Marilyn, my mother is dead, but not my father, and I have to go back to him. I have to face my life as it is, just as you must do. I know you'll understand.

Don't worry about me because I'll be fine, and I know you'll be fine too. Just slow down drinking champagne and taking pills. Eat a lot of carrots instead! Ha!

By the time you read this, Sonny and I will be on our way back to where we came from. Don't worry or call the cops. We'll be just fine.

I have my camera with me, and when I get home, I plan to develop the film and show the photos to all my friends. They'll be so envious and so happy too! I can't wait to see the expression on my father's face.

You won't be able to get in touch with me, Norma Jeane, and I wish I could explain why. Just know that I'll be seeing you in the movies, and I'll remember all we've been through together, and all we've felt together and shared together.

I'll watch your movies and I'll cry, and I'll send you my love, always.

Darla

I folded the letter, slipped it into an envelope and placed it in my camera case. I would leave it for her when Sonny and I left to search for the moonlit path that I hoped would take us back to 1998.

CHAPTER 35

The trip back to Weston took two days. We could have driven it in three hours, but Marilyn was in no hurry. On Sunday, December 26, she insisted on exploring Rhode Island and Connecticut coastal towns. I figured this was her way of healing herself; to have a few more adventures before returning to Weston and facing her life. We spent that night in a motel in New London and ate at a local seafood restaurant. Since it was Sunday and no liquor stores were open, Marilyn had been unable to stock up on champagne. The restaurant had some cheap champagne on the menu, and luckily, no one recognized Marilyn. The next day, Monday, December 27, she found a post office in New London and mailed the film I'd given her to her New York photographer friend.

We were both muted and reflective after the trials of Christmas Day. I began to berate myself for encouraging her to stop by her father's family's house, without calling first or being invited. It was a crazy plan. Why had I thought that I could give her advice about anything? The remorse and sense of failure I felt contributed to my determination to return home to my father.

Of course, I didn't mention any of this to Marilyn, and we both did our best to be upbeat.

Outside one Connecticut town, we stood on a narrow wooden dock that extended 20-feet into Long Island Sound. It wasn't all that solid, but Marilyn didn't seem to notice or care. We didn't talk, we just stared, feeling the chilly breeze rush over our faces, scattering our hair. I let Sonny explore the area and he ventured near the edge of the water, his nose to the ground, eyes watchful.

As we were leaving that lovely place, Marilyn said, in a reverent whisper, "This is what I want to remember when I'm back in Hollywood. This quiet and peaceful place. It feels like a church."

We breathed at the same time, turned and started back for the car.

When we arrived home, the Greenes' house was eerily quiet, like an empty theater without an audience. At sunset I watched fiery finger clouds stretch out across the sky, and I wondered if that was an omen, a cosmic indication that it was time for me to return to my own time.

Marilyn told me the Greenes would arrive the next day, so I planned to leave that night. If I couldn't find the time doorway, my only back-up plan was to return, but I wouldn't allow my mind to speculate about that. I had firmly set my intention on finding that doorway and I wouldn't allow the memory of Dr. Ellen Miles' repeated failures to turn my mind from its optimistic course.

We ate scrambled eggs for dinner and said little, both sensing something was about to shift. Even the air in the room seemed oddly changed, like a chilly wind that blows in after a warm, summer day.

I insisted on washing the dishes while Marilyn dried, after which she poured herself another glass of champagne and became a bit giddy. I followed her into the living room, and she rambled over to the world globe, giving it a little spin, tilting her head back and aiming for the couch.

"Are you going to call Mr. DiMaggio?" I asked, still not comfortable calling him Joe.

She sat. "Yes… why not? I miss him."

Her mood darkened. "Maybe I should have gone with him. Yeah, I should have gone with him instead of wasting my time driving to Rhode Island."

That hurt a little, although I knew Marilyn's meaning had nothing to do with me.

"I should call him," she said, reaching for the phone. "Yes, I should call Joe."

She wedged the receiver between her shoulder and ear, her finger poised, about to dial. "It's funny, isn't it, Darla? Joe and I had a falling out and now we're having a kind of falling back in."

As she waited for the long-distance call to go through, she stared into remote distances, as if she were remembering something.

I left for my room.

Marilyn made call after call, not aware of my jittery mood. At 10 p.m., she poked a head into my room. I lay on the bed, my hands locked behind my head, still fully dressed, my eyes restless, my thoughts projecting possible outcomes.

"Everything all right, Darla?"

I lifted up. "Yeah. Fine."

"I'm sorry I was on the phone for so long. I had so many things to catch up on. So many people were concerned that something had happened to me. Imagine that, a girl wants some private time, and her agent, friends, directors and producers all think she's taken a powder or something..."

On impulse, I got up and went to her. Quietly, I wrapped her in a hug, holding her close. She was surprised.

"What's this?"

"I had so much fun. Just so much fun. That's all."

We stood back, our eyes warm on each other.

"It was a blast," Marilyn said. "It was wild and fun, and a real blast. Well, maybe not that part where the father tells the daughter to go to hell, but..." She shrugged. "Who knows, maybe I'll try again in a few years. Maybe he'll change his mind once he sees I've become a real actress."

She changed expressions, from light and girlish to doubtful. "But you know, Darla, I think that when you are famous, every weakness is exaggerated. Maybe that's what that man who is my father sees."

"Don't talk like that. Don't put yourself down because of him. My mother once told me that what a person says about me, good or bad, reveals more about them than it does about me. I never forgot that, even though I was just a little girl."

Marilyn gently touched my cheek. "There you go, being all grown up again. Darla, we are going to have such fun together."

I hesitated, and my voice quivered. "Marilyn, I may not be able to go to New York with you."

"But why not, honey?"

"I may have to go back…"

"Back to the orphanage? But why? I don't want you ever to go back there, Darla. You should stay with me."

"I may not be able to, Marilyn. I may have to go back."

Marilyn stared, first with skepticism and then with understanding. She knew I was once again skirting the truth.

"It's not because of you," I said. "It really has nothing to do with you. It's just that there are people, other people, who might need me."

She explored my eyes, her eyes somber. A smile formed, and hung on her lips, and we just stood there. Finally, she leaned in and gave me another hug. "We'll talk about it tomorrow," she whispered. "The Greenes can help you if you're in trouble. We'll figure it out. And I'll mention it to Joe. I'm sure he can help, too."

I felt love and anxiety in equal measure. I felt a deep, aching sadness and, ironically, I felt something new inside; something growing, rising, struggling to develop. Was that a new me about to emerge, to be born?

It was after midnight when I crept into Marilyn's bedroom. She was asleep, curled up in a sheet. I stood by the side of her bed watching her sleep. I was happy to see she was peaceful, her breathing easy, a strand of hair covering an eye. I gently swept it into place but, being playfully obstinate like Marilyn, it refused to stay, falling, bouncing back over her eye. I smiled.

As I whispered my final goodbye, I placed the folded letter I'd written a couple of days before next to her pillow.

Wearing my winter coat, I slipped on gloves and hat, swung my camera case over my shoulder and found Sonny's leash. He was sleepy but game. He was always game for a walk.

Outside, we ventured off into the night, my ankle stronger but not fully healed. I figured it was about two miles to the spot I'd fallen into the road, where Marilyn had found me.

Sonny led the way along the narrow shoulder of the dark country road, avoiding plowed drifts of snow. The occasional car approached, its headlights stabbing my dry eyes, but the cars didn't stop, seeing I was out walking my dog.

I paused to rest a few times, speaking encouragement to Sonny, who seemed less enthusiastic about our little walk, now that the wind had picked up.

By the time we reached the area where I'd taken the tumble, my foot had stiffened and some of the soreness had returned. I stopped, glancing about, while Sonny looked up at me, his eyes narrowed in fatigue.

"I know, Sonny. I'm tired, too. Just a little further," I said, to calm a mounting fear. If I couldn't find that doorway, I didn't know if my foot would carry me back to Marilyn. And it was cold, the wind blowing day-old snow up on the slope and across the road, where one streetlamp leaned, its light gleaming on the pavement, adding to my feeling of loneliness.

"Come on, Sonny, let's go."

I started up the slope with gasps of effort, my feet digging in, struggling for traction, Sonny loping ahead, tugging on his leash. We were under a sky bright with stars, with a fragment of a moon hanging over the dark trees.

I arrived at the crest, breathing hard. Sonny shivered. There was a good sting in the night winter wind and my toes were frozen, hands tingling. I had to work fast, before Sonny and I froze to death.

CHAPTER 36

I blinked about, trying to reorient myself. Nothing looked familiar, and I wrestled with a trembling anxiety. I turned left, remembering the road where Eddie had parked his car. In the faint moonlight nothing was clear.

"Does anything look familiar to you, Sonny?" I asked, looking down at him. "Do you remember that path? Do you remember where it is?"

He looked up at me with gloomy eyes. I had to act—to make a choice—so I walked left in the direction I thought led to the road. Minutes later I came to a full stop, mouth open. There it was, Eddie's car. It was parked in the same spot as the first time I'd met him. Was Eddie here? I searched. I was astounded when I saw the silhouette of a man standing about 40 feet away, his back bent over something. His telescope?

Sonny barked, jumping on his leash. I started forward, grateful, confused and astonished.

Eddie heard Sonny's bark and he whirled around to see me. He stood stiff as a post. I shook off the night chill and moved closer. Neither of us spoke until I was nearly on him.

"What the…" Eddie exclaimed. "What the hell are you doing here at this time of night?"

"Me?" I asked. "What about you?"

He stuttered, pointing at his telescope, trying to get the words out, but he couldn't. The overcoat he wore looked worn, the tweed cap, cute, cocked coolly on the side of his head.

"I'm out here with my telescope."

"Yeah, well, I can see that. Why are you out here? It's freezing and it's after midnight. And you have a hat on. You said you never wear a hat."

"Yeah, like I don't know that it's freezing? I'm wearing a hat because it is really cold. But forget all that. Just look, Darla. Look at that sky. Look how filled with stars and planets and worlds and infinity it is. Look how clear it is—no clouds, no haze. It's a perfect night for star gazing."

I looked up into the vast bowl of the sky, shining with billions of trembling stars, dazzling my eyes, drawing me in and firing up my imagination. I lost all sense of urgency, of finding that time path, and just stared.

"Wow…" I said, moving in a slow circle. "Wow. It's so amazing, isn't it?"

"It's more than amazing, Darla. It's endless, beautiful and mysterious. It takes me beyond all thought to other times, places and worlds."

"It seems timeless out there," I said.

Eddie pointed up. "Yeah, did you know that Proxima Centauri, one of three stars in the Alpha Centauri system, is the nearest star to our sun? It's 4.22 light-years away."

"Wow," I said.

"And just think, Darla, the universe is about thirteen billion years old and the Earth about four billion years old. That means, way out there somewhere, there are mysteries and realities far beyond what we could ever imagine. There are planets that were formed billions of years before ours. That means they are billions of years older and more advanced than we are on this tiny little planet."

I loved Eddie's enthusiasm. I loved his love of mystery. I wondered if the time travel doorway I'd passed through only a few days ago was one of those mysteries. I became entranced—lost in the stars and imagination.

Eddie's voice brought me back to Earth. "Hey, so what are you doing here?"

Slowly, reluctantly, I turned my attention on him.

His hands were on his hips. Despite the cold, and the seriousness of my quest for the doorway, I felt playfully defiant.

"What's it look like I'm doing? I'm out walking Sonny."

His lips moved soundlessly, as if he were cursing. "You know, Darla, I knew there was something kooky about you when we first met. Now I'm sure of it."

"Kooky?"

"Yeah."

"Why are you so upset?" I asked, remembering the last time we were together. He'd been kind, and we'd hovered on the edge of a kiss.

Eddie stared down. "I called you a few times, but nobody picked up. Were you avoiding me?"

"We were out of town. I told you we were leaving. Remember?"

"All that time, at Christmas? And even after?"

"Yes. We just got back."

"Did Marilyn drive you here tonight?"

"No… I walked."

Eddie looked doubtful. "It's cold and it's got to be almost three miles."

Sonny's nose lifted; his ears perked up, listening. He'd picked up a scent or he'd heard something.

A little distracted, I said, "Well, why do you drive all the way out here just to look at the stars? The stars and moon are everywhere. Why don't you just step out into your own backyard?"

Eddie's eyes locked on me. "Because this is *my* place. My private place. It's quiet and away from everything and everybody. I dream about this place when I'm away at college. I don't share it with anybody. This piece of land and sky is my very own observatory."

"So did I crash your party?" I asked, with a flirtatious grin.

He held my gaze. "No, Darla. Not you. You are a kind of party all to yourself."

That warmed me to my bones. "Really?" I asked, feeling my passion ignite.

I stared at Eddie—handsome Eddie, with his fixed, serious eyes, broad sweep of chin and tall frame.

"So now what?" I asked, waiting for a kiss. Wanting a kiss, remembering that couple ice skating back in Rhode Island.

He turned shy. "What now?"

"Yeah, now," I said, my hormones making me bold.

Our eyes explored each other's eyes and lips. He came to me, lifted a hand, and with a finger, he touched my lips.

"You, Darla, bring out the knight in shining armor in me. I want to rescue you, and yet, I don't think you need rescuing."

"Oh, I don't know," I whispered in the sexiest voice I could find.

I thought, *what would Marilyn say?* A line flashed into my head, and I heard her speak, as if she were standing next to me. "A girl doesn't mind having a knight in shining armor rescue her now and then. It makes her feel pretty, and every girl should be told she's pretty."

Eddie leaned, gently brushing my lips with his. It was a roller coaster thrill, and my knees went all wobbly.

"You *are* pretty, Darla," he said, in an intimate whisper. "Maybe you need to be kissed. Maybe you need to be loved by a guy like me."

He kissed me; an open kiss, first soft then firm. I flinched in excitement, melting into his arms, feeling like a grown-up woman ready to give her brand-new, fluttering heart away. We held that kiss for what could have been thirteen billion years.

When we broke, I pulled back, my mind still, breath trapped, my chest flaming. Eddie's expression was warm and inviting. "Darla, I want to see you; be with you. You flash into my head when I'm asleep and when I'm awake. You baffle me, irritate me and excite me. I'll come home on weekends and we can do things together. All kinds of things; not just look at stars. Marilyn won't mind. I think she even likes me. And then after you graduate from high school, you can go to a college near me, near Fairfield. We can... well, you know, be together."

I stood in a confused, dreamy atmosphere, forgetting who I was and where I was. It was just like in the movies. I was in love, standing under an intimate night sky under glittering stars that were entangled in the tops of the trees.

In that perfect, brilliant and lovely moment, Sonny jerked the leash from my relaxed hand and darted off at full speed. It snapped me fully awake. I spun about and watched him tear off into the trees, barking wildly.

Then I heard it. A voice. At first just a blur of a noise, then an echo of a voice as if it were calling from deep inside a cave. I cocked an ear, listening. It was calling me. My name. The voice was calling my name.

"He'll come back," Eddie said, not wanting the magic to end. "Don't worry... Sonny will come back."

I gave Eddie an urgent stare. I felt my stomach pitch. There it was again. The call. Someone calling my name. It was my father's voice, calling to me!

Before Eddie could snatch my hand, I was off, blundering through the dark night, dodging trees, following Sonny's barking. I ran in puffing grunts of effort, ignoring my weak ankle, heading toward the sound of the calling voice.

Eddie's voice fell away. "Darla... Come back!"

My dream shattered; reality crashed in: cold wind, weak ankle, tingling hands and feet.

Eddie's voice faded into the whispering wind. "Darla... Come back."

I struggled ahead, conflicted, staring into a vague and uncertain distance. I trudged on, calling after Sonny, stumbling and cursing.

And then I saw it. The lighted path. Was it the same path I'd taken with Sonny only days before? I stopped, breathing hard. It was lit up by the moon, flickering petals of pink light.

I glanced up through the dark, reaching branches of trees, and I saw the moon, a soft pink magical globe of a moon; a changed moon from the one I had just seen with Eddie through the telescope. This moon was gliding through wisps of purple clouds, eerie and enchanting.

Was this the path? The same path? Sonny was far ahead, fading into the rush of night wind and shadow. I glanced back over my shoulder, the brittle, confused moment pulsing, breathing all about me. The woods seemed alive with a presence that sent shivers up my spine. I was a tight-rope walker, precariously balanced between two worlds, unsure of which way to fall, but I had to fall; to plunge away into the unknown.

Did I want to leave Marilyn and Eddie? Did I want to leave my father alone in a sad, shattered future?

The sound of his voice brought me gasping for air, as if I were surfacing from the depths of the ocean. I faced toward the sound, my heart jackhammering in my chest.

"Darla…" he called. "Are you there, Darla?"

I tottered off down that narrow lighted path, the moon flying overhead, sweeping across the night sky like a ragged, fleeing ghost. My feet were heavy, lungs burning from the cold air. I faltered and then froze, a chunk of ice.

There it was, a thin, blue, staticky line, appearing as a long, blue cylinder of light racing toward me. The world seemed to roll under me as I watched the light dance. At the last moment, I ducked, shouldering into it as if it were a charging ocean wave. I was stung by a hot electric shock. It buckled my knees, and I dropped face down into four inches of freshly fallen snow. The hot and cold shock punished me, and I rolled over onto my back, spent, wiping snow from my face.

"Darla! Darla, are you there? Darla! It's Dad. Are you there?"

My father's voice drew closer, loud in the night silence. Sonny had stopped barking.

With great effort I pushed to my feet and shambled ahead, following the sound of my father's voice, down the path and out into the open meadow, where moonshine bathed the snow and my approaching father.

There he was, only 40-feet away. I shouted and waved. "Dad! Dad! Over here!"

Even with ankle pain, I ran to him and, in a rush, he grabbed me into his arms and bear-hugged me.

"Where have you been? I've been worried sick," he cried, in a cracking, emotional voice. "I've been frantic, looking everywhere for you. Carol's about to call the police."

He smothered my cheeks with kisses and said he loved me.

"I thought I'd lost you, Darla. I thought you were gone. What would I have done if something had happened to you? How could I go on living?"

I choked back a sob. "I'm here, Dad. I'm here."

I wrapped my arms tightly around my father's barrel chest, burying my face in his shoulder, thrilled by his voice, by his boozy breath, by the smell of masculinity—all the loved familiarity that comforted me and anchored me in the present. 1998.

"I'm back, Dad. I'm home."

I thought of Marilyn and her father; a father who didn't love her; a father who ignored her; a father who told her to go away.

Sonny swam my Dad's ankles, barking.

"I'm home again, Dad. Me and Sonny are home again. I love you."

We held the embrace for long moments until I noticed something was wrong. I broke the hug, stung by sudden anguish. I felt my shoulder. My camera case wasn't there! I threw glances behind, down, around and up the path, into the trees. But the path I'd taken only seconds before was gone. It wasn't there. I panicked.

"What's the matter, Darla?" Dad asked.

"My camera. It's gone. I had it. It's gone! It's got to be here! I've got to find it."

Dad and I searched every inch of the ground, kicking snow away, following paths, using sticks to poke at mounds of snow. After twenty minutes, he went to the house for a flashlight, and we searched again... but we never found it.

Unable to accept that the camera case was lost, I returned the next day, wandering paths and meadows and woods but, again, to no avail. I must have lost it on the path—the path that had vanished.

Heartsick, I finally surrendered, resigned to the fact that the roll of film I'd kept was gone forever. I could only hope that Marilyn's friend would develop the roll

I'd given her and that now, in 1998, those photos had become part of the historical record.

But the photographs were not the only thing missing. Before I'd left the Greenes' house, I'd put the pearl earrings Marilyn had given me in their box, and I'd carefully placed it at the bottom of my camera case.

They, too, were lost forever.

EPILOGUE

The next morning I was sitting at my desk before my iMac computer, with 32MB of RAM, a 4GB hard drive, and a 15-inch built-in monitor, a piece of equipment that would have been utterly unimaginable in 1954.

I booted up, logged in and launched *Google*. With anxious fingers, I typed *"When did Marilyn Monroe die?"*

The answer popped up. **August 5, 1962.**

I sagged in my chair, depressed, staring blankly into the screen. So it was true: my time with Marilyn had had no impact. I had made no difference in her life, whatsoever, nor had my presence altered the details of her death in any way. I nosed toward the monitor and, sadly, I read a brief description of her life.

> *Marilyn Monroe was an American actress, model, and singer. Famous for playing comic "blonde bombshell" characters, she became one of the most popular sex symbols of the 1950s and early 1960s and was emblematic of the era's changing attitudes towards sexuality.*

I shoved my chair back and shot up, disgusted and angry. I kicked the chair and cursed the computer screen and the writer who had summed her up with that shallow, brief description.

"What the hell do you know about her?" I fumed and stormed away.

It wasn't until a week later that I screwed up the courage to do some further investigation, to see if I had left a footprint in 1954. After all, I had spent more than a week back there. Surely, I'd effected some change, no matter how minuscule and insignificant.

First, I conducted hundreds of internet searches, looking for any of the photos I'd taken of Marilyn and me; the ones she'd sent to her photographer friend in New York in 1954. I found nothing. Absolutely nothing. It was curious, bewildering and discouraging. I was sure Marilyn's photographer friend must have developed the film I'd given her. I knew for certain that she would have wanted to see those photos.

I continued the search. *Pinterest* and *Facebook* did not exist in 1998, and social media was still in its infancy, so I searched Marilyn Monroe collectors' sites, auction sites, movie paraphernalia sites and anything else I could think of. I came up empty on all of them. None of my photos appeared. How could that be? It was impossible.

As I pondered that, I sat down and anxiously shot off an email to Johnny Cash, attaching a recent photo of myself. Surely, he'd remember Marilyn and me picking him up; remember our fabulous night at the diner and sleeping in those quirky motel cottages.

Just as I was about to click on SEND, something stopped me. What if Johnny wanted to meet? I was still 16 years old, and he, 67. Forty-four years had passed, and I hadn't aged one year. He wouldn't believe me. He'd think I was out of my mind, or out to take advantage of him in some way. Weren't there crazies and con-men/women always out to swindle entertainers and movie stars? A crushing defeat sent me to the refrigerator, where I seized a quart of chocolate chip ice cream and returned to my room.

I deleted the email.

As the days and months flew by, my memories began to fade, as schoolwork demanded my attention, and new friends added social interaction; as a boyfriend or two tickled or thrilled me for a time. Oddly, my time travel adventure began to recede from the forefront of my mind, at times seeming more like a dream or a movie than reality.

But there were times, just before sleep or at dawn, during twilight states, when I would recall those days spent with Marilyn and I'd smile, and I would miss her.

Eddie often came to mind, but I swiftly pushed the memories away. If he was still alive, he'd be somewhere in his 60s. Over time, even those memories faded.

In college, when I was bored, or a bit high after a few beers, I would formulate theories about what had truly happened. I theorized that while I was out in the cold for four hours, my mind had played tricks on me. Maybe I'd gone a little crazy? For years, I'd obsessively watched Marilyn Monroe movies, and I'd identified with her early life on so many levels that I'd just imagined the entire thing. I'd always had a good imagination, and long, vivid story dreams.

Dad said that when he found me, I was trembling and so cold that I must have been close to hypothermia. Maybe I had simply gone out of my head. Wasn't that more plausible than time traveling to 1954, and meeting Marilyn Monroe, Joe DiMaggio, Johnny Cash and Eddie the stargazer, the man of my young dreams?

By the time I'd graduated from college, I seldom thought about my Christmas journey with Marilyn. Occasionally, I watched an old Marilyn movie and felt a pang of anguish and a longing, as if some truth lay just below the surface of my mind, but I dismissed it and went on with my life.

With a journalism degree, I found a job in Manhattan with a well-known magazine, writing an occasional special interest story, but mostly working with a team, developing the magazine's social media platform. I soon got bored and began writing freelance articles for hard copy and online magazines, complete with my own photos. Happily, over time, I was able to leave my steady job and make enough money freelancing.

I met a guy when I was 24 years old and we married a few months later. It lasted almost three years. Suffice it to say that he wasn't my "one and only," and neither was I his. We divorced and have remained friends, more or less.

Dad and Carol divorced the same year as I, taking their cue from me. That was the same year Dad developed heart and liver problems, and I was finally able to persuade him to stop drinking altogether. I moved back into the house with him and we had some good years until he died from a heart attack in 2013, leaving me the house and enough money to live comfortably for the rest of my life, if I wasn't too extravagant. But I wanted to work, and I needed to work. I have never been the sit-around-the-house type.

Luckily, I had success writing articles for travel magazines. This allowed me to travel and take photographs for a purpose. I was also fortunate to have several of my photos displayed at a New York gallery some years ago, and even though the show produced some buzz and good reviews, it didn't add to my professional advancement. I tried writing a novel but got stuck after a few chapters.

Now, in 2019, I live alone in the same house I've lived in since I was 16 years old, except for the years of my brief marriage. Last winter, I started an on-again, off-again relationship with a guy, but we were not heart-connected. It was more of a companionship of convenience that consisted of dinner dates, movie dates and sometimes a sleep-over. We broke up in October, and I feel more alone than ever, especially when I watch old Marilyn movies.

I still have a dog, a beagle like Sonny, named Benny, after the Elton John song, *Benny and the Jets.* He is good company, and we are best mates during long winter nights when the blues often settle in, and I feel emotionally parched and lost.

Although I still enjoy my work and my friends, now that I'm 37, they aren't enough anymore. I need, and I long for, something else, but I have no idea what that is, and that's the way it's been for a while now.

Writing this book—my Christmas journey with Marilyn—was prompted by a recent event that stunned me, jarred my memory, and shook me to the core.

I was working on an article for a financial magazine about the wills of the wealthy and famous, and what they had left others. In my research, I learned that Paul Revere left one grandchild $1, but left all the others $500. Secretary of State Daniel Webster left one grandson a snuffbox. George Pullman, the railroad mogul, left his daughter an island, while leaving his disappointing twin sons each a couple thousand dollars a year.

In more modern times, Jimi Hendrix left his $80 million estate to his adopted sister. Pablo Picasso did not leave a will, and thus his heirs—comprised of wives, mistresses, legitimate and illegitimate children—were left to figure the mess out in the courts.

These stories were ripe with possibilities, and I was sure it would be an engaging and entertaining article.

As I persisted with my research, I stumbled upon an article that literally brought me to my feet. It stopped my breath as I stooped, staring down into the computer screen. The name Marilyn Monroe caught my eye. My heart fluttered as I lowered myself back down into the chair. I began to read, my hard eyes focused, my lips moving over the startling words.

Recently discovered! *2016.*

Among Marilyn Monroe's personal items found in her Brentwood home in Los Angeles after her death in 1962 was an 8x10 photograph that has puzzled the retro movie industry, Marilyn collectors and enthusiasts. According to the 1962 inventory list of Marilyn's personal items, the photo in question was listed, but it seems no one paid much attention to it until recently. Perhaps there were too many other things to distract the public at the time: the conspiracy theories, Marilyn's personal demons, her relationship with Joe DiMaggio, along with a reported possible reconciliation, and Marilyn's many love affairs with notorious politicians—and you know who they allegedly are.

The photo in question (shown below) was found in Marilyn's lower dresser drawer, neatly framed, with no autographed signature. Marilyn must have been fond of it, as inscribed on the back of the photo, written in her own hand, are the mysterious words, "We'll meet again. I know it."

*The photo shows Marilyn and an attractive young woman, probably in her teens, standing back-to-back, hipshot. They face the camera, flashing playful, sexy smiles, obviously imitating Marilyn and Jane Russell in their famous still publicity photo for the movie **Gentlemen Prefer Blondes**.*

To date, no one has come forward to name the young woman, nor has anyone been able to identify her, and the mystery has Marilyn fans and aficionados scratching their heads.

Baxter Tate, a photographic historian with a vast knowledge of Marilyn's archives and photos, of which there are thousands, believes that the photo was most likely taken between 1953 and 1955.

A thorough historical search of Marilyn's friends, actors, screenwriters, technicians and makeup artists, along with family members, has so far been fruitless, nor have they helped to solve the mystery.

*If anyone recognizes this young girl, please contact
the writer below by email. We would love to solve this
mystery and make a lot of baffled and bewildered Marilyn fans happy.*

My pulse sped up and I sat still, moved and elated,
pleased and sad, all at the same time. So it was true!
Marilyn had developed my photos—and at least one
had survived, probably because she had kept it with her
until she died.

I stared at the photo, absorbed by Marilyn and me in
that playful pose. All the emotions and all the splendid
memories rushed in, fresh and alive, like water splashing down a mountain stream. All the joy and heart-
aches; all the hopes and wishes I'd buried in my heart
for all those years, were finally released and set free. I
was drenched in emotion and color, thrilled and giddy,
laughing and crying. It had happened! Yes, it had all
happened. I was there in 1954, and I had returned back
home to 1998.

It is my birthday, December 18, 2019, and I have
completed the book about Marilyn and me, my story.
What is left to do? What am I to do?

I sit quietly. All the faces and memories expand the
minutes and deepen the silence. When I think of Marilyn, I feel love, happiness and gratitude. I hear her girlish laughter and her whispery voice, and I'm lifted by
them.

When I think of Eddie, I feel a warm stirring across
my skin, and I'm shaken by new wonder and forbidden
possibility.

I leave my chair and make for the window. I draw
back the curtains and search the night, eerily lit by a full

moon. I squint, imagining I see a silhouetted figure standing tall in a strange, ghostly light that is streaming down from a full, pink moon, swimming through purple clouds. My breath catches, excitement rises. I bet the sky is ablaze with stars.

I've decided to take Benny for a walk, and he seems as excited as I am. We'll climb the slopes and walk toward the snow-covered trees, toward that imagined silhouette. We'll walk the same paths I walked when I was sixteen, and search for a narrow path marked by deer tracks. I'll release Benny and let him run free, and eagerly watch to see if he takes that path and wanders off into the mystery night. If he does, I'll run after him.

I glance about the house, suddenly feeling imprisoned by it. It's clear to me now. It's time for another adventure. When I shut my eyes, Marilyn slips into my inner mind, and I watch her laugh and pose, and I recall the words she'd written on the back of our photo.

"We'll meet again. I know it."

I swallow a breath, feeling courage rise; feeling that brave sense of adventure I possessed at sixteen years old.

It's December 18, 2019, my thirty-seventh birthday, and it's snowing. I slip into my coat and fasten Benny's leash to the steel circle on his collar.

I step to the small, round wall mirror, reach into my pocket and take out a tube of bright red lipstick. I open it and carefully apply it to my lips. I part and brush my hair to one side, the way Marilyn had styled it so many years ago, and then I don my hat and gloves. I smile at myself with eager satisfaction.

I look down at Benny and give a little jerk of a nod. He seems to understand, eagerly waiting to be released into the infinite wonders of a snowy night.

"Benny, you and I are going back to the trees, and you are going to find that path—the same path Sonny found all those years ago. And who knows where that path might lead? Maybe it will take us back to 1954. Maybe to 1960. Who knows?"

Benny sneezes in excitement, barks twice, and tugs me toward the door. I release the lock and fling the door wide open, my shoulders back, my head up, ready for the adventure.

"Okay, fellow traveler, the big, wide, mysterious world is waiting for us under all those shiny stars and that lovely, full moon. Let's go find that path!"

THANK YOU!

Thank you for taking the time to read *Time with Norma Jeane*. If you enjoyed it, please consider telling your friends or posting a short review. Word of mouth is an author's best friend, and it is much appreciated.

Thank you,
Elyse Douglas

Other novels by Elyse Douglas that you might enjoy:

The Christmas Diary
The Summer Diary
The Other Side of Summer
The Christmas Women
The Christmas Eve Letter (A Time Travel Novel) Book 1
The Christmas Eve Daughter (A Time Travel Novel) Book 2
The Christmas Eve Secret (A Time Travel Novel) Book 3
The Lost Mata Hari Ring (A Time Travel Novel)
The Christmas Town (A Time Travel Novel)
The Summer Letters
Time Change (A Time Travel Novel)
Daring Summer (Romantic Suspense)
The Date Before Christmas
Christmas Ever After
Christmas for Juliet
The Christmas Bridge
Wanting Rita

www.elysedouglas.com

Editorial Reviews

THE LOST MATA HARI RING – A Time Travel Novel
by Elyse Douglas

"This book is hard to put down! It is pitch-perfect and hits all the right notes. It is the best book I have read in a while!"
5 Stars!
--Bound4Escape Blog and Reviews

"The characters are well defined, and the scenes easily visualized. It is a poignant, bitter-sweet emotionally charged read."
5-Stars!
--Rockin' Book Reviews

"This book captivated me to the end!"
--StoryBook Reviews

"A captivating adventure..."
--Community Bookstop

"...Putting *The Lost Mata Hari Ring* down for any length of time proved to be impossible."
--Lisa's Writopia

"I found myself drawn into the story and holding my breath to see what would happen next..."
--Blog: A Room Without Books is Empty

Editorial Reviews

THE CHRISTMAS TOWN – A Time Travel Novel
by Elyse Douglas

"The Christmas Town is a beautifully written story. It draws you in from the first page, and fully engages you up until the very last. The story is funny, happy, and magical. The characters are all likable and very well-rounded. This is a great book to read during the holiday season, and a delightful read during any time of the year."
--Bauman Book Reviews

"I would love to see this book become another one of those beloved Christmas film traditions, to be treasured over the years! The characters are loveable; the settings vivid. Period details are believable. A delightful read at any time of year! Don't miss this novel!"
--A Night's Dream of Books

Editorial Reviews

THE SUMMER LETTERS – A Novel
by Elyse Douglas

"A perfect summer read!"
--Fiction Addiction

"In Elyse Douglas' novel THE SUMMER LETTERS, the characters' emotions, their drives, passions and memories are all so expertly woven; we get a taste of what life was like for veterans, women, small town folk, and all those people we think have lived too long to remember (but they never really forget, do they?).
I couldn't stop reading, not for a moment. Such an amazing read. Flawless."
5 Stars!
--Anteria Writes Blog - To Dream, To Write, To Live

"A wonderful, beautiful love story that I absolutely enjoyed reading."
5 Stars!
--Books, Dreams, Life - Blog

"The Summer Letters is a fabulous choice for the beach or cottage this year, so you can live and breathe the same feelings and smells as the characters in this wonderful story."
--Reads & Reels Blog